DELPHINIUM BLUES

DELPHINIUM BLUES

Stevie Morgan

FLAME
Hodder & Stoughton

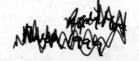

First published in 1999 by Hodder and Stoughton
A division of Hodder Headline PLC
A Flame Book

10 9 8 7 6 5 4 3 2 1

ISBN 0 340 71801 3

Typeset by
Hewer Text Ltd, Edinburgh
Printed and bound in Great Britain by
Clays Ltd, St Ives plc, Bungay, Suffolk

Hodder and Stoughton
A division of Hodder Headline PLC
338 Euston Road
London NW1 3BH

For Simon

With thanks to my children, my friends, my family and to Celia, Hilly and Sue for giving me a chance.

Chapter One

Of course I knew he was shagging someone the moment I found the Queen's 'Greatest Hits' cassette in his car, amongst the usual ones by Howling Dog Shannon, and Stinkin' Feet Brown. Obscure old blues recorded on somebody's front porch in 1937 is all that he listens to – apart from some stuff that he says is 'contemporary classical' and sounds like cooking utensils being dropped on to the concrete floor of an empty warehouse near Gatwick.

I have to hide my Michael Bolton CD in my knicker drawer and only play it when he's away on a long trip. Even Mozart is a bit too populist. When we met at college I had to flog all my Elton John and Steeleye Span albums so as to be politically acceptable enough to get him into bed. Which only left me with one Joni Mitchell and a Dylan.

I didn't say anything about the Queen album when I found it. I just imagined him playing it very loud whilst driving through wet glittery London streets going back to his flat at night. With someone sitting in the passenger seat and laughing. Putting her head right back so that her throat was hit by the lights sliding by above the car.

Actually it's not true to say I had to sell my Elton John albums to get him into bed. Getting him into bed wasn't difficult. Most of the women in Cambridge seemed to manage it. There was always some girl wrapped in Martin's dressing gown draping herself around the door frame of his college room, wreathed in joint-smoke. You just knew what they'd been doing. Or rather other people knew what they'd been doing. I knew the word for it but I had only the vaguest idea of what it actually meant.

I wasn't a virgin. Not technically anyway. I'd made sure of that at a party before 'coming up' by letting some terribly athletic boy heave up and down on top of me for ten minutes. He got very hot and sweaty and kept on asking if I was 'happy'. I didn't know what he was on about. Happy? Happy was something you were when you blew out the candles on your birthday cake or when you got your exam results and found you had straight As. Happy was not lying on a pile of coats in a freezing spare room with your tights round your ankles and a perfect stranger having an apoplectic fit on your cleavage. But I don't suppose I even knew what a cleavage was back then. Certainly not something I'd have admitted to owning.

When I met Martin all his friends had dirty Jason King haircuts and cowboy boots. Down his end of the corridor, to breathe was to be instantly stoned. Down there they existed in a haze of drugs and Neil Young. (I was too naive to realise that to endure a haze of the latter you have to be far under the influence of the former.) Down there was the kitchen where I tiptoed to boil a kettle wearing the good tweed skirt and print blouses that Mummy had bought me for going to lectures. Like a fresh prawn swimming to the cocktail factory.

Martin must have seen me as some kind of challenge. Maybe he even had a bet on it with his mate Damian. I can just imagine it.

'Hey, Marty, bet you half an ounce of Moroccan you can't get your hands inside its panties.'

Damian always referred to women as 'it'. As in 'Will you look at the tits on it?', and 'What does it think it's wearing?'. All part of his little rebellion against his mum who ran a feminist potters collective in Balham.

'Up the stakes Damian. Make it one and I'll fuck her brains out inside a week.'

'Make it two and I'll have her down on me in the back row of the Ocean.'

But maybe that's just paranoia born of what's happened. What's happening. Martin always claimed it was love at first sight. Smitten, he said, by the vision of me in my blue Donegal carrying a milk saucepan and a tin of Campbell's condensed mushroom. He's trotted out that little myth at every dinner party for the last fifteen years, looking at me blearily and slightly pissed from the other end of the table over the heads of a succession of friends. It's only now in the face of Queen's 'Greatest Hits' that I feel that Damian's misogyny seems a more likely motivation for our getting together.

Damian would have lost his bet anyway, whatever the stakes. Once Martin had sussed the entry code of my underwear – a cup of Earl Grey brought to me at my desk every evening for a week – I think even he was surprised at what happened. Some sort of peculiar congruence of pheromones turned us into rabbits. I'd never experienced lust from the inside before. I knew what it looked like from outside – the sweaty boy on the spare bed. But after Martin took me to bed I was awash with desires that filled my head with single expletives.

It was all pretty clandestine mind you. He'd sneak to my room in the middle of the night when all his mates were stoned or asleep. He never acknowledged me outside bonking hours. Would walk past me in the corridor and skirt the opposite edge of the quadrangle if he saw me in college.

That's really how I came to sell the socially unacceptable albums. I knew I had to give up tweed skirts and listening to 'Funeral for a Friend' in the dark if I was ever going to get anything I wanted, like walking down the street hand in hand.

And it worked. I started being included in the extensive all-boy Neil Young and dope fests. He allowed us to walk through town together. We even went out on dates, to the cinema and cheap restaurants where they served rice, potatoes and chips with each dish. He allowed his hand to be held.

Then, I believed he was falling in love with me. Now I think he just twigged that with me as an acknowledged member of his little coterie of self-made misfits he could shag me almost any hour of the day or night he fancied.

It's not that I minded the tweed skirt going to Oxfam. My mum-made image needed a change. And I knew that a sex life was one of the things I needed to become my dream image of myself . . . a kind of amalgam of Debbie Harry, Jane Goodall and Katharine Hepburn. But I did mind about Elton. He'd been a crucial component of my pre-university social life. For long periods the only component: finish my homework, put Elton on Dad's radiogram, switch off the lights and feel artistically lonely and misunderstood. Bliss. Or as near to it as I knew how to get at seventeen.

Getting rid of 'Honky Chateau' and 'Goodbye Yellow Brick Road' was the first stage of subjugating myself to Martin the Blond God and his Great Big Magic Wand Willy. I started conforming to his rules, which, considering that he professed left-wing anarchy, were extensive and rigid.

They still are. Or rather, they aren't rules so much as a strict code of conduct like something that might have existed in nineteenth-century Russian aristocracy or 1950s Mafia. I some-times think that Martin has big lists in his head, like the recording angel, lists of everything in the world. A list of approved things – Liberty, Levis, Labour, Lanson, Langoustine – and a list of disapproved things – Marks and Spencer, Wranglers, Chardonnay, Tories, Bacon. If you like, or think or wear or watch or read or eat anything on the disapproved list then you become a banned person. You yourself become another addition to the bad list.

The only thing that's changed with his age is that there are some things that hover between lists and are assigned according to his current state of mind. Silk boxer shorts for example – four times out of five they're 'tasteless and make you think about your tackle all the time'. But once in a while they're 'immensely comfortable, really very practical'. So it could be said that he's mellowed, except that things on the disapproved list are vilified as much as ever, even if the day before in a sunnier frame of mind he's put them on the approved side.

Which is how I came not to mention the Queen tape. Temporary hoverer I told myself. Something he picked up at a motorway service station. On a whim. 'Amusingly kitsch.' Approved.

But I knew really. It was the music of a new relationship. Something shared with someone else who wasn't me. After all it wasn't the only sign. There was the strawberry bubble bath, the purple shirt and the failure of the Magic Wand Willy. With hindsight I know that, taken together with the Queen tape, they were absolute proof of Martin being seriously unfaithful. Not just a casual away-on-a-shoot-fuck. But unfaithful in the heart. Holding hands by moonlight sort of unfaithful. Unfaithful enough to be about to do what he's about to do.

Which is leave. Leave me, his wife for fifteen years who can tell when he wants mash and when he wants roast spuds without asking. Leave his children, Dan and Frankie who laugh at all his jokes, always. Leave his home with its naturally distressed-look paintwork and lived-in garden. Leave his village where he can flirt with the postmistress and turn up to play cricket once a season and be welcomed.

The willy failure was the first sign. I didn't say anything. It's a bit like bed-wetting: the thing is never to mention it. Wash the sheets, change the pyjamas, get them comfy and off to sleep and pretty soon it'll stop happening. And you know men and their willies — it's a tricky relationship at the best of times. Start bandying words like impotence about the place and it can lead to all sorts of trouble. Tired, I thought. Stressed. Yeah he was both, shagged out and guilty as hell. And there's nothing like guilt for stopping man and willy working in harmony.

5

Then it was the purple shirt. Two-tone, purple and green, stretch silk crumpled in the bottom of his bag after a trip to America. I was gathering dirty boxers to wash when I found it.

'Wow . . . this is new.'

'Oh yeah, that. Had it for a while actually.'

'You haven't worn it.'

'I have. Up in town. You know publishers' parties. Boring stuff.'

Yeah, I know. Parties. Where you always wear those black trousers and the loose white linen shirt I bought you for Christmas because you like things simple and understated. Not purple two-tone and tight.

And last of all, just a fortnight ago, was the strawberry bubble bath. On my birthday, a great big bottle of strawberry bubble bath. When he knows I think making yourself smell of food is strange. I mean roast lamb is a nice smell, but you don't want to dab it behind your ears. I normally get a really good present. Something I really like. Something that is for me, Jess. Not some wife-present-object grabbed from one of the station shops in the five minutes before the train left.

So tonight. No yesterday now. When he said 'I've got something to tell you' and I heard a rushing sound going past my ears, I knew it was my life falling away from me. Down into the space that was suddenly underneath me. Heading for the ground ready to smash into more bits than you could stick together with a Niagara of super glue.

I have to hand it to Martin. He did a great job of explaining how his leaving us is all to do with his personal growth and development, and really very little to do with Dolores. The colour of her hair. The length of her legs. Or the date on her birth certificate. He explained how his leaving me and the kids was going to be good for us too. Great for my personal growth and development, liberating for the kids. Even Dog, our dog, is going to benefit in some way.

Everything for us is going to be the same, only better except he's not going to be here any more. He'll be in London with Dolores.

Only two things of all the many things that he told me at great length have really stuck. One was when he said he remembered why he had loved me. Had loved. Past tense. And the other was when he said Dolores's name. A caress in three syllables.

In the end, in a sort of a way to his credit, he cried himself to sleep, crumpled into a pillow at an awkward angle as if he had been dropped. I went outside to do some of that personal growth and development by lying on the lawn keening into the wormcasts. Then I got in the car and drove. Bent right over the wheel so as to see through the tears, gripping the wheel so my hands wouldn't shake. I drove all round the tiny windy lanes with a huge roaring in my head like God's own hair dryer until a black-and-white cat ran out under my wheels. It seemed all set to commit suicide. Maybe the father of its kittens had just run off with a white pedigree Persian.

Like the kids sing:

> Postman Pat, Postman Pat
> Postman Pat ran over his cat.
> Pat was nearly cry-ing
> The cat was slowly dy-ing.
> Never seen a cat as flat as that before.
> Never seen a cat as flat as that before.

Except the cat wasn't slowly dying, it was dead. I knew by the kind of wet 'crump' sound my wheel made going over what must have been some essential part of its anatomy. I stopped, but I didn't get out of the car. Everything, just everything seemed artificial. All the world around me picked out in blue and grey under the moon. The road gleaming. The way I felt inside. Martin at home in bed for the last time. And I've never in my life knocked anything down on the road before. Not even a bird.

I knew at once whose cat it was. It belonged to the couple we quite unkindly call the Axe Murderers. They live in the only house on this lane. The house with the hole in the wall blocked up with beer bottles, and huge radio aerials placed like sentinels all around its dilapidated boundary fences. He has a face like a crease in a paper bag and always wears a bobble hat. She is like a barrage balloon with eyes. They keep cats. And dead bodies. Probably.

At first, when I hit the cat I thought I must go and tell them. Knock on their door right at that moment and own up. Then I wondered how Axe Murderers would take to being knocked up at three a.m. by a demented woman with smeared mascara and the body of a beloved moggy in her arms. So I thought I'd just pick it up and leave it with a note on their doorstep. But when I got out of the car to look, the cat wasn't neatly dead, not a nice cutesy little moggie corpse all fluffy with four paws in the air. More sort of spread-dead.

You wouldn't believe how much stuff there is inside a cat when it all spills out. I'm amazed. All that inside every cat you see all the time, a huge secret world of wet tubing and pulsating pink.

So I thought I'd put the cat on something so's I could carry it up the road. It wasn't really liftable but I thought I could kind of scrape it up. There was a cardboard box in the boot which I broke up to make a kind of bier for it, by pushing it under the body and all the bits. I was very gentle and got most of the body parts on to the cardboard, but then the head fell off. So I managed to make the cat look as though the local coven have performed some unspeakable ritual with it. If I own up to the Axe Murderers now I'll more than likely be converted into one of the dead bodies they live with.

It's getting light. Birds beginning to make those first tentative 'Oh is it time to get up already?' twitterings they do before the serious business of singing begins. When it gets light things will seem a bit more real I think. I don't know if this is good or bad.

Damian, the purple shirt and Queen's 'Greatest Hits', this is where they were all leading: a godforsaken country lane at 4 a.m. with a mutilated cat body on a piece of Tesco's orange box. Jess, this, now, is your life.

Chapter Two

The light didn't help with the reality situation. I was connected enough with it all to feel as though I'd had my insides put through a very good steel blender, but I still managed to be floating two inches away from everything.

The kids woke early. They must have heard all the crying last night. But they didn't ask any questions when they came down and found me lying on the floor by the Aga. It had just seemed like a good place to lie when I got back from shoving Axe Murderer Pat's Flat Cat into a hedge. They knew that there was bad news but they didn't want to know how bad. They aren't stupid. In fact at eight and ten they are probably less stupid than they'll ever be in their lives again.

They perched on chairs by the stove like they always do first thing. Wrapped in dressing gowns and still muzzy with sleep they looked like soft and vulnerable toddlers again. Baby versions of their father, little tanned golden lions: Frankie's fine fair hair making a gauzy halo, Dan's summer crew cut already bleached white-blonde although it's only May. They're nothing like me. My genes must have been the architects of their internal organs, a surgeon looking at our livers would probably spot the family resemblance.

They were quiet, none of the usual early-morning spitting and snarling at each other. I handed them hot toast and juice and they didn't say anything about my trembling hands. Or the fact that I had bits of grass in my hair and mud smeared down my front. Maybe I'm always a lot messier than I imagine and have always had delirium tremens.

Betrayal and loss are pretty tough lessons to learn first thing on a Friday morning when the biggest trauma you've been through is a hamster funeral. I kept willing Martin to stay asleep so these last little moments of innocence, free of pain, could be stretched out.

But Martin did wake up. I heard him get out of bed. Not slowly like he normally does – swinging his feet out then sitting on the edge of the bed looking surprised and slightly offended that another day has started without asking him first – but in one movement. Maybe he'd been lying awake for a long time stretching out the moments until reality came to bite him. A single creak of the bed, then I heard his feet along the landing and down the stairs.

By the time he came into the kitchen we must all have been looking like people caught unexpectedly in the flash of a camera. You know those sorts of photos that get taken drunkenly at parties, so the faces in the pictures look disembodied, as if they've just landed there off a freighter from one of Jupiter's moons.

Maybe next year I'll be able to work out clearly what happened next. I try and put it together in my head, but the pieces fly apart like identical magnetic poles.

I know that Martin sat down between them, cramming his big body in his grubby dressing gown so that their drawn-up feet were against his thighs. Old daddy lion and the two cubs.

He told them then, that he was leaving. That he had found someone very special and he was leaving to be with her. That she was called Dolores. I'm pretty sure he didn't try giving them any of that personal growth stuff he'd pumped into me.

It was like watching a car crash into my babies. I didn't really hear anything I just saw their faces. Dan went white. Like the reverse of the moment he was born when he screamed himself pink, every new cry pushing a flush of blood further from his heart. Now, I saw him gasping to breathe and with every gasp he went whiter and whiter. First just round his eyes. Then his cheeks, his neck, his ears. At last only his lips were left livid in a parchment face. Frankie's face creased and puckered like a popped balloon. She opened her mouth and wailed. Eyes shut. Lips making a perfect o and the rest of her body limp and forgotten. Then they clung to him, each stuck to one side of his big chest looking ridiculously frail and small. And I thought how can he inflict this pain? How can he do this?

And right in the middle of this excruciatingly painful tableau, the chickens shot past the kitchen door screaming murder, gathering up their feathers like Victorian maids who've seen a mouse, chased by Dog. (Something she hasn't done since she was rat-sized and took the chicken-chasing cure: half an hour in a small coup with next-door's cockerel, a kind of avian Mike Tyson on five lines of coke.) The chickens were getting the maximum drama out of it . . . making those 'Oh my God it's got a gun' sort of noises that they do when they are seriously pissed off. Jumping in the air and squawking without any thought of dignity. Dog had clearly absorbed the bonkerness going on inside the house and had lost it in a big way. I had to go out as I thought she might have killed one of the daft birds, and when sanity returned she would never have forgiven herself. I shouted at her and threw her and the chickens in their pens. They were still all swearing at each other as I walked back up the garden.

Okay . . . so this is why he's doing it — because he has a wife who interrupts major life events to sort out dramas in a chicken soap opera.

Back inside, Martin was on the phone to his parents. Frankie was curled in a ball on the sofa with her arms wrapped round her head. Dan was doing some damage limitation.

'This isn't the worst thing. It isn't the worst thing,' he kept saying. 'If you were getting divorced that would be the worst thing.' Yeah I thought, it would. It will be.

I took them to school eventually, just to plug them into a few hours of ordinary normality before they had to plunge back into the nightmare. I bludgeoned them with cheerfulness all the way there, promises of weekend picnics, outings to the pool, trips to the cinema, safaris in Tanzania, stopovers on Mars . . . God knows what I said about the wonderful world of New Adventures that was about to open up to them. Anything to distract myself from the desire to pull over into a field and stick my head up the exhaust.

Everything looked so lovely as we drove through the lanes. It made it all seem worse. This was the little bit of rural idyll that we'd chosen for our children to grow up in. The deep set lanes running like capillaries between meadows of burnt-sienna-coloured cows and fat grubby sheep. The hedgerows tangled in an orgy of twining stems and leaves the colour of cut limes. This was the atmosphere of sweet security that allowed Dan and Frankie to disappear with a packet of biscuits at 10 in the morning with a single instruction, 'be back by tea time'. And Martin was about to wreck it by tainting all memories with loss and pain.

The village was rubbing it in too: all the houses neat and dressed for summer with tubs and window boxes already filling with eager little dots of flowers, and their occupants stepping out of front doors like figures on an ornamental clock. There was Mrs Adams at the window of her house, full of stillness and shelves steady under the load of her life-work of lurid and foul-mouthed detective fiction. Beatrice Tubb was out with her batch of ratty dogs running before her making a maypole weaving with their coloured leads. All her beekeeping gear hanging in the window of her tiny sandwiched cottage like banners. The Arnies were walking up to school, true to their stereotype of dysfunction, dirty loud and numerous: there is at least one Arnie child in every infant and junior year. A row of cars, Land Rovers and sundry muddy lane-worn vehicles stood outside school offloading kids all of whom I and Martin know by name. It's easy to learn a whole school when there are only forty-nine kids in it.

I loved these mornings for a whole set of reasons that I wouldn't admit to my high-flying girlfriends, reasons that defy my I'm-not-ironing-anyone's-shirts past: I mean I *didn't* shave my legs in my twenties as a political statement. I loved feeling my odd little bit of status and position: a married woman, caring for her children and her husband, forming some of the mortar that held it all together, the linchpin of a happy family.

So that's all gone down the tubes then.

I walked up to the school through the playground holding Dan and Frankie's hands very tightly, smiling bravely and casting off the looks of inquiry.

I delivered the kids into class and went to tell their headmistress that she was going to have to be very gentle with them for the rest of the term. Probably the rest of their primary school careers.

It was my first taste of marital breakup as performance art.

It's a shame telepathy is such a hit and miss business and only really works in the first three weeks of a love affair because choosing words is jolly difficult. I had several false starts sitting and wringing my hands whilst perched on the edge of her visitor's chair.

Saying the words out loud would make it real. Once I'd said it. Once I'd told someone else, then there was no way it could be a dream or a figment of my imagination.

'Martin and I . . .' Perhaps it's not worth telling her, I thought for a moment. Perhaps Martin is going to come back very soon. A few weeks, at the most.

'I think you ought to know that . . . The children are very upset today because . . .'

But then when he comes back telling her that will be so much easier.

In the end she helped me out 'It's not their granny is it?'

'No. No. Um . . .'

'Has Martin been in an accident?' Ha! I wish. Just as we know the children, she knows her parents by name, especially parents like us who run the cake stall, lose the egg-and-spoon race with style, and dance to every 70s disco record with the five-year-olds at the end of term hop.

'No, no. He's leaving me.'

'He's what??' Now I'd got it out.

'Leaving us,' I thought I might as well try and raise a laugh, 'found a younger prettier model. So he's trading the old one in.'

She burst into tears. 'Those poor children,' she sobbed

'He'll be coming home lots at weekends. To see them,' I said, handing her the tissues I'd brought for myself.

I'm going to have to get used to this. A lot of people are going to be very upset about us splitting up. Jess and Martin, the couple who still snogged in public at PTA ceilidhs. Martin, the big shot down from London who still found time to play with his kids and write funny pieces for the parish mag.

Shock normally ages people doesn't it? I looked in the mirror this morning and saw my mother for the first time in sixteen years, looking every bit as sickly as she did the day she died. But Martin's parents seemed to have lost whole generations when they got out of the car at lunch time today. They looked like a pair of lost kids. Disappointing for me because I'd rather hoped that two avenging angels the size of statues on the Albert Memorial were going to wield their swords and forbid him to leave.

I still had some hopes of their metamorphosing into a kind of secular Gabriel when they disappeared into the sitting room with Martin and closed the door. I wanted to hear yelps of anguish coming from him as they forcibly removed the demon Dolores from his system, but there wasn't a sound.

I couldn't stand the strain of waiting for a contrite and broken Martin to crawl from under the door so I went down the garden out of sight of the house, sat down on the grass and stared at my flower border. It's full of my favourite things just now . . . alchemillas, campanulas, nepetas and of course delphiniums just coming out. It's all about blue, even the alchemillas which are lime green are about blue. Because lime green makes blue look bluer. And delphiniums are the soul of blue.

I'm hopelessly unsuited to being a gardener really. I have no faith in the seasons, no belief that spring will follow winter, no trust that growth happens too slowly to notice. I need too much proof. I have to restrain myself from pulling things up to check that the roots are growing. But I have a gardener's dreams and obsessions: a single second when the light hits a special plant, or when dawn catches the grass just so. Gardeners are the ultimate romantics, willing to suffer, slog and sacrifice for a single moment of pure and useless beauty, a single moment of obsession. My most obsessive moments are at this time of year when the delphiniums spike miraculously all along the back of the border. I drag Martin out to look at them because after all blue is his favourite colour. But Martin likes blue shirts, blue pottery, blue curtains, blue neons. Blue things that are not alive.

Sitting on the grass in the sunshine with the bees clumsily buffeting about the opening flowers I began to make some sense of Martin's decision. Well, not sense in the real world just sense the way he sees it. It's all about style. Martin is in a profoundly stylish profession – he's a photographer, portraits, travel, features that aren't too difficult – no starving babies. When he isn't in some foreign and either glamorous or intrepid sort of place, he spends his working time in London. A weekly boarder in a flat with the sort of city view you normally see in Michael Douglas movies. He wears linen jackets and expensive shirts. He eats in restaurants, talks about shoots and image and ideas. His friends are about as likely to be interested in flower borders and the spirituality of fine delphiniums as they are in saving for their own incontinence knickers.

I too had a brief incarnation in this world of deals and opportunities, of clever talk and beguiling images. But I was in the bargain basement making TV programmes for the under-fives: scripts with no polysyllabic words and sets with only primary colours. Martin rose fast to the top-floor restaurant and ball-gown department, four pages to himself in the Sundays to display his bright, blurred, motion-smeared images. Fat front covers and long foreign shoots. There didn't seem much point in my slogging away with glove puppets and talking teddies when I could be doing the same thing at home for my own kids.

So we bought into the rural idyll. Full time for me and weekends for Martin. I could stop caring about whether my shirts were a good colour on camera or what side of bed the children's commissioning editor got out of. I could wipe my hands on the bum of my jeans and it didn't matter any more.

But Martin has been forced to live a double life and slowly the two lives stopped fitting together. A wife whose idea of dressing up is a clean pair of jeans and has a tan line in the summer where her wellies stop just didn't fit with the life he leads most of the time. Those kinds of friends with that level of glitter. And he just can't hack it any more. I mean given a choice between me in my best Gaps and Dolores in something gauzy from Janet Raeger . . .

And of course in the London magazine and paper world anyone who is anyone has got at least one divorce under their belt to talk about late at night over a half-empty bottle of Jameson's.

So he's been stolen away to the land of Media Faerie, the goblin market of career and achievement was too strong a pull to resist. Dolores is just the little microcosm of it all.

I heard the car door slam and Martin's parents driving away. No chance of a reprieve then. He probably explained all about the delphiniums and the chickens and they probably said 'Well son, you're making the only decision you can'. That's avenging archangels for you.

Martin said he would leave for London after the kids were in bed, that he'd take them swimming after school. I didn't say anything. Mostly I was crying too much to speak. I didn't know you could cry so much, cry all the time. He was quiet. Controlled. Went off to pick the kids up saying I should try and 'Calm down'.

I did try. I went and looked at my delphiniums again. But it only made me feel worse. All that serenity, everything just the same as always and inside I was containing a hurricane. I lay on the ground and screamed, with my face right in the grass so the soil soaked up the noise, and Mrs E next door wouldn't worry about her cows being disturbed. (She's very keen on peace and quiet for her cows.)

Screaming just wasn't enough. After I stopped nothing had changed. And I like proof that something has happened. Good physical manifestations. So I went inside to the big Welsh dresser where our set of matching china is kept. Was kept. Eight of everything, covered vegetable dishes, neat little coffee cups, two sizes of jug and a gravy boat. Even eight egg cups. White with a discrete little blue and red pattern. I bloody loathe it. I think we both do. But once people get the idea for a safe-bet Christmas present you're stuffed. A friend of mine has a house full of pigs . . . pig mugs, pig ornaments, pig duvet covers, pig hot-water bottles given her by loving relations because of one sartorial error ten years ago . . . a pig sweatshirt which was a present from a very unfortunate boyfriend.

I carried it all out to the garage. It took me six journeys. Then I spread two big dust sheets all along the garage wall, overlapping so as to catch all the bits. Then I began to smash the dinner service. Piece by piece. Each one thrown with loving force, so that they didn't just break, they exploded. I'd really stopped caring about Mrs E's cows by this stage.

I thought about each piece carefully as I threw it. I put something on every plate and into every bowl. The big vegetable dishes were loaded, one with the thought of Martin running his hands through Dolores's long red hair; another with the nights of celibacy ahead of me; the last with the children's faces as he'd told them he was leaving. Even the egg cups contained some little memory or resentment . . . one had Martin's mouth in, soft and mobile; another had the recipe for his favourite dessert; another the washing and pairing of his socks for fifteen years . . . tight squeeze that was.

I must have been screaming and crying as I did it because there was water dripping off my chin and my throat burned at the end when there was nothing left to smash.

Dribbling too perhaps. Attractive.

It still wasn't enough. I picked up a piece of the broken china and drew its point down along the length of each forearm. I wanted to do it really deep to have something as bad on the outside as the pain on the inside, but I stopped at shallow. I could just imagine how angry Martin was going to be when he saw the cuts, anything less than very purposeful suicide he would see as 'attention seeking'. And anyway, topping yourself on your own drive when your kids are due home isn't a great plan.

And then I panicked. Shallow they may have been but the long red lines were producing enough blood for it to be running rather than dripping or trickling down my arms. Any second Martin and the kids would be home and here I was leaving nasty dark pools on our very expensive Bath-stone drive. I threw the shard of china away, jumped in the car and drove to Sarah and Alex's house.

Their house is pretty high profile, on the one main street in the village. And after school this morning everyone will already know. There's no way me doing a wheely stop outside their door then standing on their doorstep bleeding was going to be missed. But I've never minded gossip. I'm grateful for anyone taking an interest in my life.

Sarah was home writing lectures. She's a bright girl Sarah and tough as shoe leather. She clocked the arms, the tears, everything in one glance and had me inside with my arms under the cold tap of her kitchen sink almost before the net curtains opposite had even twitched. She could be on *Casualty*.

She didn't ask anything until she'd bandaged me and had me sat down with a mug of something hot in front of me that I sipped without tasting

'What is this?'

'Tea with two sugars'

'Oh.'

'This is the first time anything's passed your lips today isn't it?'

'Yes.'

'Must be bad.' She knows I'm naturally greedy.

'Mmm.'

'So do I get any clues or are you simply going to let me guess why you've sliced your arms open and landed on my doorstep?'

'Martin's leaving. He's found someone else.'

Sarah isn't given to speechlessness. She was silent long enough for two people to walk past her window, read the poster advertising the School Barbecue, and walk on.

'Jesus. And I thought there was one man whose brains were too big to fit in the end of his penis. Just shows how wrong you can be. Jess I'm so sorry. Has he actually gone?'

'Tonight. After the children go to bed. He's taking his car to London. I've got to go back now. Feed the kids.'

'Can you drive?'

'Oh yes, very very quickly, and straight into the nearest wall.'

'Jess!'

'No no. It's okay, I've no intention of giving him the satisfaction of claiming on my life insurance.'

'We'll be round later. I'll tell Kath and Gerry. We'll all be round.'

I took a long time to get out of the car. The pools of blood had been sluiced away and the drive was flooded with vaguely rust-coloured water. When I walked into the kitchen I could hear

James and the Giant Peach on the video in the other room. Martin was next to the stove pushing fish fingers around a pan in a petulant sort of way. I stood, bandaged and snivelling, waiting for what he had to say, like a dog knowing it's about to be kicked. He managed to look like a large blond storm cloud even with the indestructible Cinzano plastic apron covering his nice London clothes.

If ever there is nuclear war I will survive it under that apron. My mother gave it to me when I left home, it was trendy and acceptable she thought, because it featured alcohol. It has clung to us like an unwanted friend who has halitosis, bad teeth and unacceptable political opinions. It has been used to carry logs, patch ground sheet leaks and, I remembered as I looked at Martin in his Liberty blue shirt and cream Armani trousers, as fancy dress: he wore it and nothing else to a party in 1979. Hard to imagine that the semi-naked youth who danced to the Village People's 'YMCA' with all the actions, was the same as this Martin, looking at me as if I were a patch of cat sick on an Afghan carpet.

'Go and change your jeans. They're covered in blood.' I never knew Martin could get so much ice into his voice.

I didn't say anything. What can you say when aliens steal your husband?

There's a gap in today after that. I know we fed the kids. Sat down at the table with them even, whilst they ate. I know Martin got them bathed and into bed. I know that when they fell asleep, grateful to escape the waking world, he left. Carried two bags out through the kitchen door in silence. I know I walked with him. Held his hand through the window of the car and felt it slip from my grasp as he pulled away.

But I think all those things might have happened to someone else. You never know your luck do you?

'Fucking hell' is the next thing I remember. 'Fuckin', fuckin' fuckin' HELL!'

'Look at the bloody state of 'er!' Gerry's a Braintree boy, he doesn't mince his words.

'Get 'er feet Kath.'

'Nos'rightcanwalk.' I got up from the drive and, dangling between Kath and Gerry, got to the garden bench by the back door and slumped. The garden was wobbling gently in front of me, like a blurry jelly. Quite pleasant really. It was still warm, an hour of daylight left. Gerry paced the patio like a boxer before a fight. Kath sat down beside me and held my hand. I burst into tears.

'Fuckin' fuckin' hell,' said Gerry, and gave me a wodge of tissues from his pocket.

'We saw him drive off,' said Kath

'Yeah. Sarah told us he was off at eight-ish. So we waited up the lane until 'is car went past. Didn't trust meself to come before. I'd've fuckin' popped 'im one.' Gerry kicked the door frame for emphasis. There was a moment's pause as he winced. He'd forgotten he was wearing sandals. Then slowly and sedately the opposite side of the frame fell on to the paving.

'Oh fuck!'

'Well done Gerry you big dipstick,' said Kath.

There was something cheerfully anarchic about the door frame dismembering itself – a kind of 'to-hell-with-it-all'. I stopped crying.

'Kath, I need to get very drunk. I think I'd like us all to get very drunk.' Just get plastered before the next wave of crying, I thought. Like a good whack of gas and air before the next contraction.

'I'll get the booze. You two can forage . . . there's about twenty million French sticks in the freezer.'

'Sarah's bringing a casserole round.'

'Good,' I said, 'we'll have a wake.'

Suddenly we were all infected with the spirit of the broken door frame: 'Aah, fuck it.'

I went to the dark little cupboard where Martin's wine rack is. It's Martin's wine rack because Martin cares about wine. I just shove it down without it touching the sides too much. 'You can drink anything from the top two rows,' he used to say, 'but please don't touch the stuff on the bottom.' The stuff on the bottom is Interesting. Carefully Chosen. Some of it even Laid Down. I've never felt anything but affectionate indulgence for Martin's bit of wine buffery, his last innocent pleasure when everything else had been sacrificed to Success. But standing in that cupboard this evening I felt fury, how dare he tell me what I can drink or not drink in my own house? I felt vindictive. I felt like a bottle of something very Interesting and extremely Carefully Chosen. Something Laid Down for a Special Occasion. And God knows today was a special occasion. I pulled out three bottles of white and three of red from the very bottom row of the rack. They were all dusty and all French. He'd been saving them, poor lamb.

Sarah and Alex arrived with a casserole dish that could have concealed Ali Baba and all his mates, full of a chilli that snarled at you from underneath the lid. The sort of chilli that bites at least twice. We lit every candle we could find and ate the chilli like fondue with the casserole in the middle of the table and us spearing its contents with one or two of my million French sticks. No plates any more. I say we. I didn't eat. I couldn't, which was a shock because nothing, nothing puts me off my food. I'm the only person who can gain weight with a dose of gastroenteritis because I eat to comfort myself for feeling so lousy. I'd get fat on cholera. But I did drink and cry and talk. Told them all about Personal Growth and Dolores's hair and birth certificate, about the kids' faces, about Martin's perfect chest hair, and how Damian could have won his bet if he'd ever made one, and about Queen's *Greatest Hits* and the strawberry bubble bath. I think I probably lost some of my audience about then. So I drank a bit more. We all drank. We drank all of Martin's bottom rows and quite a few of his middle ones too.

Gerry, who was Martin's partner in wine buffery, looked at the bottles lined up around the kitchen. 'I do feel bad about it y' know. I mean just look at that lot! I was wiv 'im when 'e bought that Chablis. 'An' 'e's 'ad that Rioja set aside since a year last Christmas. For 'is fortieth 'e said. I jus' feel. Y' know. Bad.'

'Shut up Gerry,' said Kath

'Yes Gerry, you're not sympathising with the bastard are you?' Sarah isn't liberal in her personal life. She's a side-taker. Also, her first husband ran off to Rio with one of his second-year students. So she knows about long hair and birth certificates. From the moment I was on her doorstep bleeding, she was ready to put Martin's wedding tackle in a blender.

'Well, 'snot sympathy exactly. I jus' . . . Oh I dunno.'

'It's just what?' Kath is very disturbed about Martin. They're similar. High-flyers. Copers. Organisers. Not, she thought, deserters.

'Well. E's jus' done what every bloke wants en 'e?' Gerry's accent begins to need translation after about a bottle and half. "E's 'ad the 'appy families bit righ'? An' nah 'e's shagging some bint wiv legs who's half 'is age.'

'No, actually Gerry,' Alex's Beeb English gets more cut-glass with drink just as Gerry's gets blurred, 'shagging some bint half his age, as you so tactfully put it, is not what every bloke wants.' Well at least not what Alex wants. Sarah is second-time round for him too. His first wife did a runner with a long-distance lorry driver.

I lifted my head off the table to contribute to the debate.

'She's not half his age. She's twenty-nine. Old enough to bloodyknowbetter.' I put my head down again. And then the phone rang.

It was Martin. I took the cordless phone outside into the dark to concentrate on his voice. I was sober, instantly.

'I think we've both been rather emotional over the last two days,' said my husband the Space Alien. The Aliens clearly get their model for human speech from Home Service Newscasters, circa 1954. Yeah, bit emotional Mart, gets like that after loving someone for nearly two decades.

'Yes,' I said. 'Can you hold on for a moment please?' Now my voice seemed to be courtesy of BT's speaking clock. All very weird. I held the phone from my ear for a moment, so as to be able to breathe. 'Okay go on.'

'I just wanted to make my position quite clear. I'm not thinking of this situation as temporary. Even if I finished with Dolores tomorrow, I'm never coming back to you.'

'Just a moment.' Breathing really was impossible with his voice in my ear. I held the phone away again and breathed deliberately, thinking quite hard about how to do it.

Finished with. What a funny phrase to use. I hadn't heard that since school. 'I finished with Kevin last night. I told him when we was down the rec.' 'Oh have you heard? Gary's gonna finish with Penny today. At afternoon break.' Finishing with someone was what you did at fourteen.

'So you think it won't last with Dolores then?'

'That's. Not. The. Point. I feel it will last. But even if it doesn't, I'm not coming back. I've never felt really comfortable with you. I feel that you've . . .'

Had to breathe then. I couldn't tell him to wait again. He was already getting very peevish about it, I could tell. After a few gasps I put the phone back to my ear . . .

'. . . and no sense of yourself. You've lost your spirit of adventure.'

'Well it's hard to have adventures in school hours. Simply can't get back from the Arctic by 3.30.'

'This is just what I didn't want. This kind of exchange.'

'Well I can't say the husband I love running off to a Nookie Nest in Westminster is what I wanted either.' I was losing the BT overtone and sounding horribly like a Monty Python housewife. I did some more breathing. I was surprised to hear him still on the line when I stopped.

'Jess . . . are you still there?'

'Depends where you mean. Martin. Why are you doing this?'

'Because of you.' And then he hung up.

I'd been standing and now I was lying down, looking up at the sky with the phone still gripped in my hand. It was a perfect blue velvet night and it smelled of summer. Martin had succeeded. He had made his position clear not so much by what he had said but how he had said it, his voice some kind of high-tech alloy of industrial diamonds and that kind of very dense ice you get from the bottom of glaciers. This must have been what Franklin felt like when he realised that he'd found a direct route to Baffin Island, not the back way to Hong Kong. What migrating animals feel like when what they thought was the Pole Star turns out to be the Southern Cross. I'd had the map of my life upside down, back to front and inside out.

I had that sound of air rushing past my ears again as the best twenty years of my life sailed through the night air over the hedge, and Mrs E's veg patch, and sank to the bottom of her slurry pit.

'Oh fuckin' hell! 'Ere, Alex, Kaff, Sarah . . . come out 'ere give a 'and. She's done it again.'

That wasn't so long ago now. A few hours perhaps? The chaps went home to relieve the babysitters, but Sarah and Kath are still here. Kath is in bed beside me and Sarah is on the floor. Kath is snoring in a very genteel ladylike sort of way but I don't think Sarah is even breathing. Sarah's life forces are a bit tentative at the best of times, after the amount of booze we've all had tonight I think they must be well nigh extinguished.

This kind of intimacy is rare for a grown-up. You sleep with your mates when you're a kid, giggle yourselves to sleep after hours and hours of talking incessantly about absolutely nothing. Then when you're a grown-up you sleep with your husband, very little giggling or talking to be had there for most people. We three have slept together once before. Last summer on a weekend camping trip. All girls and children. Kids piled into one tent, talking and giggling, mothers in another doing the same. We lay awake and talked in the dark with owls hooting outside.

'This'll be what it's like when our husbands are dead and we're in a home,' Kath said.

'We can lie in our little beds with a tube in every orifice. Food in one end and out the other and you won't even have to move,' I said.

'Oh God, what a relief, no more sex, just blanket baths.' Sarah was genuinely wistful.

I must be odd, I thought. I plan to use my zimmer frame as a sex aid. I don't want to outlive fucking my husband.

I think they were frightened to leave me alone tonight. But I wouldn't kill myself with the kids in the house. It's one thing to have a dead mummy, but to find mummy dead is something you don't get over with a bit of therapy and some homeopathic remedies.

It's my second night without sleep. I feel strange, as if I've been transferred to a new body that I'm not familiar with, that does things that my body doesn't do. I never sweat: this body is bathed in the stuff. My heart only picks up speed if I've been running for twenty minutes: this heart beats like a demented voodoo drum. And there's something wrong with this body's muscle control because it trembles constantly.

I can't sleep, and I can't operate this body I seem to be in to do much else, so I've got no option but to sit here and think. Remembering. And by some cruel trick of memory the very close and the very distant are right next to each other. Or perhaps the last two decades or so really are in Mrs E's slurry pit and lost to me forever. Somehow all the years in between the now and the very-then have been wiped clean, so that firsts and lasts for Martin and me are lined up in a parade of compare and contrast. First kiss, last kiss. First meal, last meal. First date, last date. First sight, last sight.

Just forty-eight hours ago we were in this bed together. Like we always were. We got undressed. Laughed. Joked. He even said he loved me. What happened? Where did it go?

UFO. It's the only rational explanation.

Chapter Three

The house is full of flowers and I spend all my time on the phone. I perform all tasks — pinning out washing, cooking for the kids — with a cordless phone scrunched on to my right shoulder up to my ear. I'm getting curvature of the spine.

If we hadn't moved from town all the people who I phone and who phone me would be here in the house demanding food and explanations, and given that my ability to put together a meal is currently stretched to the limits by fish fingers and peas, that could be tricky. There are simply too many thoughts required in a correct sequence to make proper meals. Getting something out of a packet and putting on the stove is very nearly too complicated. Yesterday I got a packet of peas out of the freezer and then forgot about them until this morning, when I found them in the airing cupboard. I've no idea how they got there. And there'd be no flowers. You usually only get flowers instead, not as well as a person. So curvature of the spine is a fair swap.

I don't know what else I've done for the last five days except be on the phone, telling and retelling the same story of Martin and Dolores to relatives, friends, work colleagues. Where they met, how long it was before they fell in love, how he tried so hard to give her up and couldn't, how he left us for her. I can almost do it on automatic pilot — I can say the words without feeling it's too much to cope with. I tell it like a love story, the greatest love story of the late-twentieth century. It'd better bloody be, if me and the kids are going through this amount of pain, it had better be worth it for someone.

It's not just the telling of the story of course. There's Comment and Analysis. Comment from whoever it is I've rung up to tell the glad tidings, or whoever has rung me. Analysis from me, either in conversation with someone or endlessly, endlessly inside my own head. The analysis isn't up to much if I try and look at it clinically. It mostly consists of me telling myself in one form or another that this can't happen and that he will come back. Or rather that this isn't happening and in a minute it will stop and I'll be able to stop feeling like this, crying all the time and putting frozen peas in with the pillow cases.

I look at why it's happened. And mostly I think it's my fault, I'm on a never-ending escalator in my head passing by posters with adverts for what I've done wrong. If I'd gone on wearing interesting underwear and been less grumpy about his work, if I'd asked him before painting the kitchen green, if I'd never got a dog, if I'd never flirted with his friends, if I'd never said anything mean about his relatives. If I'd never had that one night stand at the end of series party. I know it looks like it's his fault, that he's done that thing that every other man seems to do as they get to forty. But that's because only I know all my sins.

But maybe I feel that just because I've spent all my adult life believing that he was right and I was always somehow wrong. Wrong inside. Bonkers. Irrational. Emotional and demanding. He told me once 'Jess you require unreasonable amounts of love.' Maybe I do. Like a difficult plant, an orchid or something. He's gone for something that thrives on neglect, blossoms if you fail to water it, produces new leaves in the poorest soil.

There's constant noise in my head. All that debate going on the whole time but it's still a relief to get some sort of comment from someone else. Comment straight from the heart down a phone line.

My, our, old friend Flic was the first. She rang just after the weekend. The first day I had alone. Two days ago now.

'Whaddya mean he's run off with the true love of his life? I'm still here!'

She was Martin's assistant for a year or so. They flirted all the time. I thought they might be bonking. Certainly had the opportunity: two shoots in Moscow.

'Who is she? What does she look like? How old is she?' Flic was indignant.

'Thank you for asking after me Flic. I'm very well considering the circumstances. I haven't cried for ninety minutes.'

Yeah. They must have bonked. I knew Dolores wasn't the first.

'Jess don't be pissy. I can hear from your voice how bad you are.'

Well, Flic only fancied him, she didn't want him. 'Cute but dumb' was her nickname for him.

'Okay. In order. Dolores: TV researcher. According to Martin's lengthy description she's a sort of Katharine Hepburn/Claudia Schiffer crossbreed.'

'That was nice of him, to tell you just how beautiful she is. 'Spect he told you how long her legs were.'

'Only to the nearest inch. 31 inch Levis. Size 8.'

'Age?'

'Do I have to?'

I didn't want to tell Flic this. Somehow I feel more responsible for my age than for anything else. As if it's my fault that I'm thirty-nine and past it.

'Twenty fucking nine.'

'Okay so now I know what to say. Dick 'ed. Said it before. Still true. Dick head.'

Whatever the conclusions of my ongoing analyses, it's nice to get pronouncements like that. They make it all so simple. Wrong; here. Right; here. With a nice clean line down the middle. Though why the rights and wrongs bother me I don't know. Why should it make it hurt less if Martin is Wrong? Objectively judged to be Wrong by a jury of his peers and hitherto best mates. However right I am and wrong he is in anyone's eyes makes no difference. He's still got his hand on the inside of Dolores's lovely thigh, not my claggy old badly stuffed cushion of a leg.

Not that my thighs are like badly stuffed cushions, it's just that I feel they are in comparison with what I imagine Dolores's to be like. I don't know if her reported beauty makes it better or worse. I mean, what would I feel like if he'd run off with some old boiler even uglier than me? I always felt particularly sorry for poor old Di in that way. I mean you spend half your fucking life at the gym and the hairdressers and having your bum high-pressure hosed on the inside, so that you look better than you did at twenty, and the stupid bastard goes and shags something that looks like a pony-nut sack.

Chris is another person whose feelings about Martin and Dolores's affair of the year might be mixed. Chris would dearly like to get his hands down my knickers. Anywhere near my undies would do for starters. Even a fingertip up a jersey sleeve would keep him happy for quite a while. I'm not belittling it. It's just that I find it almost incomprehensible that anyone could fancy me that much. Well, at all at the moment. Now I think that Martin only did because I fancied him, and because he was kind of fond of how I made him laugh, and because I was always pretty keen on bonking. But I'm grateful for Chris's lust even if it isn't exclusive to me. Chris just wants to get laid. If things go on like this I may be very glad of that in six months' time.

He rang yesterday afternoon, whilst I was in the middle of putting the tent up in the garden for the kids. I'd walked round the outside of the tent four times before I remembered that the next thing to do was put the pegs in.

He was incredulous. But not terribly helpful. 'How does he do it? He's got two women in love with him and I can't get one past first post. Jesus. It's just not fair.'

Chris is attractive, dark, strong in a wiry sort of way. Bit of a short arse but that never stopped Tom Cruise did it?

'What's the matter with the man? God knows you'd be more than enough for most people.' I wasn't quite sure how to take that remark. 'Jess this is terrible. Do you know the last time I made love? Three years ago. I have not been fucked in my forties. And there he is with two women. Two women.'

Chris only has one fatal flaw (apart from patches of complete self-obsession); he's camp. Hot-blooded hetero though he is, he comes over as a raving bum bandit luvvy.

'Jess, my dear girl. You are going to have to be so so strong.'

I've never been able to bring myself to tell him and he just doesn't realise. People are forever telling him that they always 'assumed he was gay', and he's forever saying how incompre-hensible he finds it.

'I'm so angry with him. I don't think I'm going to be able to be civil if I see him in London.'

And I'm forever saying that I don't know how anyone could imagine he was licking the wrong side of the stamp. So what with that and his wanting access to my panties I feel kind of responsible for Chris.

'I can't bear to think about those two sweet babies of yours. How could he leave them just for a bed warmer?'

It doesn't help that he's a fashion photographer, 'shirt-lifters to a man' or so Martin claims.

Of course the assumption everybody makes, that I tell the Love Story to, is that it's all about sex. That Martin, as Sarah so sweetly put it, is keeping his brains in the end of his willy. And maybe it is all about sex, but not in the way they assume. They say things like:

'I mean your sex life can't go on being wonderful after fifteen years can it?'
and

'He'll get fed up with just sex. He'll want to come home for a good dinner.'

and

'Wonderful sex isn't everything in a relationship.'

All said to make me feel better. And what they all imply is that all that the nearest Martin and I ever got to a simultaneous orgasm was sipping cocoa at the same speed. And what I can't tell most of them is exactly how far from the truth that is.

Was.

From the time Martin won his theoretical bet with Damian, sex was how we worked our relationship. We bonked our way through everything. Career crises, financial disasters, grief, joy, loss, fear, sunburn, toothache and morning sickness. We fucked in my parents' bathroom the afternoon my mother died; we fucked in the hospital the night before Dan was born; there isn't a flat surface in this house that we haven't fucked on, against or under. I see us everywhere I look, like a continual pornographic hologram.

After nearly twenty years of practice at anything you get good and we were brilliant at sex. We could do it anywhere, any time, at any speed or volume. Left alone together for any period longer than fifteen minutes it was generally what we did. I thought of sex with Martin as my hobby.

So when Sarah said on the phone this morning, 'The sex will get boring for him eventually. Just like it does in a marriage.'

'But sex wasn't boring in our marriage. He didn't leave because of sex.'

'Well no, not boring, but you know you don't swing from the chandeliers with your knickers off when you're forty do you?'

'Look Sarah. Can I tell you something? You know your bonfire party when we all leant against your wall in the dark watching next door's fireworks?'

'Ye-es.'

'And Martin had his coat round me?'

'Yes.'

'Well. Just imagine what you can do inside a big coat like that.'

'But I was standing next to you.'

34

'And remember at our drinks party at Christmas when Martin went out to fetch logs? He didn't get further than the kitchen. He put me up against the pantry door and shagged me stupid. That's how the French bread got burned. And whilst you and Alex were having tea at that yellow book garden last summer I was in the middle of their ornamental artichokes giving Martin the blow job of a lifetime. And on the ferry to Cherbourg at half term I'd come twice before we were even out of Poole Harbour. So don't tell me that Martin has left me for more exciting sex. Better legs. Longer hair. Firmer tits. Appearances. Image. Okay?'

I feel bad that I hung up on her. She was trying to make it better. But it isn't better. Can't be better. Because she's right. It is about sex. Sex as a shorthand for life, which is what it's always been for Martin. But I'm right too because it isn't the mechanics of what he does with Dolores that have made him leave. It's what fucking her symbolises: youth and freedom. City Lights and the Future. Fucking me symbolises the Past, all the long history of our time together: the antithesis of glamour, caring for kids who are throwing up at two a.m., eating toast in your jim-jams in front of the telly, drying socks on the radiator. Dolores's body isn't a map of a relationship. Mine is like an Aboriginal landscape, every ravine, outcrop or plain has its story: my ridiculously small hands, pudgy, calloused with gardening, that Martin has always found funny. 'Little girl's hands. Tomboy's hands,' he used to say; the flobby bit of skin under my ribs that never recovered from first Dan's then Frankie's feet pushing and stretching in impatience to be born.

Dolores's body bears no marks, perfect and smooth as a blank page.

But the most important part of Dolores is that she isn't me. She isn't inextricably tangled with children's lunch boxes, flower borders and demented chickens.

When I'm not on the phone talking about Martin and Dolores and how awful it all is, I'm in a kind of dream. I know I do things like boil kettles and make beds, but I'm not really there when I do them.

I'm not at all clear what the kids are doing either most of the time. It's been half term and sunny. I put the tent up on the bottom lawn next to the chooks and that's where they are with sundry visiting friends whose parents come and drop them off . . . too embarrassed to look me in the eye. They're busy escaping from it all: making dens, fetching endless supplies of KitKats and Penguins and all sorts of stuff they wouldn't normally be allowed to take out into the garden. There are no cushions left on any of the sofas and the airing cupboard is emptied of blankets and pillows.

I looked into the tent today and it's like a sort of mini opium den, layer upon layer of breast-like softness into which they can burrow. They spend all day in there roasting with the tent door zipped shut and Dog outside barking herself to distraction.

I see them when I do serious crying. I cry a lot. Most of the time it's just something that I do whilst I'm doing other things, as if my eyes are kind of passively leaky. But a couple of times a day crying becomes an all-absorbing activity. The sort of thing that I can't even be on the phone for. The kids seem to have a sixth sense for these times. They run from their canvas and upholstery womb and plaster themselves around me as if they are quite literally holding me together. They don't cry themselves, they're too intent. They hug me to ensure their own survival, to make sure that someone will still be there to tuck them in and make spaghetti bolognese just the way they like it. So their hugging is concentrated and purposeful. They will me to be Okay.

They haven't done much of their own crying yet. They still have that shell-shocked look about them. I've seen it at bedtime, on the couple of nights when they haven't been sleeping in the tent with a pile of biscuits and a few friends. Frankie won't even let me say the word 'Daddy' or 'Martin', without diving under her duvet and singing Boyzone songs at the top of her voice to blot out the sound. Dan is, as the Californians say, 'in denial'. Along with his mother I suppose. He's determined that Martin is coming back. He keeps saying that Martin still loves me. That this is all just temporary. My son's whispering husky voice at my ear telling me just what I long to believe acquires the status of some mystical prediction. I come away from his room feeling that I must leave the kitchen light on when I go to bed just in case Martin comes home in the middle of the night.

But of course if he came home in the middle of the night now, I'd be awake anyway, because sleep is one of those things I used to do. It's entered the realms of the past historic, the tense that I never understood in French lessons. In less than a week, sleep along with everything else of Martin's life with me has moved into the past historic. I say things like 'We used to have people to dinner on Saturdays.' 'I used to see Martin off from the station.' I'm beginning to sound like a 1950s French grammar. The implication of the 'I used to do X . . .' construction is that it's something that happened for a while but now will never happen again. As in 'I used to have a husband . . .' or 'I used to have sex . . .'

If sleep stays in the *passé simple*, Martin will have to come back to get the children because I'll be seeing little pink elephants flying round the light fitments and being spoken to by the toaster.

I'm already feeling odd all the time and I used to be such a talented sleeper. Put me in a dark place and off I'd go. Used to drive Martin potty in cinemas. I've barely seen the last reel of anything.

Losing the knack for sleeping changes everything. There's nothing to divide one day from another. Nothing to make anything simply stop for a while.

I do have a very clean house and an almost weed-free garden though, because there's so much time if you don't sleep. At midnight my mind is still racing around like a rabbit on caffeine. I clean the tops of door frames, and take books off shelves to dust behind them. This house has never known true hygiene before and all the furniture and the windows are looking a little surprised. Another week of this and Christian Barnard could be doing transplants on my lino.

But the habits associated with sleeping and going to bed die hard. About one-ish I feel I could do with a bit of a lie down. I get undressed, slowly and deliberately folding everything. I put on what I refer to as my pyjamas, but what is really a selection of hugely baggy T-shirts, and leggings washed so many times that the Lycra has gone to meet its maker. This delightfully sexy nightwear is probably one of the reasons that Martin left. He always claimed to have no liking for lacy feminine concoctions with the warmth-giving properties of a strip of Sellotape on a husky's bum. But I bet he's developed one now. I mean you don't have a name like Dolores without having at least three lace teddies to sleep in. And one or two basques I'll warrant.

Anyway. I brush my teeth. I get into bed. And I lie there fantasising about boils growing on Dolores's bottom; about fungal growths on her thighs; about genital warts, herpes and halitosis. I visit upon her a selection of the embarrassing, the uncomfortable, and the socially unacceptable. Spectacular flatulence is a good one, piles is great and alopecia is delightful. I don't imagine her with anything life-threatening. If she's going to die I want to be the one to do it with a trusty piece of good cold steel.

Sometimes this is soothing enough to let me sleep. But never for long because in my dreams Martin is starring in a Quentin Tarantino movie: wearing a black suit and setting about me with a medium-sized filleting knife. I wake up wet, soaked in anxious sweat as if someone had cunningly tipped a bucket of water over me.

Then I have a few moments in intimate contact with the reality of Martin's departure. For a few long excruciating seconds I feel with every cell that he has gone, my skin crawls with horror as if something from a Stephen King novel had laid down on top of me.

So I get up. But I don't have the necessary coordination for cleaning door frames at three or four a.m. All I can do is pace. I walk up and down the kitchen, round and round the table, holding my ribs with my arms and surprising myself with the strange little noises that I make.

And then it's six a.m. Only an hour before I can ring someone and talk about it all again and again.

Chapter Four

Grief is like a parallel universe where almost anything is possible. Gravity could take Tuesday off, estuarial worms could speak Mandarin Chinese, I could fall into the arms of a fox-hunting Tory. And as one of these things has actually happened today, I'm prepared to believe in a six-day week for Newton's Theories and intelligent life under a worm-cast.

When I say fall into the arms of I don't mean anything remotely romantic. I mean really 'cry on'. Which is what I did in the middle of the lane coming home from school this morning. I cried all over a Tory quite uninhibitedly.

I used to love that little tootle back home from school . . . Sisyphus's skip down the hill done on wheels to very loud and tasteless rock music. But nowadays it's a slower affair. A mere postponement of the moment when I walk back into the house to be reminded of Martin by every object I lay eyes on.

So when my neighbours' Range Rover pulled up alongside and rolled down its window I was grateful.

Not really my neighbours'. My neighbour is Mrs E. But the only people she ever talks to have four legs and udders, so she's not much use. So my nearest functional neighbours are three fields away. James and Mary. They live in a whacking great pile of a house that's been in James's family since before underwear was invented. It probably started as an up-market mud hut and it's been added to by every generation since, in a relaxed eccentric sort of way. James and Mary live in the middle section of it, with old paintings of things that their families have owned . . . country estates, ships, prize Hereford bulls . . . and archaeological layers of Persian rugs. At either end of the house they store things, Chippendale dressers and badly stuffed fox heads and James's fabulously ancient dad with all his various shotguns that have been with him since birth.

James is a barrister and Mary is a fanatical gardener. They have grown-up children who do worthy things for the Empire in Foreign Parts. I've never seen Mary in anything but calf-length tweed skirts and Sensible Shoes. She wears Puffa jackets in the winter and Lady Di shirts in the summer. At weekends, James wears green moleskin trousers and huge Aran sweaters which Mary knits for him. The Hunt meets in their courtyard four times a season.

We go, sorry we went, to their drinks party every Christmas, but I see Mary out walking the dogs, in the lanes and fields, and we smile and swap any recent news headlines in our lives,

Me: 'Martin is in Russia/America/Israel/France for two/ three/five weeks.'

Mary: 'Pip/Roger/Bruno [dogs] has had fits/ canker/ bad paw.'

Then we make a couple of feeble and overly enthusiastic jokes about the weather and part awkwardly until the next time.

I mean, they read the *Telegraph*, and only know the word Gay in the context of Gordons. I could never really see them as kindred spirits.

But that was in the Old Universe. This morning was in the New.

'Long time no see,' said Mary as the electric window zizzed open. Heartily jolly as always. She must have been a head girl. Or hockey captain. I never even managed to make milk monitor at primary school.

'How's that absentee husband of yours?'

There's no good way to answer this. No point in trying any kind of softening preamble. The most I can manage in these situations is a blurt. With or without tears. This morning it was with.

'Very absent. He's left me Mary.'

'The bloody fool!' This was said with such shocking force that I gasped, as if I'd been slapped. 'Pull over into that gateway,' she ordered me in the voice she used to terrorise her Jack Russells. I've seen them hop to with tails held determinedly between their legs when she uses that voice, so I knew it was a good idea to be submissive. I pulled over and before I'd switched off the engine she'd opened the car door and virtually lifted me out of my seat.

'What a stupid stupid man to leave you and those lovely children.'

I never imagined I would be so close to the intimate workings of Mary's body. Pressed into her arms like that I could feel the boning of her corset under the light lambswool sweater, and smell the pink powdery smell of her scent. Mary is a big upper-class Norman and I'm a titchy troglodyte Celt, so when she hugged me I thought my ribs might crack.

And that's sort of why I burst into tears because I got that feeling of being temporarily safe in the arms of a person much bigger than myself – the kind that you get when you're a little kid. I've spent ten days crying, and talking, and having my arguments listened to by all my good liberal left-wing buddies. They are kind and concerned, but they have their lives and their jobs. Daytimes are lonely. And when I do see my friends, like all members of the British middle classes they are pretty iffy about physical contact. An arm round the shoulder is a big deal for them.

What I really needed was someone to hold me very tight and let me blub. Just like my mum or dad would have done had they been available via any means other than an Ouija board. And of all the people in the known and unknown universe, the person to do it for me turned out to be Mary Walton-Naseby. Née Hornchurch.

Once you've smeared snot and dribbled over somebody's shoulder, little details like political affiliation and vowel sounds really don't matter any more. And there's not much point in trying self-conscious routines about the weather or the state of your dogs' digestion. So when I disengaged myself from Mary's ample and impeccably upholstered bosom we smiled quite unselfconsciously at each other.

'Thank you,' I said.

'That's quite all right my dear. A jolly good cry is absolutely necessary. Now, James and I will pop round this evening. Just for a short while. We won't intrude.'

And then she was back in her Range Rover and off down the road. Another good deed done for the Empire.

So today turned out to be a Better Day. I didn't even go inside the house when I got home post Mary. I decided to avoid looking at the Martin and Jess holograms in every room, and to spend the day outside in the garden that was always really mine. If I were ever famous and asked to do that 'Room of My Own' business in the Sunday paper I'd have my garden. I could tell them as much about every plant I've put in as the pretentious gits they interview tell them about their Etruscan nose-pickers or their kitsch novelty seaside gum dispensers.

I decided to do something to prove that I could manage without Martin. Hah! He could spend his whole life rooting around inside Dolores's lace teddy for all I cared. Mow the lawns I thought. Use that great big symbol of thrusting phallic power, the motor mower.

We, I, have a lot of lawn. I'd like to plant things in, around, and all over it, but you can't when you have kids who want to reenact the 1996 cup final, do Evel Knievel bike stunts, and play Scott of the Antarctic in the Cabouchon two-room family tent.

But in spite of the large lawnage and me being self-appointed Head Gardener, I've always managed to get by without ever having to use the mower before. Martin does the mowing because he's the Man and pushing things is what men do . . . like the only household chore he's ever really up to doing cheerfully is vacuuming.

Martin's absences are either not quite long enough for the lawn to transform into savanna with jungly bits, or happen in winter, when all that mowing would achieve would be to flatten the worm-casts.

So before today I'd never started or driven our mower.

I got it out of the shed with that familiar graunching scraping sound. It was weighty and awkward, but hey I'm an independent girl, I can move heavy objects without a husband. Then I checked the petrol level, successfully remembering which of the little bits the petrol was in.

Then I had to start it.

Hold lever A tightly against bar B.

Okay.

Pump three times on button C.

Ah . . . can't reach button C whilst holding lever A. I lean over bar B . . . the bit you push or hang on to as it goes forward on its own. My fingers are six inches from button C. This machine was designed for someone whose legs and body added up to a lot more than sixty-two inches.

Try it backwards. Thread body under bar B, lean back limbo fashion to button C.

Fall over painfully on to the knobbly bits on top of the engine.

Lateral thinking. Pump button C first.

Yes!

Now hold lever A against bar B. Fine.

Next step. Pull smartly on chord D to start the engine. Release lever A and depress lever E. Move forward.

Pull . . . smartly . . . on . . . chord . . . D.

It has to be faster and smarter than that: PullSmartlyOnCh-ordD . . . PSOCD.

All I can do is pull . . . smartly . . . on . . . I don't even get to the end of the chord because my arms aren't long enough.

More lateral thinking. I can't PSOCD because I'm not strong enough and the chord is too high for me to pull my weight against it.

So if I can make myself higher . . .

I stand on a bucket, holding chord D and throw myself backwards.

The bucket tips and my other hand comes off lever A.

I tie lever A to bar B with string.

Climb back on to the bucket and throw myself violently backwards into air, whilst clutching chord D.

I hit the ground with some force, but I have started the engine.

Get up. Untie lever A, depress lever E.

Yesss.

Off I go. Woman and machine in harmony. Up and down making those nice stripes you see on cricket pitches.

Then the grass box is full.

If I stop and remove the full box I'll have to do the standing on the bucket routine all over again. Next time I could break some ribs.

I tie lever A again using the one-handed knot technique I developed earlier.

Tentatively remove the grass box getting very close to the still flailing blades, and have a brief fantasy about Martin finding my bloodied and mangled corpse amongst the grass clippings. (If only I hadn't left she would never have tried to do the mowing alone. Woe is me.) I tip the mound of warm green clippings into the chooks pen, instantly rendering six other living beings orgasmically happy.

Replace the grass box. Untie the lever and start another stripe.

I could write a little booklet for the RHS: Mower Starting for The Smaller Woman. Mowing for Midgets.

I have broken the Ancient Taboo of Mowers, that they shall only be operated by person of the male sex. All through my childhood my dad went out To Mow The Lawn as if it were some moral imperative, some duty to appease God and save us from the damnation of sloth and idleness. Nothing could be allowed to hinder him from his labours, or from his uninterrupted rest in front of the snooker afterwards.

Now walking up and down in the pleasantly soporific noise and mildly narcotic fumes I realise what a glorious little piece of escapism he had afforded himself by laying a third of an acre to grass, and vowing to keep it up to the standard of the wicket at the Oval. Mowing is really very pleasant indeed. No one can talk to you because of the noise and no one could expect you to do anything else whilst you're mowing. No wonder Martin was so keen.

By midday my mowing is done. My garden looks gorgeous, my fingers are at last truly green and I haven't cried once since Mary enveloped me at twenty past nine.

A very much better day.

Waiting for Dan and Frankie in the playground at the end of their school day used to be one of my great pleasures. Especially now in June, when the house martins swoop over the rooftops of the village below, and the hedgerows are the colour of fresh peas, I'd stand and natter, about the next PTA ceilidh, about BSE and beef prices, about remedies for nits, about frocks and funerals, about recalcitrant relatives, hopeless husbands and witless wives. Sometimes I'd have a real friend to talk to, Sarah or Katherine, Gerry or Alex, but mostly just one of the other familiar but little-known faces. All of it felt like another sweet Sisyphean moment.

Nothing Sisyphean about it now. Crisis and trauma are like a kind of invisible leprosy, people can't bear to come close in case some bit of you drops off scabby and green into their laps. There were no real friends in the playground today, just acquaintances whose eyes slid over me like they did yesterday and the day before, like oil over Teflon.

Their eyes didn't slide off completely. They looked at my back. Searching for flaws and failure. Watching for some obvious defect that will explain away the fact that Martin has left me.

'You know I never noticed it before, but she's got one shoulder lower than the other. Now what man would put up with that?'

'Of course you can just tell by lookin' at 'er that she can't cook. He's never had a decent meal in fifteen years of marriage. Think of that!'

'I went to her house once and the kitchen floor was filthy. Men don't like a slut you know.'

'I heard she was sleeping with her builder. She'd go with anyone. You only got to look at her to see it.'

Because if they can't see some mistake in me then the same thing might happen to them. One day they might just wake up and find the warm patch beside them in the bed gone cold and empty.

I'll wait in the car tomorrow.

At last. The kids roared out festooned in a chaos of bags and half-done paintings. Dan and Frankie are always last. Always have been. But today they weren't. They have been falling into the arms of Tories too it seems. They came out deep in conversation with another brother and sister pair, Andrew and Angela Riley.

'Mum can Angela come to tea?'

'Mum can Andrew come over and play football?'

'If that's okay with their mum, yeah.' I tried not to sound or look too gobsmacked. I need to save embarassing my children until their adolescence. It would not have been a good time to say 'The Riley kids? Are you serious? You hate them. Professionally. Angela tied your hair to the fence Frankie when you first started here. And Dan, don't you remember what Andrew said about Man U?'

Then the penny dropped. This new-found friendship is a part of the Alternative Universe. Mrs Riley, Jo, is another desertee. But her husband only ran as far as the other end of the village where he is living with a twenty-year-old riding teacher called Melanie. Nobody talked about anything else here for six months last year. Jo went from a handsome curvy thirty-something to a wraith-like ninety-year-old in a month, and the kids started looking like hunted deer. Yeah it was fine for them to come over, I knew without asking.

And I knew where to go to find Jo. Waiting in her car outside school. Founder member of the leper colony.

Frankie and Angela played Suicide Barbies when they got home, making the dolls have a gruesome variety of horrific mutilating accidents, falling from moving bicycles, out of upstairs windows, drowning in the pond. The girls were obviously having such a good time that Dan and Andrew muscled in too. Soon they were happily creating scenes of tragedy and carnage that would have given Attila a lump in the throat. Frankie and Angela made the accident happen and did the sound effects for the injured and expiring Barbies, whilst Andrew and Dan were the news crew covering the events.

If they hadn't invented this game weeks ago when we were still doing happy families, I'd be seriously worried that this was some twisted expression of shock and trauma.

But they didn't stick at it. The next time I glanced out at them to check that they were all still alive even if their Barbies weren't, they were looking like a grown-ups' counselling session, sitting on the grass under the apple tree. They were listening to each other without anyone rolling around with the giggles or pushing anyone else over. Each child taking a turn. It took me a moment to cotton on. Then I knew without hearing what they were saying. I could just imagine.

'Did your mummy cry all the time when your daddy left?'

'Oh yes. But she doesn't cry much now. Only at night.'

'Do you think your daddy is going to come back?'

'No. D'you think yours is?'

'Maybe. Yes. Oh I dunno.'

It was chilling. They looked so strange and unchildlike, weighted down somehow. Slowed and stunted to an adult gravity before their time. These four little people trying to survive and make sense of the breaking of their lives. Like goldfish in a tsunami.

It reminded me of those reports you hear of starving children who just don't play any more. And I got really angry for the first time. Angry that they are being exposed to an adult dose of pain and being deformed by it. Like a foetus exposed to some drug in its mother's womb. All this hurt is going to be knitted into the fabric of who they are, like the frozen crystal in Kaye's heart just setting him up ready for the Ice Queen to steal him away.

I got so angry I rang Martin for the first time since he left. I used to ring him every day. Twice some days. Three times. Four.

I didn't ring him at Dolores's. I don't want to know how good she sounds. He told me she has a lovely voice. I rang his mobile, the number must be imprinted into the ends of my fingers. I got his ansaphone, with his brief and businesslike voice.

'Hi! This is Martin Harvey's answer service. If you want to leave me a short message just do it after the beep.'

I've heard it so many thousands of times, that message. For days sometimes it was all I had of him.

Today it sounded just the same. Anyone ringing him wouldn't know that the life behind that voice is so changed. Or maybe it isn't for him. Maybe being in London with Dolores has been his real life for a long time. All he's done is just snip off the little atrophied bit that's me.

'Beep,' said the ansa service.

'I think you should know what sort of state your children are in.'

The 'sort-of-state-where-they-are-sitting-quietly-under-an-apple-tree-with-friends'. Doesn't have much of a dramatic impact does it? Rather than leave a pregnant silence I hung up.

Jo didn't come to fetch her kids. Her mum did. I was glad. I don't want to talk to Jo. I don't even want to have to think about her. I have this awful feeling that in a year, I'm going to look like she does: permanently wary and rather too thin, as if something were taking bites out of her all the time. She looks as though she's got a PhD in weeping. I'm just starting on the O level and I never want to be that highly qualified.

Being friends with Jo would be admitting that we're in the same boat, the little sinking skiff out of which both our husbands have jumped. Permanently. I want to go on believing that this is all going to stop way before I get to being like Jo. I want to go on believing that Martin is coming back. That maybe the next time I drive up to our house he'll be here waiting.

It started raining after Angela and Andrew went home with a kind of determination that made me think it could last for a long time. So Dan and Frankie were driven in to have a conventional tea indoors with a conventional bedtime to follow it. It frightens me how few of the ordinary details of life I seem to notice any more. I cooked them a meal just hours ago and I can't remember what I made. I know I sat down with them at tea time and read them a story whilst they ate. But I don't know what I read. I kept each of them company in turn as they bathed, sitting on the side with my feet in the water. I remember their bodies, smooth and solid, perfect and completely beautiful. But I don't remember what they said, chattering on about their day in school, about Angela and Andrew I expect. But I don't know. I try to think. Try to hold on to it, but it feels like clutching at water.

It fills me with panic because I think I might really be going mad with all the shock.

Sitting on Dan's bed tonight, scrunching his duvet around him and Dinosaury, (his transitional comfort object is a soft toy version of that creature in *Jurassic Park* that spits poison in your eyes and then eats you. I wouldn't have one of those in bed with me), I realised that I couldn't remember tea time, that more than an hour of my day, that had only just finished passing, had gone like water into sand.

I don't want to start believing I'm a coat hanger or that I've just had tea with Beethoven. I don't want to be locked up, away from my kids with Martin gloating over how he always said I was unstable.

So I cried more than I usually do at tucking-in time tonight. And Dan did his stuff about how 'Daddy still loves you' and Frankie said her stuff about 'It's never wrong to cry Mummy'. And in turn they twined their insubstantial arms around my neck and did for me what I should be doing for them.

That's why when Mary and James came round they found me curled up by the stove with a tea towel over my head contemplating my total waste-of-spaceness as a parent to grieving children. I must have looked like Yasser Arafat with a hangover. I hadn't heard them come in, so the first indication I had that Mary had been as good as her word was when Dog started whimpering with delight, something she only does in the presence of men. It's the testosterone. It addles her brain.

James very gently pulled me up from the floor and unwrapped the tea towel.

'Good God,' he said beaming bravely, 'I thought it might be elephant man under there.'

James was still in his rather too tight work suit. Mary must have hustled him out through the door the moment he came in.

'We've brought this,' said Mary plonking a very large bottle of champagne on to the table.

'And we are all going to drink it,' said James ripping off his tie and loosening his collar with an ostentatious and ceremonial struggle. 'Do you have any champagne glasses?'

I didn't say a word. The sight of James and Mary with the fattest bottle of champagne in the world amongst the chaotic debris of my kitchen filled me with a kind of awe. They looked awkward and rather out of place and I saw for the first time that for all the toffs' bravado they were really rather shy, rather sweet. They had stepped into the house of the antichrist, the territory of a labour-voting, hunt-opposing, *Guardian*-reading bloody lefty. It couldn't be comfortable for them but they'd done it out of a real desire to help. I fetched the glasses and blushed internally for all the things I've said about Tories . . . that they eat their own young, keep twenty-pound notes in the bath, and only read Jeffrey Archer and Dickens.

James popped the cork, and standing rather stiffly round the table we drank the first glass straight down.

I decided to be brave too. I mopped up the last of the tears on my tea towel and took a deep breath.

'Have you eaten?' I noticed the slight paling beneath the skin as both Mary and James suppressed a flinch as they visualised the sort of meal that might come from a kitchen like this: jars of pasta, olives and – Good God! – pulses clearly on display; a filthy floor and a table covered with books, from *Asterix in Algeria* to *British Erotic Verse 1966 to 1984*, interleaved with unpaid milk bills and lurid junk mail advertising nose-hair curlers and fluorescent garden flowers.

'No . . . but we wouldn't want to put you to any trouble.'

' 'S no trouble. It could be an adventure. I haven't managed anything more complicated than opening the oven and putting something in it since Martin left, but let's have some more booze and I'm sure it'll be fine. Do sit down and talk to me whilst I cook. I've got bacon in the freezer and there's lots of eggs from the chooks, is that okay?' James and Mary beamed, genuinely and without any associated bravery.

'That would be marvellous.'

'Mmm. Haven't had a fry up for ages. Not allowed them at home these days.' James nudged Mary in a way that could only be described as coquettish. And coquettish is difficult to do when you are six-five and into forty-four-inch chest waistcoats.

'I'll fill us all up.'

I cooked a huge mound of bacon, fried all the chooks' productions for the last three days and piled it in front of them. I explained why they each had a back copy of *Elle* magazine as a plate and they applauded. Mary produced a second bottle of champagne from the Range Rover (they could have a case of it stowed in the back). They asked about Martin. And I told them about the love affair of the late twentieth century. But with a record amount of not crying throughout. And then I heard about them. About James being nearly expelled for running a small brewery concealed amongst the 125 lockers of the Lower School. About Mary rubbing callouses on her thighs whilst riding across Kenya on the back of her boyfriend's motorbike (so she didn't always wear calf-length tweed). How they met, covered in mud after a gale blew down the marquee on a hunt ball and they had to crawl out under the fallen tent poles.

For three hours I had a glorious escape into Planet James and Mary. Kids making nuclear devices in the treehouse, and being sent home from school for putting tarantulas inside the PE mistress's frilly tennis knickers; James's father trying to shoot the milkman after a particularly long session with a Laphroaig bottle; Mary decorating the kitchen with 100 red roses and 150 candles for James's birthday and having to call the fire brigade when it all got out of hand.

Then the phone called me back into my own little ruin of a life. It was Martin. He wasn't the happy bunny you'd expect him to be when you consider how he's living in bliss with the true love of his life. Luckily I was pretty fortified by the second bottle of fizz, so I didn't simply hyperventilate and crumble.

'What the hell do you mean by leaving emotional messages on my ansaphone?'

'Well it's a bit of an emotional situation. And I thought you ought to know that the kids aren't very happy.'

'You're just saying that to make me feel bad.'

'You feel bad? Oh dear. Poor you. Well, stop doing what you're doing and feel good. Leave her. Come home.'

'Don't be ridiculous. I've made this decision and I'm not about to go back on it.'

'Oh! Was that the sound of a stamping foot I heard?'

'Jess, grow up. Listen. Just LISTEN. You can't ring me up and leave me messages. I have a new life separate from you. You can't have access to me any more. Tell the children I'll ring them in the morning. Goodbye.' There it was again. The ancient ice from the bottom of some Alaskan glacier. The fizz-induced bravery couldn't withstand its stabbing. I can't get over how much polar icecap he has got into his voice in just a couple of weeks. Within moments of the dialling tone returning to my ear I was being scraped off the floor by James and Mary. What is the matter with me? Permanent low-level amnesia and fainting fits like a Victorian Virgin. I'm beginning to feel like the rag doll I had for my sixth birthday: she developed a sawdust leak from behind her ear that was resistant to all forms of mending, so the contents of her head and body gradually leached out, soon she was not much doll and mostly rag.

They propped me up in a chair wedged against the table and Mary fed me sweet tea until I could give more than monosyllabic responses. Then James began to ask me 'sensible questions'. About how long Martin had been gone, where he was living, what I was going to do for money.

'I've got the joint account still. I mean he's not a total bastard. He won't leave us destitute.'

'Jess my dear,' said James with the very best of legal bedside manners, 'in my experience under these circumstances men are as reliable and trustworthy as the average puff adder. You must get some sort of legal advice. At the moment there is nothing stopping him running off to Timbuktu, leaving you with nothing but debt and the contents of your fridge. In the longer term, he isn't legally bound to pay for anything beyond the children's maintenance unless you fight for it.'

'But that's assuming that he's not coming back. And he is. He is. He'll miss being a family. I know he will.'

'Jess,' Mary took my hand in her big smooth paw, 'James and I have seen this many times, friends, family, colleagues, people in the hunt and in the village. There are two common courses of events: the first is that the men simply don't come back. The second is that they come back, and they are not wanted.'

'But I'll never stop wanting him. And he will come back. I mean, I'm sure I've heard of people who get divorced even and then get married again. If I give up believing that now I'll die.'

Mary didn't have to say 'Well-just-tell-me-that-again-this-time-next-year', her face did it for her. It must sound like so much melodrama to her. And it is melodrama but what frightens me is that inside me it feels true. I'm not going to kill myself, not in the opening veins into a warm bath sort of way, but I've noticed now that when I'm in the car alone I don't take care. I drive very fast because there's no reason not to. When I pass bridges on the motorway I think 'Just a turn of the wheel and this could all just stop. I could switch off the pain'. And it's a definite temptation. Matter-of-fact, grey and ordinary as a Monday morning. If my heart gives up on Martin comple-tely, like my head has, I'm frightened of what I'll do.

But whatever Mary and James thought, they were very patient. They didn't ask any more practical questions. They waited for me to stop snivelling and then they small-talked me back to life. Dogs, garden, minor village gossip, social events. Mary was in her element, 'Could you get a baby-sitter on Friday night?' she asked.

'I don't need to. It's my first weekend without the children. Martin's coming to pick them up about seven.'

'Marvellous. Then come to Francis Weaton's party, it's his fiftieth, he's invited half of the world.' Francis Weaton eh? I am being admitted to another social circle via Martin's departure. Francis is part of the village old school, but he's not as catholic in his social tastes as Mary and James. Farming families, hunt buddies, business partners, old county professionals are who he mixes with, not liberal in-comers. At least when he's not off spending his inheritance in St Moritz, or Florence or New York. Famously rich and single. Probably a great big frilly girl's blouse, to be still unmarried at fifty.

'There'll be music and dancing, about 150 people I think.' Well as a first solo outing it will at least be interesting. Who knows, maybe there'll be a spare gorgeous millionaire with a passion for herbaceous borders and small women. I really like the idea of being completely pampered, of losing all anxieties to do with my material well-being: not that Martin is a pauper. He earns a lot but with no security. I never plant anything that might take more than two years to flower. Maybe he's been so busy bonking Dolores that he hasn't got any money. Maybe there's nothing in the account and even now the building society are out there waiting to pounce on my flower beds. Yeah, a millionaire would be good.

'Okay. Can I see how I feel?'

'We'll just come and pick you up. Around eight.'

I smiled at James. 'All right. You may have to cope with a few nervous changes of clothes whilst you wait, but come at eight.'

They went home to their dogs after an extremely warm farewell, for British Tories they're amazing. They hug like Mediterraneans.

Now I'm pacing again. But not making any noises or crying. Pacing a little more constructively. Trying to think in a forward direction, in a straight line, not wiggling and branching off into analysis or doubling back into memory.

James is right about practicalities. I've got to start planning. I need a job. I need to earn. At best it'll shock the hell out of Martin when he comes back if I've organised my life, and at worst I'll be ready to support us if he does run off to Timbuktu to take pictures of the Tuaregs with Dolores on the back of a camel.

But the only things on my CV are programmes about counting from one to three and naming two things beginning with 'a'. So getting a job means returning to the realms of monosyllables and soft toys with attitude. However gloomy it makes me feel, it is at least vaguely possible. I have an ex-boss who took over as head of the regional TV station down here and I read in one of Martin's media trade comics that they're doing lots of children's stuff for one of the networks. I'll write and plead. Maybe five years full-time making cakes with Smarties on and hanging grey school socks on the radiators is some sort of qualification.

I'm trying not to think about the coming weekend. I'll see Martin. Then I'll be here alone. I don't feel there are any constraints on what might happen. He could arrive, fall at my feet and plead forgiveness. He could phone from New York on Saturday to tell me he's abducted the children. He could turn up with a gun and shoot me, or I could elope with a gay Tory millionaire. Any of these things seems possible. For the sake of my sanity I must inject a little more structure into the empty shell of the weekend: I'll buy paint and decorate my bedroom. Change it round to be unrecognisable as the place where I made love with Martin, slept beside him, lay awake and listened to him talking in his crazed and driven sleep.

Chapter Five

'I can feel your bones Mummy,' Frankie said this morning in bed. She was curled into my right side and Dan into my left. They fit into me like jigsaw pieces. The only thing that changes as they grow is that their feet reach further. Tucked under my shoulder, Dan's feet are level with mine. Frankie's started chin-side of my ribs and now both their toes skim my calves. They don't grow fast. It's slow, gentle almost. Lets you into the next sort of being a parent easily. Like aging. It's quite kind, just a few wrinkles more each year.

It was raining again. Heavy as a monsoon, making the countryside look disappointed. All those big green fleshy leaves, holding themselves out to the sun, and getting rain. It hasn't stopped since Monday. I'm glad of it. I couldn't bear all that happy indifferent sunshine. This rain feels like sympathy. Or if not sympathy, then at least it's appropriate.

'Yes Mum, I can count your ribs, and the bones in your tummy.'

'Nobody has bones in their tummy.'

'Well you do.'

I'd been asleep. Really asleep for at least five hours. They woke me as they got into bed, so I had company for that moment when it all comes back. They had climbed into bed with me like they used to do every morning when Martin was away, and there was room for them.

I think for them it's still like that, Daddy away on a work trip, like normal. Crossing off the days until he gets back. Once he wrote messages to us all on the calendar. 'Only two weeks to go now.' 'One swimming lesson and three days at school until Daddy is here!!' and 'Yippee Daddy gets home tomorrow.' And it was always 'yippee' too: the house specially tidied. Kids specially cleaned and told to be good. Food specially cooked. Candles specially lit. Underwear specially matching.

Some times of year are 'Martin coming home times' because they've so often been the seasons when he's returned from a long trip: like blossoming chestnuts always used to give me butterflies because it meant exam season, and the smell of burning leaves always meant 'Grandpa' because he devoted the last ten years of his life to bonfires. The horizontally cutting cold of early March makes me think of walking up the lane, listening for Martin's car, wanting him to find me first, before the children. Picking blackberries in the turning weather of mid-September, the weft of bramble leaves waving bronzed undersides in the wind means 'Martin's coming home.' It was like a magic spell to say those words, the salve to all hurts, the solution to all problems.

I loved the rituals of his returning: dirty and tanned, tired and laughing. Coated with a kind of mysterious glamour, smelling more of himself than ever. Watching him unpack his bags with the debris of some exotic place clinging to the clothes: dust from African bush, cigarette smoke from New York bars, hieroglyphic laundry marks from Tokyo. Presents for the children cushioned inside dirty shirts. I loved the canvas holdall with lots of little compartments holding Swiss army knife, and folding cutlery, a miniature towel – everything with an accustomed place and a role to play in his life away from us, where we couldn't sustain him. His little shuttle away from the Mother Starship. Of course as it turns out, it was more of an escape pod, and in one of those little compartments there was probably a regularly restocked supply of condoms.

*

The kids were right about the bones, as I discovered when I came back from school to find something to wear for tonight, the Francis Weaton do. I threw open the doors leading to my fabulous and extensive collection of evening wear hoping, as I always do, that the fairies will have visited its innermost corners and sprinkled magic moondust on the selection of old tat in there. I haven't bought anything new for going out in since we moved here. What's the point? Wear a dress and tights to the places I go and either a dog will leave paw marks down the front or I'll sit on a jam sandwich that some child left on a chair last November, or I'll have to walk through three hundred yards of slurry to get to the front door.

Two bright overshirts, a pair of shiny black leggings, a suit bought for a job interview fifteen years ago, and a tie-dyed velvet top with only a small hole. I tried them all on, and although overshirts are meant to be loose, there's a difference between casual draping and looking as though you're wearing a dust sheet. Even the leggings were too big, with nasty baggy folds round the crotch. The velvet top, bought baggy to hide the multitude of sins perpetrated by time and two pregnancies made me look like a six-year-old in Mum's frock. Whose were these clothes? Had I filled them a fortnight ago? I felt as though I'd shrunk, wizened up like a pea out in the sun.

I stripped them all off and looked at myself in the mirror. Even my underwear was baggy, and yep there were the ribs, and the 'tummy bones' sticking out at each hip. It's not true what Wallace Simpson said about it being impossible to be too thin. It's especially not true when none of your clothes are as thin as you are. I didn't so much mind going to the party looking like a bag lady, but the real highlight of the evening was Martin fetching the kids. That's what I had to dress for. The brief meeting at the back door, that could turn things round in a moment. He'd see me looking stunning, different, strong and in a split second realise his mistake. But not dressed in leggings like track-suit bottoms and a green shirt large enough for me to camp out in for a week.

Whatever the state of the bank balance the only solution was a retail one.

Five and a half hours before picking up the kids, enough time to trawl ten chain stores in town and find the one perfect thing that would restore me to Martin's heart in a single glance.

This could be the most important shopping trip of my life. For once I'd have to do it properly. The mistake I always make when I shop for clothes is I look awful. I'm not going to see anyone, so I don't bother with even a clean pair of jeans. And let's face it, that's as much bother as I do these days. But I do see myself, and after ten minutes of it I'm so depressed that I'd buy anything that fitted approximately just to stop having to confront my image in the mirror.

So today I had to try and like what I saw. I put my favourite jeans on. Luckily clean. And my favourite T-shirt. Both baggy now but okay for that. And some make-up. Really bright lipstick and something to make my skin look like skin rather than dishcloth material. My best black lace-ups, still shiny, and a shiny black belt to pull in the jeans. Tolerable for quite a few viewings.

I was in the car ready to leave when I saw my hands on the wheel. Just the one finger with rings on. Diamond solitaire engagement ring, fine gold wedding ring and the eternity ring that was last Christmas's present; eight tiny blue diamonds scattered in a plain gold band, the most beautiful thing I'd ever owned. I'd looked down at it through finding all the Signs . . . the Queen tape, the strawberry bubble bath, all of it . . . and thought 'No, 's alright, he does still love me'. Now there it was flaunting its beauty against the red roughness of my stumpy little fingers, sneering at me 'Fooled you! Tee hee,' it said.

When you think jewellery is talking to you it's time to take action. I dragged all three rings off my finger and dropped them into the deepest zipped dungeon of my bag. No one was going to buy me gold any more, so I'd buy myself some silver.

When it came to it, I couldn't get the joint account cheque book to cope with buying something as frivolous as a dress. And such a lot of money for something so small, just a couple of metres of blue silk, so insubstantial you could shove it in a handbag and still have room for a first-aid kit, a disposable nappy and a spare pair of tights. The sort of garment that would only do one sort of job, whereas my other clothes are multi-skilled – everything from planting bean seeds to church fêtes and Christmas parties just depending on how clean they are.

I spent half an hour in the changing room turning round and round, taking it on and off, calculating how many pairs of wellies, children's shoes and herbaceous perennials I could buy for the same money.

I imagined Martin tut-tutting as he found it on his bank statement, telling all his friends how I was spending his money out of spite. I left the frock on the counter all wrapped up and ready to go while I ran down the road to the building society to extract some of the last of what I called 'my' money, squirrelled away whilst I was working. I ran back up the road clutching nice starched and ironed tenners, and paid for it in cash. Walking from the shop with the scrap of dress coddled in its nest of tissue paper at the bottom of a very large stiff bag, I felt as if I were carrying some rare secret animal, something that could wake up and grant me three wishes if I was kind to it. Like Jack escaping down the beanstalk with the giant's harp, sleepy and willing to come quietly.

Having got away with buying one thing, buying something else didn't seem so scary. There was a new-age shop on the way back to the car, with a window full of wind chimes, rainbow candles and crystals on leather thongs. And rings. For a tenth of the cost of just one of the little blue diamonds on my eternity ring I kitted out a good selection of my fingers with large chunks of shaped and patterned silver. Martin was going to be very surprised.

I drove to pick the kids up playing the radio at full volume, with the window down as the sun came out from the last rags of cloud.

Dan and Frankie were wound up like little springs in advance of seeing Martin. I'd been looking forward to greeting them at the school gates, eager to share the news of my repackaging. Able to smile for the first time in two weeks. Desperate to have a little scrap of normal jollity with my kids. But they got into the car without speaking, eyebrows in a straight line. I decided now was not a good time to tell them I'd blown half a term's worth of dinner money on a new frock.

I could see their faces in the rear-view mirror, distorted with neat aggression. How many hundred yards would we get before they exploded? About three.

'Stop staring at me, Derby.' I don't know why innocent Derby has been selected as this year's worst insult, but it has. It can hold a remarkable amount of venom in the hands of an eight-year-old girl.

'I'm not staring at you, Durr.' Durr? I don't know where they get them from. Sometimes having children is like watching one of those Desmond Morris programmes about how other cultures use winking and giving someone the thumbs up to signify 'I've shagged your sister, and your mother is a prostitute'.

'Yes you are. Pig-face.' Okay. Good. At least that's something I can relate to.

'Pig-face yourself.'

'Fatso.' Oh dear. That was the light-the-blue-touch-paper insult. Dan didn't even reply. I glanced up to the mirror and caught his purple face as his boot flashed over the back seat and caught Frankie in the leg.

Since Martin left the escalation to violence is almost instant and my disciplinary ability has blown out of the window along with everything else. There seems to be nothing I can threaten them with any more – going without your favourite telly night doesn't hold much terror when the worst thing you can imagine has already happened.

I stopped the car, with a deliberate jolt so that the shudder would at least physically prevent blows for a moment.

'Stop that right now or we'll sit here until you do.' There was a temporary halt to hostilities and I drove off. Inside thirty seconds they were at it again, Frankie gurning at Dan and Dan doing that horrid tongue under the bottom lip thing that I think means something very obscene if you're Italian. Frankie cracked first and kicked Dan on the knee. Tactically in these situations Frankie has the advantage, with longer legs in relation to her body, so she can scrunch herself into the door out of Dan's leg range and still clock him one with her boot. That's in normal times. Today Dan just undid his seat belt and threw himself across the back seat on top of her, flailing punches anywhere he could. He's short but built like a miniature prop forward from Pontypool, so in this situation he has more than a tactical advantage. If he lost all self-restraint he could hospitalise her.

I stopped the car again and shouted. It didn't even ripple the surface of the conflict. They were in all-out nuclear war. Total Armageddon, mutually assured destruction.

I got out, opened the back door and tried to haul Dan off her. It was hard to do. He weighs about the same as an Alsatian and he struggled like a dog does when it's mad for a fight. I pulled at him and screamed. Tried to stop him hitting her and her kicking him. In the end, the only way I could do it was by grabbing his ear very very hard. It's an unfamiliar activity for a parent to be inflicting maximum pain, but it worked. He tried hitting me of course, but I kept hold of the ear and twisted and eventually he stopped struggling.

Frankie just lay on the back seat howling. I sat her up and checked her over, a black eye maybe and some bruises but nothing more. Dan instantly started crying about his ear, about how cruel I was, about how all I wanted to do was hurt him, about how I hated him. Then Frankie started crying again. 'You didn't have to hurt him so much Mummy. You didn't have to drag him,' she wailed, as if she were saying 'You didn't have to maim him for life you sadist'. This it what it's like being a UN negotiator between the Serbs and the Croats I thought, you end up wanting to Kalashnikov both lots.

Then I tried to get Dan back in the car, so we could at least get home and kill each other in privacy. He wouldn't get in and every time I tried to grab him he flinched and jagged away from me in a wonderful pantomime of mock terror. As if my touch was a white-hot poker.

'I don't trust you not to hurt me,' he said rolling his eyes. Get your RADA audition now boy I thought.

After ten minutes of calmly explaining over and over the events as I saw them:

1. You were about to kill your sister
2. So I had to pull you off
3. You are so big ear-pulling was my only option
4. I didn't intend to hurt you
5. If I didn't love you I wouldn't be doing any of this I'd let you kill her and spend your life behind bars,

Dan was still telling me all I wanted to do was hurt him, and Frankie was still wailing at me for 'dragging' her brother. I finally lost it completely. It was a physical sensation, I felt an iron grid inside me being raised and something very wild getting out. Like Basil Fawlty in front of his broken car, I stamped and shouted in time with my words.

'Yes of course you're absolutely right both of you. My only aim is to inflict pain and misery on you. That's why I give you hot milk on your cereal every morning, and let you sleep in my bed. That's why I iron your school shirts and make cakes shaped like dinosaurs.' I picked up my bag at this point and swung it repeatedly by its handles so that it crashed into the car door, as punctuation.

'It's why I'm here and your (crash) father (crash) bloody isn't. All because I hate you both so (crash) bloody (crash) much (crash).'

Now we were all wailing, but at least it got Dan into the car. We drove the rest of the way in sobbing and whimpering silence.

I felt like molten lava, all my tears just fizzed into air the moment they hit my skin.

This, this was what I had been left with. Whilst Martin was off doing Personal Growth and Advanced Shagging with nobody's socks to wash, or breakfast to get, or life to organise but his own, I was here beating my car with a handbag. What was the point of imagining another life for myself inside blue silk frocks when this was what I had to deal with?

I was nearly at meltdown by the time we got home. The kids were still crying.

'Okay, get out of the car and go and get changed. If there's any more fighting I'm going to kill somebody.'

'Yeah you probably will,' Dan said as he ran off inside.

'You're just taking it out on us. Just because Daddy left you. It's not our fault,' Frankie shouted as she slammed the car door.

Remember Frankie is eight. I should. But I didn't. I grabbed her wrist.

'Yeah? And what do you think you and Dan are doing trying to kill each other? If you're so angry why don't you go and be angry with the right person.' I threw her wrist away like a stick and she staggered sideways and hit her head on the car window. The look of real fear on her face will be with me on my deathbed. She didn't even cry out. She just ran.

I slid down the side of the car with my head in my hands and slumped on the damp paving stones. The afternoon sun was making up for lost time and drawing the moisture out of everything, the stones, the soil, the leaves. I could smell the growth and summer over the hot dirty smell of the car's flank. They were right. I was right. We were all working out our anger on each other. Instead of clinging together, we were blowing each other apart. And Jess, Jess the Mummy and Grown Up was worst of all. Now I understood how terrible things happened, how women smashed their babies against radiators, how people drugged their children and jumped off bridges at dead of night holding them in their arms.

Dog bounced up and started talking to me in her funny selection of growls and whimpers, rolling on her back begging for attention. Good timing Dog, a minute ago and I might have kicked you into orbit. Time to get up and sort out the mess I'd created.

I couldn't find the kids inside the house. I had calmed down but they probably hadn't. I was about to start on the garden when the phone rang. It was answered immediately, and I assumed the machine had clicked in early, so I picked it up. But a conversation was already going on. The kids had the mobile somewhere and they were talking to Martin.

'Okay I can talk now. What's the prob?' Martin's voice cool and businesslike, slightly irritated.

'It's Mummy,' Dan's voice trembling, tearful and angry. 'She's gone mad and she's threatening to kill us.'

'What???'

'We're hiding in the garden now.'

'Look Dan just tell me what happened.'

'Well, Frankie and I were fighting, in the car. Just playing. And Mummy suddenly stopped the car and dragged us out and started shouting. She pulled my ear,' frantic whispering in the background from Frankie, 'and pushed Frankie over.'

'And where is Mummy now?'

'She's lying down by the car.'

'Okay. I'll be home in um two and a half hours okay? So here's what you do. I'm sure she isn't going to kill you. I want you to ring Gerry and Kath or Sarah and Alex. You know their numbers?'

'Yes I think so.'

'Tell them what happened and ask them to come round.'

'Okay Daddy.'

'And in the meantime keep away from your mother.'

'I'm sorry to interrupt,' I had to head off the international crisis management that was about to ensure. Martin might phone the police for all I knew.

68

'Jeezuz Jess, what the hell are you doing? What is going on there?' Martin was spitting acid.

'Nothing. It's all fine. We've just had a row because we're all so upset.'

'And you think eavesdropping on their conversation with me is acceptable do you?'

'I wasn't I just picked up the phone. I didn't know they were talking to you.'

'We'll discuss this later. Are you calm enough to assure me that my children are safe? As you know they are the most important thing to me.'

'Yes Martin.'

'All right, kids? Dan?'

'Yes Daddy.'

'If you're still frightened phone the police okay?'

'Jessica, I'll see you at seven.' Wow . . . sulphuric and hydrochloric mixed.

'Right.'

I hung up. I don't know if they talked for longer. I went to my bedroom and opened the windows to let the air in. I called out to the children across the garden that it was safe to come in when they wanted. Then I lay down and let the weight of everything press me into the bed.

This was how it happened: 'I haven't spoken to my mother since that day' and 'My father just came and took us away. She slit her throat the next week' and 'I've been on the streets since I was ten'.

They must have crept in avoiding all the creaky stair boards because I didn't hear them until they were sitting on my bed.

'Mummy?' Frankie spoke first.

'Yes love?'

'We're really really sorry. Dad's gonna kill you.' She collapsed on my front in tears, closely followed by Dan.

'No I'm sorry. I'm so sorry about it all. I'm sorry about Daddy leaving and us all being so angry. I'm just sorry.'

And there we lay twined round each other until we were cried out. It felt like a long long time.

At last Dan could look me in the face and said, 'It's like those mine fields Mummy. When one goes off you have to poke the ground all around to make sure there aren't any more.' Well there's a future for him in psychology at least.

By the time were were through with all that it was twenty to seven. I had twenty minutes before Martin was due to arrive. Probably with a strait-jacket for me and a care order for the children, but I still had to give the dress strategy my best shot. He'd have time to think about all the business with the phone whilst he drove here, to realise how much damage he had done, how much we were suffering. How much I loved him. Maybe all he'd need by the time he arrived to tip the floor and slide him back to me was the weight of me in that new dress, looking as he'd never seen me before.

But there I was in the best jeans and T-shirt I'd worn all day and that Martin had seen almost every time he came home from anywhere for the last five years. The kids hadn't been fed. Their clothes for the weekend were in the multicoloured jumble of clean washing on the spare bed. Prioritisation was necessary.

Spent, but cuddled and contrite, the kids were prepared to cooperate with almost anything. I slammed two bowls, a pint of milk and a packet of cereal on to the table and they set to eating without a murmur. I ran upstairs with a poly bag and shoved a pretty random bunch of clothes from the spare room chaos into it, hoping that there would be something for each of the kids amongst it all.

Fifteen minutes left. I showered in two and a half minutes but managed to slice myself in three places shaving my legs – something I only realised after I'd left bloody stains all along the landing carpet. I put my fingers through the first pair of tights I tried to put on and had to sit on the bed and do deep breathing before my hands were steady enough to try another pair. Eight minutes left. I dried my hair but it only ever goes right via the monkeys-and-typewriters principle so I had to wet and dry it again before it looked okay. Five minutes to seven. I cut my losses on the make-up front and decided to stick with lips only. Mascara at this stage and with this amount of general body tremble was too high a risk. I was likely to leave myself needing corneal surgery if I tried getting anywhere near my eyes with that lethal weapon – the pointy little brush thing you have to use. Seven o'clock. But hell, Martin was always late. He's only managed to catch trains since they've been privatised. Not today. For the first time in our married life, Martin was bang on time. I heard him come through the back door and greet the kids, checking that they were okay and that I hadn't lopped off any limbs or gouged out eyes.

More deep breathing. Just zip up the dress, slip on the shoes and go downstairs.

I lifted the dress from its tissue paper and put it on feeling sorry that there wasn't time to savour it more. It felt wonderful. Transforming.

Now: shoes. What shoes? What shoes did I have to wear with this glorious little slip of petal-textured nothingness? A choice of trainers, black lace-ups or calf-height DMs.

I had been to every shop in town, found a perfect dress that was unlike anything I had ever worn in my life before and had managed not to notice that I didn't have any shoes to go with it. No tottering high heels, no slaggy slingbacks, nothing dainty and feminine. Only shoes that were completely consistent with what I really was, lumpy, low-heeled and workaday.

'Jess!' Martin called up the stairs. 'I need the children's clothes.'

'I'm just coming.'

Nothing for it but to brazen it out with the post-punk look and pretend it was all planned. I put on the DMs and tied a bright blue ribbon of Frankie's that had been wrapped round the knob of my dressing-table drawer since she left her girly phase two years ago, into the middle of my hair. More deep breaths and down I went.

Not much hope of miracles now, but you never know.

A kind of involuntary emotional sleight of hand had kept me from imagining what seeing Martin again would be like. In my vague fantasies about him falling at my feet I'd seen him as he used to be. Mine. My Martin about whom I assumed so much. Standing in the kitchen now, he wasn't mine at all, and with all the assumptions proved ill-founded he seemed as unknown as any other man.

Just like me he was wearing new clothes. Cream cotton chinos and a loose black linen shirt. Both of us already metamorphosing into something different, Darwin's finches evolving in isolation on separate islands. Only I was the one up the evolutionary dead end destined for rapid extinction.

He looked his best. Ten out of ten. Drop dead gorgeous. I hadn't done that. Dolores had. I remembered Kath saying to me jokingly before Christmas, before the Signs appeared, 'Who's Martin bonking, he looks great?'

'Me,' I'd said with a little internal glow, 'nobody new, just me.'

What a sap. How could I have believed that I could make him luminesce like this? I wasn't enough, not even in the cute frock, with skinny legs and new look fingers. Especially not with ten-hole Doc Martens, no high heels and a miniature vertical pony tail.

The kids were hanging on to him as I came into the room. Dan cuddling an arm, wrapped around it as if it were a holy relic. Frankie was having her head stroked as she clung to his hips. I thought my heart was going to break my ribs.

'Your stuff's upstairs kids,' I said, 'in a Tesco's bag in my room. Just run up and check I've put in all you want.'

They melted off Martin without a word.

Dan whispered, 'Are you all right?' as he went past me.

'I'm fine sweetie.'

'They may be a few minutes I'm afraid,' I said, in my best talking-to-elderly-visitors voice, 'I don't think I did a good job of packing.'

'Fine. There's no rush,' he said in his best talking-to-useless-junior-editors voice.

I edged around the table, so the DMs would be concealed. I'd given up on the falling at my feet fantasy pretty much the moment I'd walked into the kitchen, but I didn't want to go for voluntary humiliation. We could hear the sound of the kids running about upstairs, fetching clothes they actually wanted instead of the first things that I'd laid my hands on.

Tension without electricity. I hadn't planned the moments to stick like this, the way spotted dick used to stick to my spoon at primary school dinners, making me retch with every forced mouthful.

I piled up the bowls, closed the top of the cereal packet.

'I don't think cereal is really enough for an evening meal for two growing children,' Martin said. There it was again, the shard of polar icecap. So Martin had had his fantasies too about this meeting, planning how he would instruct me in the care of his children. Give me a good telling off about being over-emotional. Looking at him I could see it. He was popping with all the things he'd spent the journey planning to say. And now all he could manage was a jibe about catering quality.

The dress hadn't filled him with renewed desire, but it had made me unfamiliar. A person who could bite like other people, not simply Jess who would never fight back. So at least the gossamer silk had given me a little protection, a little courage.

'And I don't think one parent is sufficient for a household. So we're quits.'

There was a split second of goldfish silence before the kids thundered down the stairs and gave Martin the excuse not to speak. Loaded with bags of clothes and toys and books, as if preparing for a term at Mallory Towers, Martin hustled them through the door and out.

The house was very quiet. An hour before James and Mary would come. My first hour of evening without the children. Without responsibility, without purpose. What could I do? Some name tapes needing sewing on to Dan's new sports kit, or I could make some soup for the freezer. There was a pile of household bills to sort. But if I did any of those things then that's what I would always be doing whilst the kids were away, just waiting for them to come back and get me out of my box again.

I took off my dress. I poured a large gin. No tonic, but the kids lemon barley was okay.

I ran a bath. Soaking in a bath was hard. I'd schooled myself for years to do the whole thing from kit off to mascara on in twelve minutes so to simply lie in a bath and relax took discipline. I managed eight minutes. I'm aiming for fifteen next time.

Slowly and deliberately I did all the preparations I had been determined to do to beautify myself for Martin. Somebody else would get the benefit now. Me.

Chapter Six

Francis Weaton was turning fifty in style, not just one marquee but a whole Bedouin settlement of them clustered on the south side of the house, from the French windows and terrace, to the huge barn with tented walkway tunnels connecting them. He'd clearly taken very good advice about the weather because the rain wasn't going to matter inside that lot. The lighting was weather-proof too, because all the strings of coloured lights were blazing out across the valley as we swooped down the hill in Mary and James's car. Even in the rain it looked jaunty, fairgroundish, exciting. Mary hadn't given it a good enough billing and I began to feel that maybe Martin wasn't the main event of the evening after all.

We parked in the muddy field (very glad of the DMs), and huddled up to the front door on either side of James's substantial and comforting bulk under a golfing umbrella to rival one of the Weaton birthday tents. The entrance to the party was via the marquee erected over the terrace. Arched over the opening into the tent was a construction of tangled willow like a great wave, woven with thousands of tiny blue fairy lights. It gave us all the feeling that we were entering into some magical domain.

'Well,' said James, 'he has pushed the boat out.'

Inside there was more abstract willow sculpture with more of the blue fairy lights, pulsing at various rhythms so that the wave shapes looked alive and sent patterns of light shooting over the ceiling. A beautiful boy in a doublet and hose costume in every shade of blue stepped up to us with a drinks tray. There were others like him everywhere, in fantastical gear, with short slashed-sleeve jackets, strange velvet hats like ornamental gourds, all with hose and some with codpieces. Some had tiny gauze wings on their backs, others had fabulously decorated and jewelled masks. All had a quality of fragility about them. Fairy-like. Hmm, I thought, so this is Francis's coming-out party then.

There was no access for guests into the house. The beautiful waiters slipped from behind a velvet drape that must have covered the French windows from the drawing room on to the terrace. Francis was clearly keeping the inside of his house private, separate from this one-night-only created world of magic.

'Oh that's a shame!' said Mary, when she realised we were solely under canvas for the whole event. 'I'm sure you'd enjoy his house Jess. Full of strange pictures. You'd love them.'

Like new Narnians, fresh out of the wardrobe, we wandered through the reception tent into the main marquee, softly lit by candelabra hanging from the roof. It was laid out like a giant sitting room, with little groups of sofas and armchairs clustered around pools of light from standard lamps. At the far side on a little raised dais was a grand piano with a dapper dark-haired pianist burbling away some embellishments around a Cole Porter core. Already people were perching on the seats, sipping champagne and taking canapés off the trays offered by the faerie boys. It was starting to feel busy, alive. Looking around there was a high proportion of Laura Ashley taffeta and pointy court shoes, but there was also the sector of Francis's friends who matched the decor of the party: men with unusual dinner suits that had been chosen from a number in their wardrobes, women with evening dresses that might once have been down a catwalk. I began to feel that the DMs really could be a fashion statement rather than a tragic mistake, and that wandering single in the field of this particular party was going to be fun. I could take on whatever personality suited me, not one provided by two decades of parties with the same person.

I finished my champagne and reached for another as a boy with a golden mask and rose-coloured wings passed by with a pink tray. I'd been wandering dreamily on, but Mary and James had stopped to talk to someone they knew and were perching on a yellow settee with orange cushions. Mary came after me and took my arm. 'Jess, do come and meet Felicity.'

I wondered why Felicity had been singled out for my introduction, rather than the rest of the group of eight or so all talking animatedly – probably about hunt balls and buying land. Mary lowered her voice, and I found out what was special about Felicity. 'Felicity's husband left her four years ago,' Mary told me as she manoeuvred me into the corner of the sofa next to a tall woman in a green taffeta frock. She was very handsome, in a strong sort of way. She glowed with a kind of sinewy physical strength so that although her frock was loose-fitting, I felt she might just burst out of it by accident. She had big dark eyes, shiny black hair with almost no grey swept up from her face, weathered skin from years of being outside all day with stock and horses. Her make-up made her look sort of gilded. Polished.

She smiled and shook my hand. 'Mary tells me you've just joined the deserted wives' club,' she said in a very posh voice indeed.

'Does it have a large enough membership to be a club?'

'Oh, you *are* a new member. Yes, my dear, I'm afraid it does.' It could have been a patronising thing to say, but she said it so softly and so sadly that I felt a chill between my shoulder blades and a sudden hard clearing in my head. This was it then, this kind of shiny bravery in the face of sadness was what I had to look forward to.

'I'm so sick of telling people about me,' I said, 'tell me what happened to you.'

'Well. I live up on the moor. I have forty acres of grazing there. My husband and I used to breed horses. I still do breed horses. Four years ago I found him in bed with one of the stable girls. She was already pregnant with his baby. They live together in the village with their child, children. He and his tart have just had another brat.' The colour pulsed more intensely into her cheeks at the words tart and brat. I got the feeling that these words hadn't even been in her vocabulary before her man betrayed her. 'That's all there is to say really. He doesn't want to know our three children now.'

'Doesn't he see them at all?'

'He sees them. Sees them as you see anyone who lives in the same area. You run into each other. But he doesn't visit them, or ask them to visit him. He greets them like strangers.'

Felicity's pain was as apparent and as unhealed as mine. She was like a newly-severed limb. How could she have gone on bleeding like that for four years?

'Have you divorced him?'

'I can't. I love the bastard.'

We talked on for a while. About her children. About the horses. Her life was busy, ordered, productive. She had friends, an active social life, goals to aim for with her work. But no lovers in spite of her high-coloured good looks. And an emotional wound as open as a stigmata. I felt like Scrooge cowering before his own lonely and unmourned grave. I couldn't wait to get away. She asked me about Martin, but I slid out under the questions. I didn't want to join the club, least of all tonight in my new frock and my daring footwear. As I made my excuses and went off in search of another drink I felt her eyes on my back burning like a branding iron: 'You think you're different but you'll learn.' I knew Mary watched me go too, planning the next opportunity to introduce me to another woman 'in my situation'.

I found some more drink, half a bottle of champagne that I blagged off one of the Pucks. I carried it off by the neck, swinging it discreetly at knee height and walking insolently.

Women who wear DMs with their party frocks don't stay down after their husbands leave them. Oh no. They aren't still crying after four years, because they find somebody else. Maybe not at their first party, but soon. Well inside the first year. Probably.

I wound through another two smaller marquees, one was the food tent lined with sides of smoked salmon and towers of meringues and pineapples, but food doesn't really compute with me any more. Another was a magic tent, where guys in smart suits like encyclopaedia salesmen, and a girl in a sequined mini-dress were mingling with the guests and pulling birds and eggs and Belgian chocolates from behind their ears and out of their cleavages. Dotted amongst the strangers were people I knew vaguely, village stalwarts, couples I'd had stilted conversations with at Mary and James's drinks parties. I smiled, joked, laughed, flirted and moved on, as they took in the clothes, the champagne bottle, the atmosphere of recklessness.

I found the dancing tent at the end of a long fairy-lit tent-corridor. The dark draped walls soaked up any illumination so that the disco lights looked like they were shining in space. A few adolescents, probably relatives attending this very grown-up party on sufferance, drooped around the edges, uncomfortable in smart clothes. It was still early so no one was dancing. Except the DJ, a fat man with a big black pigtail and a Hawaiian shirt with green parrots all over. He was boogieing daintily around his little space with that lovely pendulum-like balance that some fat men have, and mouthing along to Talking Heads. Drop me in the wad-der . . . the waar, der, er, errr. Bending and pirouetting, like one of the tutued hippos from *Fantasia*.

This was perfect. An empty dance floor and a DJ who could probably be persuaded to play almost any piece of disposable pop I cared to name.

I could get myself hours of mindless dance oblivion right here.

Martin didn't really like dancing. Too uncontrolled for his tastes. But at college he'd liked to watch me dance. We'd exchange glances of one hundred per cent proof lust as he leaned against the wall with his cronies and I threw myself around happily to The Clash or Elvis Costello. Occasionally as 'adults' after college, we'd go to a party somewhere and I'd dance and he'd lean and maybe look a bit. But my taste in music got worse as far as Martin was concerned, I began dancing to all sorts of things on the disapproved list: Madonna, Abba, East 17, the Cranberries. After all you can't actually dance to Stinkin' Feet Brown's 'Greatest Songs Of Human Misery' can you? I gave up in the end. I simply couldn't cope with the disapproval. So with Martin I was permanently dance-starved. Pushing the kitchen table to one side and turning the CD up loud with your kids just isn't the same as a real dance floor with lights, volume.

And a fat DJ in a loud shirt.

I offered him the last of the champagne. Close up his face was tanned and weathered, hard to age but no spring chicken. He swigged from the bottle one handed and put on another Talking Heads, 'Slippery People'.

'Can I ask you to play some things?'

'You can ask, sure, I may not play 'em. But you can ask.' He was American, and an American with a sense of humour, which was pleasantly exotic.

'Okay. They're pretty trashy requests. Not up to the standards of a Talking Heads fan.' Flattery and champagne, it had to be a winning combination.

'You don't like to dance to Talking Heads?'

'Sometimes. But I want something else tonight.'

'Like what?'

I needed to think of something I'd like to dance to that would put my terrible musical taste in a slightly better light, I felt too self-conscious to jump straight in with 'Cherish', 'Magic' and 'Give Me a Man After Midnight'.

'I've lost my nerve now.' Adding flirting to the champagne and flattery that seemed to be working.

'Okay I'll make you feel better: there are some Queen tracks I'll play, and I even like.'

'Thank you. I'll work up my courage to ask for Queen later. I've just thought of something to start with. B52s 'Loveshack' or 'Rock Lobster' . . . 'Loveshack' for first choice though.'

His eyes lit up. 'You got both. But now you have to dance.'

The hour and a half that followed could turn out to be the highlight of the rest of my life.

Morgan, the fat DJ, (from Virginia, whose Mom worked at the White House and whose brother was an alcoholic, as I found out), played my dream top 50. The records I can never remember from a standing start on my own, but as one record finished he'd yell out, 'What about "Oliver's Army"?' or, 'Would you dance to something new, like Hansen?' or, 'Are you ready for that Queen track right now?'

He dredged things up from my memory I didn't even know I had in there. Things from before I'd censored myself to suit Martin, things from out of my car dancing fantasies. The Clash, oddly, got the droopy teenagers dancing, and after that they didn't want to stop, so when Morgan played Abba's 'Dancing Queen' and came out from behind his ranks of lights and decks, we danced with outrageous abandon together. Old Lag, Fat DJ and Spotty Adolescents.

Not in a million years of months composed entirely of sunny warm Tuesday nights could I have had such an experience if Martin had been with me.

At last the rest of the party got pissed enough to dance and found their way to the tent. The floor filled up and Morgan had to play things to suit his audience: why do the upper classes like The Rolling Stones so much? I carried on dancing squashed into a corner by the lights and the speakers by men with ties undone and shirt fronts untucked, women with wonky lipstick and wild hair. The drink had clearly been very freely flowing in the other tents. Over on the other side of the dance floor I could see James and Mary strutting their stuff pretty darn funkily – I remembered the Harley across Kenya – with a very thin blonde woman in a kind of Lurex catsuit.

As 'Honky Tonk Woman' came to an end Mary spotted me. She waved and powered her way through the dancers towards me. 'There's someone I want you to meet,' Mary said as soon as she was in earshot.

I had a premonition about the skinny gal in the spangly all-in-one.

She was Lucy, ex-Roedean and Classics graduate who had ridden to hounds very dashingly as a girl but ended up with a sheep farmer from Perth. I didn't ask how. I suspect it had a lot to do with all-girls schools, a lack of brothers and a catastrophically high exposure to male pheromones at a sensitive age, and anyway there's only so much information you can exchange over full volume 'Brown Sugar'. The ill-advised nature of this match only became apparent to Lucy when her bit of Aussie rough found he really did prefer sheep to anything in life and threw her out with their kids. By the sound of things she could at least be thankful her children didn't grow up bleating. Anyway, they came back to England with nothing. Here she was three years on, dependent on Daddy and Mummy, chain-smoking and too skinny to bother with a bra.

How many ghosts of Christmas yet to come were there?

I squirmed back through the crowd on to the dance floor where, warmed up by the Stones, Francis's assembled followers were ready for something else, so Morgan hit a rich vein of Glam Rock. I've always had a soft spot for Mott the Hoople and even The Glitter Band.

As more and more people danced, my status as unpaired female of still shaggable age came to the notice of the various sharks that swim in any party pond. Four or five drunken and dishevelled men came and invaded my dancing space and started conversations. Trying to talk next to a speaker with enough whack to fill the Albert Hall doesn't strike me as intelligent behaviour, and anyway when I'm dancing I just want to dance. But I'm terminally polite, I can't just turn my back or shout piss off, or even just look at the floor or dance with my eyes shut. I smile sweetly and yell back.

'And what music do you like?'
and
'I said WHAT MUSIC DO YOU LIKE?'
and
'No I don't have any Chris Rea.'
and
'Oh accountancy. How sensible of you.'
and
'Yes, my husband is a very lucky man.'

Martin did used to rescue me in these situations. In fact it was the only time I'd get to dance with him. At the end of an evening when some guy with double vision would threaten to engulf me in an embrace as the smoochy music started, he'd step out on to the dance floor and cut in. For a man who never hit anyone Martin has a hugely impressive air of violence about him, so they always stepped aside. I loved it. Same as my hens do when the cockerels fight.

But tonight, when the smoochy slow stuff started, I didn't have any defences when a tall grey-haired guy with the complexion of a coronary candidate just walked up and grabbed me. In a polite well-spoken sort of way you understand. He asked permission to dance with me. And then just grabbed. He was a good dancer mind you – raised on ballroom I guess – and I'm rubbish at that stuff. I step on feet, I try to lead, I'm ugly and awkward. He held my hand very tightly and held my body very close with one hand on the small of my back, very firm and very controlling. I wasn't prepared for what it produced in me: A Seven-Bore of lust, revulsion and memory.

It was wonderful to be touched, to be held so obviously sexually after the kick in the guts rejection that Martin had doled out. Anybody would have done – knock-kneed and bowlegged with a face like a lorry's exhaust – I wouldn't have cared for that first five seconds. Anything male and vaguely potent would have had the same effect on me.

There's no way he missed that immediate response because as I brushed against him he had a hard-on like the Gower Peninsula, and started moving his hand down over my backside and pulling my hips closer. But after the first five seconds, a few discriminatory faculties kicked in: he had halitosis, and three chins and he'd never been much of a looker I guessed. I had a sudden vision of this guy's body in bed with me, and of Martin, my lovely blond bear Martin: light catching the hairs on the back of his arms. And I really hated Martin at that moment for taking himself from me and leaving me with this old tub of overheated Spam to fuck instead. The terminal politeness stopped for once, I broke away and pushed my way out into the fairy-light corridor where a flap of tentage had been unlaced. I dived through it and outside.

After four hours in fairy-tent-land it was a shock to be outside. It wasn't raining but it was very dark, everything smelled wet and washed out. Even the smell of the soil had been drowned out it had rained so much. I couldn't see, and I couldn't hear anything beyond the post-disco ringing in my ears. After ten paces of fast-forward blundering I stumbled into a low wall and my dress snagged on a kind of anti-burglar prickle bush, probably genetically engineered to bite. I shut my eyes and stood still, waiting for my night vision to kick in and help me out. A hand fell on my shoulder and I screamed.

'Gee I'm sorry.' Not Cardiac Arrest Man then, but Morgan with a torch, come to be knight in shining armour, well wobbling blubber anyway. 'I saw you were getting a little upset, and I saw you run off so . . .'

'What about your disco?'

'I have a half-hour tape I can leave playing if I need a break. Anyway those people are so gone they wouldn't really notice if I played the Stars and Stripes.'

'I'm caught on this bush, could you shine your torch so I can disentangle myself?'

'Oh sure.'

I began to try to tease it free, but my hands and my arms were shaking so much I had to stop.

'Are you okay? I mean should I fetch somebody . . . ?'

'No don't worry. I promise not to throw up on you or have a fainting fit. I'm not ill. I'm just, upset I suppose.'

'Okay, okay. Look, you hold the flashlight, I'll do the dress, right?'

'Right.'

Morgan's daintiness seemed to extend beyond the dance floor. He had small hands that were quite at home with silk hemlines. He handled the material with professional care and without the slightest glint of lasciviousness at being so close to my legs.

'You're not a DJ full-time are you?'

'Naa. It's just a hobby. A favour for Franny's birthday do. I'm a costume designer.' Ah! Of course, one of Francis Weaton's gay friends. It all fitted in — the lights, the costumes, the lovely fat-boy dancing.

'Are the beautiful boys all yours then?'

'Excuse me?'

'The fairies, I mean the waiters.'

'Yeah.' He smiled and freed the last piece of hem from the bush. 'There you go. Nice dress. Yeah. I borrowed them from the production I'm doing now. Lock stock and barrel . . . the costumes I designed, the waiters are my actors. It's a new *Midsummer Night's Dream*, my company's doing this summer. Travelling with it all over.'

'I'd love to see it.'

'Really?'

'Yeah.'

'Well young lady . . .'

I laughed.

'What's so funny?'

'No one's called me that in twenty years.'

'Well I can't think why, seeing you boppin' about on that dance floor tonight.'

'You're very gallant.'

'What I was about to say when you found "young lady" so funny was that I have a ticket right here, for the Ettington Arts Festival in August. Take it.'

'Thank you. That's very kind.'

'You've stopped shaking.'

'I have.'

'Then I'll say goodnight. I have a disco to run. And it's a fearsomely serious operation. If you wanna stay out here, why don't you keep the flashlight. Bring it back when you come to the show. I don't need it, my mom made me eat a whole truckload of carrots last time I went home.' And a whole truckload of cream buns too, but still he balanced his bulk gracefully through the shadows and disappeared through the tent flap. So kind, so gentle. Shame he was also So Fat and So Gay. But at least another little social venture to look forward to. I tucked the ticket carefully into my bra. No pockets in silk frocks, it's their only flaw.

I didn't want to go back in and face Cardiac Arrest's Gower Peninsula again, or Mary and James's concern for my welfare manifested in another Introduction. I had told them I'd find my own way home. Anyway, Morgan was clearly bowing to market forces and playing end of evening grope music.

I had my DMs, I had Morgan's 'flashlight' and it was only four miles to home. It wasn't raining. I'd walk. In an hour or less I'd be there.

Out on the dark wet lanes I turned off the torch. Scrag ends of navy blue cloud ragged across the sky like torn bits of witches' underwear. The moon showed through sad and ill-looking, a little uncertain of its ability to shine, diffusing its light thinly from horizon to horizon, and picking out silhouettes sharp as broken glass. With two hillsides between me and the party the only sound was the orchestra of running water, every tone from piccolo rivulets to bass gush of the overloaded stream.

I love night. It's intimate, subtle. Day is just so obvious. Night is to day as radio is to television.

I've missed the night this last ten years because, unless you're a traveller, with your family accommodated in a selection of old transit vans, you lose your acquaintanceship with the night when you have kids. You have to be inside joggling colicky babies on shoulders, keeping shampoo out of eyes, trying to remember the future tense of 'venir' and how to do quadratic equations. Or just simply being there to ward off nightmare monsters, freak fires and wandering nocturnal child molesters. You can't wake at three to find moonlight on the duvet and decide to walk up the road to feel the Earth turning. At least not if your partner in parentship is in New York.

So I was grateful to Cardiac Arrest for causing an early departure on foot. And I was, briefly, grateful to Martin because all the pain is stripping off my skins, like Nitromorse on old woodwork, and I feel more alive. Tonight, standing on the last hill before home, I felt the air on every square millimetre of skin, the moonlight inside my eyes, all mixed in with the memory of Martin's presence, solid and sweet, and for a few moments free of the sickly coating of loss and anger.

I was of course simply pissed out of my head, on the best part of a whole bottle of champagne. I must have been, because when I got home I rang Martin's mobile number from the phone by our bed. It would be off so I could leave a message on his answer service.

I thought.

It rang three times and Martin answered already irate.

'I knew it would be you. Do you know what time it is?'

'I'm sorry, I thought your phone would be switched off, so I could leave a message.'

'Okay. So what's the message? You do realise it's twenty to three?'

'I'm sorry. I just wanted to say that I love you.'

'You were going to leave that on my ansaphone?'

'Yes.'

'To make me feel bad?'

'No!'

'You can't do this Jess. Keep leaving me emotional messages. Quite apart from anything else they're irrelevant. I'm turning the phone off now. Don't ring again.'

It was my own fault. I set myself up for it. I had no right to be crying. I wondered when my love for Martin had become irrelevant. For how long had he seen it as an obstacle to what he wanted. So much more convenient for him now to be hated rather than loved. You can leave someone who hates you and know that you are doing them a favour. You know that they will rejoice in having the top on the toothpaste and never again having to find used matches in the box. You can even indulge in feeling a little put upon, because it's unpleasant to be despised. But leaving someone who loves you is irritatingly messy.

I looked around our room. Nothing had changed since he had left, except that one wardrobe and one chest of drawers was empty. It looked as it had always looked to me – Our Room, in Our House. How long had Martin lain here and seen it as the place he used to sleep, the bed he used to make love to his wife in? Weeks? Years?

I had the distinct sense of living inside an old freezer that had been chucked on the tip. He didn't want it, but I could have it.

It was half-past four and really quite light, by most people's breakfast time I could transform this room, into a room for my life. Not just something Martin saw as irrelevant. I dried my face, stripped off the dress and pulled on some class-three clothes . . . holes, grass stains and paint spatters, and began moving furniture.

For six solid hours I was completely manic. I shifted both wardrobes, the double bed and two chests of drawers. I painted the white walls and all their memories with a layer of the deep sunset pink left over from the backdrop of the ballroom scene of the Christmas Panto in school. Not pink like icing or babies' booties, but pink like the heart of old roses. I put my whole body into every stroke of the roller, bending low and stretching to the limit of my arms to take the sweep of colour over the whole height of the wall. By eleven the walls had two coats, the ceiling one, and I was feeling very strange: throbbing inside, so that every heartbeat shook me.

I went downstairs. The back door was open and Dog was lying outside in the first sunshine for more than a week. I sat down next to her on the warm paving stones and she wagged a sleepy tail. I lay down, and the ground pushed up to hold me as all my energy dropped out like a discharged battery.

'I don't fuckin' believe it. Every bleedin' time we're 'ere, you give us bloody 'eart failure!' Gerry said and took another pull at the whisky for the sake of his nerves. He and Kath had dropped round to ask if they could take me out for tea, and found me stretched out on the patio with Dog sprawled on my stomach whimpering melodramatically.

'I don't do it deliberately Ger. I just fell asleep.'

'Yeah well, next time tell that dog of yours to lay orf the Greyfriars Bobby act. I thought you'd given the bastard the benefit of yer life insurance.'

'Here, drink this.' Kath handed me a mug full of something hot which didn't taste of anything except heat.

'What is it?'

'Tea with honey, can't you tell?'

'Nope. My taste and smell apparatus doesn't work any more.'

'I 'ave to tell you Jess, you look like deaf. Honest.'

'Thank you so much Gerry. Well I feel fine. I slept again. That's twice this week. And I have started to convert my bedroom into a tart's boudoir. Martin would loathe it.'

'He would. But I think it's wonderful.' Kath eased herself a little further into the deck chair. The subversion of Martin's decor was giving her great pleasure on my behalf.

'I'm putting the bed under the window so I can look at the stars before I go to sleep. But I need to give the walls one more coat, then I'm going to paint the woodwork distressed gold. I'm going to get up and finish it in a minute.'

'No you're bloody not.'

'Yes I am. Just because you want to paint the world magnolia doesn't mean to say everyone has to.'

'It ain't the colour I mind. It could be black wiv a mirrored ceilin' for all I care. 'S your room. But you ain't doin' it.' Gerry sat up and poked a finger into my chest for emphasis, then sat back. 'We are.'

'Yep. I'm going to nip home to get our painting clothes in a minute and we'll finish it off for you. Then we'll cook you supper and tuck you into your new bedroom.'

'An' no bleedin' arguments. Righ'?'

'I wasn't going to argue.'

I do wonder what was in the hot whatever Kath gave me, because I fell asleep again. I think Kath might secretly be a witch because her house is full of books on herbal lore and she gets the gardeners at The Court (where she works) to grow all sorts of weird stuff. Anyway when I woke, it was getting dark. That's late in June. I was still in the deck chair but covered in a duvet. The kitchen door was open and Gerry was standing leaning on the lintel with a glass of wine in his hand. He was telling one of his stories about Toffs. Gerry is well known to the toffs of the area, the people with houses like Mary and James only bigger and with no bonkers relations decorating their rooms, and no plaster missing off the outside walls.

'She 'ad this paintin' righ'? Wiv gondolas and crowds and that. Soffink 'er dad Lord Wassisname gave 'er. Nice piece. Copy of a Canaletto, Victorian I s'pose.' For all his working-class hero bravado, Gerry knows about things, objects of all sorts from chairs and candlesticks to paintings and porcelain. 'Anyway, I says to her " 'S nice. East India Docks innit?" and she says "No silly it's Venice." ' The amount of laughter was too much for even a very drunk and loving Kath to produce alone. I made a bit more effort to focus and I could see Mary and James in the kitchen with her. James sat at the table with his feet on another chair, Kath and Mary were chopping things and going back and forth to the Aga. They'd never met before, this side of an exchanged wave in the lanes, and now here they were in paint-spattered shirts and holey trousers, cooking, boozing and swapping stories. What's more, while I had been asleep they had all been painting my room.

I didn't move. I didn't reveal that I'd woken. I just watched this little social miracle. The red-hot ex-Commies and the true-blue Tories enjoying each other in this serendipitous sort of way. I felt almost as I did the day Dan made Frankie laugh for the first time and they stopped being just a baby and a toddler and started being brother and sister.

Kath and Mary, with a little aid from the bottom of my freezer and the chooks' eggs, had made salmon and hollandaise and potatoes. We ate outside, and they drank whisky and water after we finished the wine. James and Gerry lit a bonfire under the apple tree when it got cool and we sat around drinking more and telling stories: Gerry about eccentric nobles, and James about criminal peasants. Mary, Kath and I about 'ghastly things our kids have done'. Just when we were getting sleepy, Alex and Sarah called by *en route* home from some academics' work do of Sarah's. Having limited themselves to very polite topics of conversation all evening they were ready for some ribaldry. Somehow we got on to the subject of outside weeing for girls.

'It's part of my family heritage. My mum taught me and all my sisters how to do it without splashing your knickers. I love it,' said Kath, 'just show me a decent bush and I'll wee behind it.'

'But what do you do about paper?' Sarah wouldn't dream of exposing any private part of her body anywhere but behind several securely bolted doors.

'Just wave your bum in the wind to get the drips off.'

'You should try it Sarah. I've had some of my greatest moments of communing with nature whilst weeing outdoors.' I said to Sarah's horror. 'You know that sense of playing your part in the nitrogen cycle.'

'Tell 'em about that parked car in Covent Garden, Kaff.'

'Bloody hell Ger, you always remind me of that.'

'All righ' all righ'. I'll tell 'em. We was comin' 'ome from the pub one night. 'S before we 'ad kids, righ'? And Kaff's a girl for the pints ent you Kaff? Anyways. She says "I got to do a wee Gerry",' here Gerry perfectly imitated Kath's rather sweet and cultured voice, 'and she lifts her skirt and drops her knickers by this parked Jag. Nuffin on 'er side of the road – all on mine. Few pedestrians like and a big jewellers. So I'm waitin'. And she's takin' for ever, righ'. And then vis copper comes up and starts eyein' me up.

'What's your business here sir?'

'I'm waitin for me girlfriend.'

'Oh yes,' he says, 'at midnight, sir outside a closed jewellers,' and at that moment the lights on the Jag go on and it drives orf, and there's Kaff, wiv her skirt round her tits and her knickers round her ankles and her bum in the air. This copper he didn't even flicker, he just said "Your girlfriend sir?" and walked orf.'

'Well, I think Mary can top that one,' said James with a definite glow of pride.

'Oh James. You weren't even there!'

'Oh tell the story Mary!'

'All right. It was an awfully long time ago . . .'

Yet again Mary revealed a more colourful past than any of us by relating how she'd 'spent a penny' in broad daylight in a traffic jam on the Champs-Elysées. And not discreetly under a long skirt like gals in crinolines at garden parties, but by hitching up her tight white sixties mini-dress and trying to keep the splashes off her white suede thigh boots.

With Martin here none of this would have been possible, not the spontaneity, not the acceptance of favours, not the risky cocktail of people. This was something new, and totally mine.

I rolled into the duvet as it was just getting pearly around the eastern horizon. Surrounded by the smell of the new paint my friends had put on for me I felt almost hopeful about the future. Maybe Dan and Frankie wouldn't grow up to be drug addicts, maybe it wouldn't be the end of the world if Martin didn't ever come back. I couldn't really see the colour of the walls or the glint of the paintwork, but I knew when it was light enough they were going to look sensational.

Chapter Seven

I'm usually bad at making decisions. The living room has one blue wall, one green and two moth-eaten flock because I couldn't make my mind up about the colour. It's not that I avoid decisions, after all if I did that, the walls would be all moth-eaten flock or all magnolia. No I know what choices I have, it's just that I can't make them. Usually that is. But now isn't 'usually' any more and I've made three decisions in twenty-four hours.

And one of them has been to divorce Martin.

It happened quite suddenly on Sunday when he brought the kids back.

I was expecting them any time from five, so by four-thirty I was hyperventilating and having to sit down every few minutes to keep calm. I pottered about outside trying to feel as if I wasn't waiting. Snipping shoots that didn't need snipping, dead-heading flowers that were still alive, watching the chooks doing nothing in particular and checking their egg box every twenty minutes. I was about to give up trying to look occupied and pace instead when the car pulled up through the gate, just as I was walking across the lawn towards it. Seeing Martin sitting behind the wheel I couldn't help smiling like I used to do at him and giving a pathetic little wave. He looked back at me as if I were some Photography graduate hassling him for a job. He certainly didn't smile.

The kids almost fell out of the car and raced towards me telling me both together and all at once everything they'd done at the weekend. 'We went to the cinema and swimming and shopping and Daddy got me these new shoes and this Oasis cassette and he's taking us to Greece and he's got a video camera,' and over the top of this wave Martin looked at me with a kind of smouldering hatred, if eyes the colour of the summer sea can be said to smoulder. He'd only been angry and contemptuous on Friday, I wondered how he'd managed to convert it to hatred in just two days.

Of course I know how really. He's rewriting history just like me. I'm painting hearts and flowers around my memories and occasionally expanding them to accommodate Dolores. The difference is that he's been doing it for a lot longer than two days, probably from the very first time he met Dolores. And he isn't doodling hearts and flowers. He's been flicking through his album of mental snapshots of me, making little additions. At first it was just a few doodled pairs of glasses, reasonably flattering in their way. Then it was the odd zit. But now he's progressed to full beard, moustache, horns and where my legs are in shot, cloven hooves and a tail.

Some photos are better with me completely painted out, like Trotsky before they finally did for him with the ice pick. In these Martin stands alone, beaming into the camera with his two beautiful children and a big gap to the left of frame. Given time Martin will be telling people that I threw him out because I was having an affair.

On Friday I'd imagined that two days of looking at nothing but the two children we made together might soften his heart, but it seemed to have made him more determined than ever to rid himself of the she-devil who spawned them.

So anyway, I went on smiling, we both went on saying nice polite stuff to the kids whilst I served us a cup of tea and some juice and biscuits for the children. All the time the children chattered, and above it we regarded each other through an ice age of silence. He gulped his tea so fast it must have inflicted second degree burns down most of his oesophagus, and got up to go.

As he leaned over to kiss them each goodbye he was so close I could feel his warmth, smell his skin. Still wearing too much aftershave. I wonder if he tainted Dolores's bread with it when he cut slices from a loaf in their love nest, same as he used to taint mine. It's the one thing about him that irritated me, having to eat toast and Marmite with a hint of Nino Cerruti.

I had a full long moment at each kiss to look at his head as his eyes were turned down. The curls still looked ready for me to fit my fingers inside them like rings. I could feel the hair deep between my knuckles even without touching, nothing seemed to have changed and yet everything had. I was never going to feel the shape of his skull under my hand again.

I want him in the same way you want sleep or food. It's a wanting that can't be compartmentalised, I can't shove it away somewhere and lock a door on it because it influences everything about me. He's an addiction. He replaced something in me, some constituent of my body chemistry that my cells have come to rely on. I'm never going to stop wanting him as long as I see him and smell him and hear him. As long as my body gets a tiny fix to keep it addicted. Cold turkey is what I've got to do, I have to lock my life against him until the screaming and the stomach pains, the hallucinations and the nausea stop.

It's either that or do this for the next fifteen years. See him like that. It would get easier of course as time blurred out the shock. We might even sit and chat like the old friends we are. And sometime, between lovers or after a row with Dolores or simply when he was feeling old and low, we'd go to bed. And in the morning he'd need to reject me all over again, 'make his position clear' once more and I'd be back down at the bottom of the pit again, but this time with limbs missing and no light to climb out to.

Stuff that for a game of soldiers. I'm just not doing it.

So in the time it took him to kiss the children goodbye, I

made two decisions: one was to get all his things out of the house in the interests of my short-term sanity. And the other was to divorce him in the interests of my long-term survival.

And who knows, when he gets the cardboard boxes full of clothes and books and CDs plus the letter from the lawyer, it may shock him into coming back!

I was going to begin the operation of complete Martin-ectomy as soon as the kids were in bed, but the excitement of the weekend had evaporated like the bubbles out of a fizzy drink. They left behind a rather bitter brown residue which I had to try to clear up at bedtime. It took two hours to get them to sleep.

The strangeness of going to stay with Daddy as if he were some exotic uncle was too much to cope with all at once. Dan wasn't ready to give up on being with Mummy and Daddy together at the same time.

'We could have days out together,' Dan said forlornly as I tucked him in. 'You and Daddy and Frankie and me. Daddy wouldn't mind. He still likes you Mummy. He still wants to be your friend.'

It took me half an hour to explain why that wasn't possible and in the end we were both sobbing.

Then I trotted along the landing to Frankie's room.

'He's not like Daddy any more Mummy. He's Martin, but he's not Daddy,' she said tearfully. 'When I have children they won't have a grandpa, they'll only have a granny.' Trust Frankie to go for the melodrama. She's her mother's daughter after all. But she was really crying. And so was I after the long explanation of how Martin WAS still her daddy and loved her just as much as ever, if not more. And how he would make a wonderful grandpa . . . just as long as her offspring never actually called him that.

I know I have to give Martin a good press to the kids, to reassure them of his love and his continued utter devotion and loyalty. I can't say all the things that roar around my heart like

Millwall supporters after eight pints of lager. Things like, 'Yeah he loves you so much he's run off to live with his tart' and 'Yeah he loves you so much he'll take you bowling. I'll just make breakfast for you every morning, remind you about piano practice, fold your vests, darn your socks, and clean you up when you've been sick in your bed at three' and 'Yeah he loves you so much that I'm allowed to do the babysitting so he can go and fuck Dolores.'

It was good for me to see the kids so abject and confused because it made me murderously angry. If Martin had popped back to fetch his stereo when I came downstairs at ten on Sunday I'd have killed him, just sunk my only good Sabatier knife straight in through the natty top pocket of the linen shirt and minced his body for the chooks. Good yellow yolks they'd have after a meal like that I daresay.

But he didn't, so I paced about the patio for a while in the dusk. Taking deep breaths, smelling all the smells of summer as the earth began to breath out and relax after sundown. I sat with Dog and stroked her back and she stood still, wagging her tail slow as a hypnotist's pendulum with her eyes half shut. We went down the garden and stood by the chooks' pen to hear all the little talking in their sleep noises, so full of comfortableness.

After ten minutes of wondering about chicken's dreams . . . encounters with worms like juicy spaghetti, sitting on a clutch of eggs that hatches in seconds . . . I felt calm. Well maybe not calm but resolved anyway. Ready for the first stage of clinical removal.

No major surgery can be done without anaesthetic so I administered a controlled dose of alcohol. It had to be controlled because we'd run out of anything I really like and could be uncontrolled about. So I poured four fingers of whisky into a mug and drank it down in one whilst holding my nose.

I started on his clothes. A wardrobe full of shirts and jackets and the occasional punctuating suit layered like archaeological strata. Old ones never actually thrown away, just superseded by new, laid on top, the quality of the cloth and the profile of the labels charting his upward progress on the career ladder. Every garment had a story that I knew, a snapshot image of Martin attached as clearly as if a Polaroid were pinned to every pocket. Here was the cream Van Heusen of his father's that had been his only 'work' shirt for a year. Here was the Liberty's blue shirt he had worn on holiday in Brittany standing on the shore, the shirt, the sea and his eyes all the same colour. And here underneath another was the Armani linen shirt I had bought him for Christmas that I thought was a mainstay of his London Media wardrobe.

I felt like Mrs Caterpillar looking through Mr Caterpillar's discarded skins the day after he turned into a moth. If it hadn't been for the booze and the child-induced Sabatier tendencies, my cold turkey decision would have dissolved there and then in a little pool of acid tears. I folded everything neatly and packed it all into cases. What wouldn't fit I put in bin liners with carefully written labels around their necks. 'T-shirts self-coloured', 'Shirts 1985–1989', 'Shirts 1993–1995', 'Socks, black and coloured'.

After two more fingers of medicinal whisky I was set for another night of manic activity. By one I had sorted novels into his and hers, (Gabriel Garcia Marquez and Martin Amis for him, Helen Dunmore and Wila Catha for her), taken down all pictures with particular Martin associations, removed all his awards and trophies.

He'd already taken both the books of his own photgraphs, *Colour It Africa*, and *West Coast Visions*, but his pictures of our life were still on the walls, up the stairs, on the piano, over the bath. I took them all down, his stylised primary bright view of the world, his creative cataloguing of the children. From Frankie's peach-blossom skin luminous on a bed of dark green shawl, to a surreal vision of Dan in the sack race at school, his red T-shirt so bright it enveloped him in fire. I thought Martin's pictures had shown me the view through his eyes, but all the time he'd cropped his experience to put on the wall. I'd only ever seen the framing he'd chosen for me to see. Looking at his orange Colorado landscapes now, I just wondered who had been standing behind the lens with him.

By three, I had disconnected the complex and long-loved stereo . . . the speakers he'd driven a hundred miles to pick up, the deck he'd walked the length of Tottenham Court Road to find . . . and taken all the Athlete's Foot Kelly and His Miserable Mates-type records and CDs off the shelves.

By four, Martin's personal possessions plus a fair division of pictures, and jointly owned bits like nice pottery and little sculptures were stowed in a raft of cardboard boxes and bin bags in the middle of the living-room floor. The empty shelves had a ransacked look and the spaces on the walls had a corpse-like nakedness, but the first stage of radical surgery was done.

I went upstairs to my bed and slept like a stone for two straight hours. At six the kids wormed into bed beside me hot and soft and still smelling slightly of their father, waiting to be coaxed and moulded into the start of another week.

The next stage of Martin extraction had to be done without anaesthetic because it doesn't create a good impression with lawyers to stagger into their offices at ten a.m. after a quarter of a pint of Jameson's. The legal procedures of a divorce were going to be like the chemotherapy treatment of a tumour: makes you feel bloody awful at the time but saves your life in the long run.

I'd rung James and Mary first thing in the morning whilst I made hot Weetabix and toast for the kids.

'Jess, are you all right?'

'How did you know it was me?'

'There isn't anyone else I know traumatised enough to ring at six thirty.'

'Oh, I'm so sorry. The kids got me up. They were hungry. I didn't look at the clock.'

'Don't worry my dear. I've been up making strawberry jam since five. What can I do for you?'

I held that image of Mary for a moment, in her kitchen, presiding over a vat of bubbling jam, her winceyette dressing gown basted around her ample body.

'I need a lawyer.'

'A divorce lawyer?'

'Yes.' I didn't want to say the D word in front of Dan.

'My dear girl. Are you certain?'

'Yes. He's like a gangrenous foot . . . if I don't chop him off all of me will turn green and smelly.'

'I must say I'm sure it's the right decision. I'll ask James for his opinion on the matter and I'll call you back in half an hour. Are you sure you don't need a little company?'

'I'm fine Mary. Your jam needs you.'

'As a matter of fact I'm having problems with my set. Anyway, cheerio for now.'

So, four hours later, stone-cold sober, in a clean pair of jeans, with polished DMs and an ironed shirt, I was ushered into a consulting room at Marbel, Mays and Marchant to meet James's recommendation, Bertie Taylor. I couldn't imagine what Bertie might originally have been short for – Beatrice, Bethany, Elizabeth – but she used it at the top of her faxes like an ordinary name: Miss Bertie Taylor. Sounded a bit music-hallish for a divorce lawyer, but James said she was the best in the county. She'd fitted me in on a cancellation she said, but I suspected it was at James's pleading.

'Miss Taylor will be in shortly. Do take a seat.'

You could tell it was a room used for matrimonial stuff because the only thing on the table was a huge box of tissues. I was going to try not to need them. And so far it looked good . . . shaking, nervous but not ready to cry. This had to be done like dissection, not a person but a body; not a marriage but a contract. Just tease out the organs, follow the arteries to their source and keep spraying on the formalin. James had said all I'd have to do was answer questions at this stage, very basic easy questions like 'What is your name?'

'Mrs Harvey,' Bertie Taylor burst through the door and started talking in one exploding bubble of energy, 'I'm so sorry to have kept you waiting.' Immediately I felt like a small jam doughnut beside a large two-tiered iced cake. Messy, insubstantial and soft edged, beside geometric and purposeful formality. This was the archetype of successful womanhood: physically solid, no truck here with fashionable fragility, style without flash but with lots of power. Even the hair in her blonde bob looked like it did what it was told. Her shoes probably shined themselves, fearful lest they should miss a spot and incur her disapproval.

'I understand from James Walton-Naseby that you wish to take divorce proceedings against your husband. Am I correct?'

'Yes.' Oh well, so the first question wasn't too difficult then.

'I need to start by taking a few basic details.' She was like a big lifeguard pulling a drowning dog out of the canal, firm, kind, but with no tolerance of struggling, whining or barking.

She asked my name. Martin's name. The address of the marital home. Martin's new address. None of those felt bad. But they were just marking the dead skin for the incision: 'Are there children of the marriage?' That was it, the cut to the bloody inside. The children of the marriage, everything else could be sliced and apportioned back to two single people, but Dan and Frankie were made of the marriage itself. To wilfully destroy that seemed like the most fundamental of betrayals: raising Pinocchio as a real boy only to tell him that in truth he was always made of carved wood, as dead as a chair.

I did need the tissues. Almost half a box, by the time we got to the grounds for the divorce.

Hobson's choice.

Irretrievable breakdown? No, not as far as I was concerned. I wasn't going to give Martin the material to construct a fictional tragic marriage with which to impress his friends . . . 'we were both trapped. Just . . . trapped by it. Divorce was the only way'.

Two years' legal separation? Two whole years unresolved and in the pending tray. I could be on a zimmer by then. Forget it.

Adultery? Not grounds for divorce in my book. It's always seemed silly to throw away a marriage because of one episode of extreme bonking. He could install Dolores in the spare room and shag her there just as long as he didn't leave me and the kids.

But the reason he left us was Dolores. Or so he said. So adultery was the nearest approximation to the truth.

So: 'Divorce on the grounds of adultery with an unknown woman?'

'Okay.'

Eventually Bertie explained to me all the practical details about the dismembering of the body of our marriage. She gave me forms to fill in, advice on financial survival, getting control of our bank account. Finally she said, 'You will be surprised how strong you will become.'

'Yeah,' I said through the twentieth tissue, 'I bet you say that to all the girls.'

For the first time in two hours she laughed, and her hair went a little unruly. But only for a moment.

The kids went to Kath's after school, she sweetly said she'd keep them overnight. They were glad to get away from me for a while, to have a little rest from me being miserable. Anyway I didn't want them to be home when the van came to take Martin's stuff away. The driver was a friend of Gerry's who did delivery jobs and happened to be free to take it all to London for me. Today. Gerry fixed it in ten minutes first thing this morning.

I rang Martin at his publishers as soon as I got back from Bertie, while I was still feeling strong and tough.

'You can't do this Jess,' he said, 'you can't just tip my stuff out on to the street.' He couldn't shout – I could hear other people in the room with him.

'I didn't tip it out on the street. I have packed it all very neatly and carefully. Clothes, books, records CDs, stereo, and your bike. It'll be arriving at Dolores's flat at about eight thirty this evening. I thought that would be convenient for you after work.'

'You can't do this Jess. This is totally unreasonable.'

'Martin, what is unreasonable about sending your belongings from where you don't live to where you do?'

'You should have consulted me first. It's very inconvenient.'

'I'm sorry Martin. But this friend of Gerry's offered such a cheap deal.'

'I don't care. You'll just have to cancel him.'

'No Martin, I'm not going to do that.'

'Jess. JESS, YOU CAN'T DO THIS.'

'I just have.'

And I hung up. And I didn't cry.

I didn't even cry when Gerry's mate had loaded it all into the van and driven away. This was a 'logical conclusion' and Martin has always been really big on 'logical conclusions'.

'The logical conclusion of that argument Jess, is that we should all live in mud huts' 'Jess, for God's sake can't you follow anything to its logical conclusion!'

Thinking of Martin's 'logical conclusions' stopped me thinking of his hand in the small of my back, the things he wrote in birthday cards, 'Jess, my darling love. You are far more than I deserve.' 'The Happiest Of Birthdays, all the love in the Universe, your Martin.' And the way he couldn't sleep on Christmas morning: awake at five, desperate for presents and fairy lights, shaking the children at six, unable to wait any longer, 'Wake up. It's Christmas,' as if it was the first time ever, as if someone had just put the baby with the Colgate ring around his head on top of our chicken shed.

It made me more resolved to give him a few logical conclusions of my own. Like the logical conclusion of saying you don't love me any more is that we get divorced. The logical conclusion of moving in with Dolores is that your stuff moves out of here.

Making decisions seems to make me feel better. One reason I could manage to wave goodbye to the last evidence of

Martin's shared occupancy of this house was making decision number three.

Last week, after James told me to beware of Martin disappearing to Timbuktu with the pension fund, I dug out my CV from some ancient dusty computer disk at the back of the desk drawer. Our new computer (yeah, that's one thing of Martin's I didn't pack up and send. Inability to use computer games as child sedatives would be intolerable at the moment), treated it as if it were doggie dos but just about managed to translate its antiquated and degraded information into something it could deal with. By the time I'd tarted it up, added a few exaggerations and been extremely economical with the truth about how I've spent the last five years, it looked okay. An executive producer reading it fast on a Monday morning, in a good mood and after his second cup of coffee, desperate for anybody to help with the workload, might think about ringing me. I printed it out and sent it off to David Herring, without the least expectation of a reply. With about as much hope as buying a single lottery ticket.

It's the wrong sort of name for a TV mogul. I always thought David should be called something like Troy Masters or Conrad Ritblatt. Something more thrusting at least, because David was really into thrust, especially when it came to juicy female researchers. He'd been a producer at Media Magic when I'd started grovelling on the studio floor looking for missing teddy eyes. Everybody knew he had his foot firmly on the rungs of the management ladder, and his eyes fixed firmly on the very tippety top. He combined knowing all the secret handshakes with real ability, because he kept getting jobs he wasn't qualified to do, and then doing them. By the time I left he was a senior commissioning editor with a glass-walled office and a desk the size of a small continent, and six months into the job he was ready to jump into a bigger pond.

I knew all his career leaps since, because I had followed them in the TV industry comics. David did so well because he understood that the TV business is like the Mafia, it's business combined with the law of the jungle: deals, alliances and loyalty enforced by fear. I never liked David – ambition that naked is pretty unattractive, it's like having a great big erect penis strapped to your head all the time – but I always felt quite at ease in his company, because I never regarded him as anything other than a kind of automaton. He was as easy to understand as a machine.

And now he was the biggest cheese in the fridge at Charlatan TV, top dude at the company which controlled four of the channel three regional franchises. And with their HQ thirty miles down the road from me.

This morning, just after I'd put the phone down on Martin, David the Big Fromage rang. Well not the man himself, his assistant (twenty-three, five eight, size twelve blonde Gina Davies look alike I guessed), could I come in that very afternoon and see Mr Herring? I'd just look in my diary I said, Oh yes he's in luck I have a window at 2.30. (Yeah and 3.30, 4.30, 5.30 and every other bloody 30 for the rest of my life.)

Jezuz. What did David Herring want with me given that he doesn't have pity or idle curiosity on his hard disk? How did he think I could be useful? Well whatever it was, if it paid, I'd have to do it. If I could just avoid apologising for my CV, my appearance, my age and my having children to care for, I might be in with a chance.

The quality of his suits had gone up, and there was a nasty little incipient softness around the middle of his naturally skinny body, but apart from that he was pretty much the same. Maybe the tiniest smidge of grey in the shiny brown hair, the suggestion of greyness under the dark eyes but nothing more. In a silent room his body might hum, it's so full of racing nervous energy.

'It's great to see you Jess.' The same flat northern voice too. David's no Oxbridge product hauled up to the top by ropes of knotted house ties. He's raw from the ranks, a boy with nothing to get him out of a Barratt box but his own wit and hunger. 'I was really very sad to hear about Martin.' Wow, a triumph of technology, David Herring sounding genuinely compassionate. So genuine in fact that if I'd listened I'd have been on the mat telling him about the parlous state of my undies' drawer. I just had to pretend that I was Mrs Brazil Nut.

'Well David, you know it's an occupational hazard with you media men. Let's get down to business shall we? I'm sure you didn't ask me here to share your condolences.'

'Ah Jess, you haven't changed. The straightest girl in telly.'

'And you haven't changed either David. The most ambitious boy. So what's the deal?'

Now David turned on the charm, persuasive soft-spoken, lots of eye contact. Whoever it was who had put together this bit of software knew what they were up to. It was most lifelike. And terribly revealing. He must want me to do something. He must need my cooperation. Nothing like a little power to make a girl feel good.

'We are making a new pilot strand for daytime TV, for the network. It's called *Pets and Their People*, it explores the essence of the relationship between humans and animals. We have some terrific stories lined up, the man who gave his wife llamas for their twenty-fifth wedding anniversary, the girl who sleeps with fifteen rats in her bed. But it needs a strong presenter lead, somebody who the viewers can identify with and who can get people to talk. And that's where you come in.'

'David, all I've ever done is interfering with soft toys in front of a camera.'

'Yes. But what Media never spotted, and I did, was that you were completely at ease on camera. You never turned a hair. I'd be willing to bet your pulse rate didn't even go up. And you've always been able to get people to talk Jess. You knew the life story of every person in that building.' David leaned forward, eyes on maximum laser-beam setting. 'And you picked up all those mice and hamsters and things on *Mr Bounce* and,' suddenly a note of real school-boy wonder came into David's voice, 'that tarantula without even flinching.'

Well, flattery is nice even if it comes from a machine. I didn't say anything, I knew if I opened my mouth I'd tell him how terrified I really was, all the time.

'Jess, I thought of you as soon as this thing came up. It was just fate that your CV landed on my desk. I feel you'd be so right.' Flattery is nice but only when it is vaguely believable. This wasn't.

'You must think I walked in here out of an incubator. You're telling me that you have a pilot series for a network slot and you don't have a celebrity presenter lined up? Instead you want to use an ex-*Mr Bounce* presenter who hasn't worked for five years. Will you tell me what's really going on?' The laser beam went off, the charm shut down. The machine sat back in its chair.

'Okay. I hate the idea of the programme, but they think they want it. And it is potentially a lot of work for us, two half-hours a week for twenty-eight weeks of the year. And, given that we've just lost the *Treasure Trove* show for Channel Four and we have staff sloshing around like bilge water, we need it. But they want the six pilots by August, and the budget is shit for the pilots although it's a bit better for the real thing. We have eight filming days for six half-hours. We put our money into getting a presenter who would definitely turn out the goods, Monica Mostar, but she pulled out yesterday. So now we have an inexperienced director and no presenter and the crew booked for the day after tomorrow. I need you Jess. I'm pretty sure you can do this really well. It could be a good break for you.'

'No, it won't be David. You know if you get the contract for the strand you'll get some celeb to do it.'

'Yes, that's true, but all the same Jess it could be a route back.'

'Why are you bothering to sort this out? You're too high up the ladder.'

'It's a favour to the Director. We're . . .'

'Close?'

'Yes. Yes. Close. Anyway she was in the shit and I knew you wouldn't do it for someone you didn't know.'

'Touching David. Truth is, you know and I know that I'll do almost anything to get back to earning at the moment. How much a day?'

'Two hundred.' Two hundred for eight days. Mortgage and food for eight weeks, if we didn't have the heating on, buy any clothes or go anywhere. Not enough.

'Don't bargain David, you're not in a position to. You have a crew booked for Wednesday. Why don't you just give me what was in the budget for a presenter?'

'Because I'm using what we save to do more post-production on it, polish it up a bit.'

'Polish less and pay me more. It's not worth my while for less than four hundred.'

'Okay. Four hundred. You'll get written confirmation by fax today and a contract by Friday.'

Damn, he gave in too easily. Should have asked for six. I bet Monica Mostar wasn't doing it for anything the cheap side of fifteen hundred.

I almost ran out of Charlatan doing maths in my head. Four hundred a day! More than three thousand quid in the bank by the end of the month. That could last all summer. So Martin and Dolores could run off to Timbuktu. Well until October anyway.

I was well down the road, carried along with fantasies of financial independence and plans to open all bank statements and bills without fear when the panic set in.

I pulled into a layby and got out. How was I going to do this? Stand in front of a camera for the first time in five years? Impossible. It was difficult enough the first time round, and that was without wrinkles and a wardrobe of clothes like worn-out sacking. No use wearing a blue silk frock to meet a llama. And what was I going to do about the kids after school? Doing nearly twenty-five minutes of telly in one day was going to mean filming until light stopped play. I lay down on the grass taking deep breaths until I could see the sky again and hear the *sschwapp sschwapp* of passing cars.

It would all just have to be all right. The kids could go to Kath's or Sarah's, maybe Jo's even, after school. It was just eight days after all. Monica Mostar would get the real gig . . . more than fifty days filming at four hundred a time. With money like that Martin and Dolores could emigrate to Alpha Centauri if they wanted.

Chapter Eight

Being at eye level with a Great Dane's testicles isn't my idea of having a good time. Huge and taut, like comice pears made of flesh, and covered with little tufts of ginger hair they swished past my nose every time the animal did another circuit of the tiny garden.

The first filming day for *Pets and Their People* had got off to a difficult start. Basil and Bono didn't like strangers, least of all strangers with cameras and odd black boxes of equipment. They would only stop their stentorian barking if we all sat or crouched.

'They're just big babies really,' said Janice, their owner, as they walked up to Rob, the cameraman and snarled, babylike and endearing as a rabid wolf.

I perched on the kerb of the path with Janice beside me making streams of excuses for her pets' ceaseless aggression and waiting for an opportunity to interview her on camera, preferably with dogs' faces rather than bollocks in shot.

There were huge dog turds like giant slugs everywhere, lurking in every tuft of grass. We'd all stepped in them at least twice whilst setting up and avoiding Basil and Bono's dear little snarls. We were all deeply unhappy. It was eleven o'clock with not a single moment of usable footage in the can and we had two more stories to do before bath time.

Judith, the director, was twitching with anxiety, obsessively putting her long blonde hair (David Herring as predictable in his female choices as ever) behind her ears and crossing things out on her clipboard in brightly coloured felt-tip. Only Steve, the recordist, looked content, propped against the wall as far from the dogs as he could get and still monitor the sound from our radio mikes.

'Come to Mama,' crooned Janice for the fiftieth time, and instead of continuing their ball-displaying circuit, Bono and Basil did come to her. I was at last acceptable it seemed, and as a sign of their approval they were going to lick and slobber all over me.

'There you are, just like babies. Oooz Momma's ikkle babee ven?' said Janice.

'Okay turnover. And. Action.'

'Janice, tell me about Basil and Bono here . . .' If I'd had any residual nerves, being eye to eye with both ends of a Great Dane would have killed them.

Even before the ginger tufted genitalia it had been a difficult day. Dan and Frankie were ready for mutiny from the moment they got up and remembered that this was the start of eight school days from hell, having to do without Mummy to pick them up and get their tea.

'I'm not going to school. I'm just not. You can't make me,' said Frankie at twenty-five past eight from under her bed. 'I won't be picked up by strangers and have to be in their house just so you can do stupid work.'

Where should I begin? With the fact that Kath and Gerry and their kids Joe and Louis are hardly strangers after six years of friendship? Or with the fact that without the stupid work we'll have to sell the stupid house and be on the stupid streets? Last night I braved the bank statements and the bills. Martin moved fast and his pay cheque didn't go into the joint account last month. He seems to have put in nothing else instead, so as of Friday when the mortgage gets paid we are in big debt. Or with the fact that it is now gone half-past eight and I have eighty minutes of driving to do in an hour to be on location in time? Or with the fact that it's not my bloody fault this is happening?

'Frankie, I'm so sorry. But it's only for a few days that we'll have to do this. Come on sweetie. Please.'

'No, go away. Go to stupid work. I'll stay here.'

'Frankie you're eight. It's illegal to leave you alone in the house. I could go to prison.'

'Good.'

Of course when one child is being foul the other wades in to display virtue. Dan stomped up the stairs and burst into Frankie's room, school bag on his back ready and waiting.

'Come ON, we'll be late. Frankie you Durr. Come on.'

'Get out of my room. I hate you I hate you I hate you.' Frankie emphasised her words with a stream of missiles.

'You Durr Frankie!'

'Dan this isn't helpful. Go and wait downstairs.'

'Don't be horrible. I'm trying to help.'

'You aren't helping. Get out!'

'Don't push me. Don't take it out on me because Dad's left.'

'I'm not. Just do as you're told for once.'

'Don't be horrible to Dan too, you old cow.' Frankie wriggled out from under the bed and stood before me brazen and jeering. 'You're always horrible to everyone. Come on Dan, let's get in the car.' They flounced down the stairs together. What now? Scream? Laugh? Sob? No, just get in the car and get to work.

Of course by the time we were at the school gates, they were sorry. Full of hugs and kisses, looking into my face for signs of upset. Then out of the car like escaped larks, leaving me feeling that the working day had already been ten hours long.

But still I drove off with relief. Freed for a day from parental responsibility, given goal and purpose beyond going home and wondering if I should ring Martin and remind him that his name is still on the mortgage if we default.

I drove with the window down in spite of the spitting rain, to smell the wet summer of bent droplet-laden grasses and water-filled flowers. Underneath the coolness and the misting of cloud and showers, summer was still happening, relentlessly pushing on with a dour straight mouth through June, hoping for a better July. Like me, head down through the present hoping the future might be okay.

Then I put the radio on. It was a mistake, but I could have turned it off when I heard the first few notes and knew what it would do to me. The Bangles, or the Bagels as Frankie calls them. Prince's little protégés they were. All girls, with cute harmonies, clever west-coast lyrics and dinky sentimental tunes. Just the sort of thing Martin loathes. And here was the song he hated most of all, full of rhymes like shine and mine, memory and set-you-free. Corny stuff about eyes meeting and the loss of love.

It did for me. In seconds Martin's eyes were in front of me. Dolly-blue as my mum would have called them, looking over a little wrought iron table in a Toronto café. For a moment oddly formal, smiling at himself for being a touch nervous. He even cleared his throat. A detail that made my eyes prickle every time I thought of it.

'Jess, I want you to be my wife. I want us always to be together.'

He looked, in my memory, like he meant it. We'd remembered it together as if he had.

But he's thrown it away because it didn't mean enough to him. Now it only existed in my head like that, perhaps no more real than some scene held from a movie. Less true than a story.

All of Martin, all of my life with him, would be just a memory if he never came back. Just a memory with nothing carried forward into today or tomorrow to show that my past was ever real. No shared past, no building on a history. No old jokes that no one else understands. No thread. No continuity. My memories just the same as a pile of book-club novels with their spines shot.

And now here was the bit in the song about the lover's voice losing its warmth and affection. Oh God why didn't I just switch the bloody thing off? I'd always loved his voice. A raspy deepness underneath the grammar-school RP. Down phone lines from across the world, in the pitch dark of bedrooms, and even from the depths of anaesthetics, it had warmed me through and through. And now it warmed another woman and would never speak to me again.

At last the final lines: What's the point of it all? What's the point of surviving and being tough if all you want is the person you can't have? Trying to rebuild something was a waste of time. Those friends of Mary's at the party, they'd survived, but the biggest thing in their lives was still the great gaping hole in it. Nothing had replaced the trauma and bleeding, no new limbs had grown back.

I'd always said to Martin that if I was ever in a crash or something and survived, but without being able to do anything like walk or stand up, he was to shoot me. I wanted all of my physical life or none. I want all my emotional life too, or none.

Through the streaming tears I saw I was driving at ninety-five and it didn't seem to matter.

All that melodrama because of a song with a tune and lyrics about as sophisticated as 'Three Blind Mice'. Martin, who likes music as random notes played every three seconds or as some old gin-soak coughing his guts up down a microphone, would never fall for such a thing. So why did he leave me for someone who likes Queen?

If that is what my brain is going to do every time I drive to a location driving into a motorway pillar at ninety really is going to be a sweet release.

Of course it did matter that I was driving at ninety-five, because it meant that in spite of the under-the-bed scene I still got to work on time.

The RV (that's crew-speak for rendezvous) was at a Little Chef down the road from Basil and Bono's place. It's easy to spot film crews. Theirs is the big car with lots of rather sinister black and silver boxes in the back which look large enough to have major portions of human bodies inside (legs in that long one, torso, spare head, assorted arms, fingers left hand, fingers right hand, etc). The driver, the cameraman or woman, wears expensive outdoor clothing – top of the range Berghaus jacket, a Patagonia fleece, Rohan bags; the passenger will look similar, but will be talking (and probably smoking). This is the sound recordist. Off duty they talk incessantly because they spend their working lives having to shut up and listen to everybody else through their earphones.

The accompanying director is more variable. More stylish, (black Calvin Klein jeans or Levis, leather jacket) or messier (holey sweater with cake crumbs), usually more attractive, (the arrogance necessary to do the job promotes a kind of physical self-confidence) definitely more animated. Usually to be found standing close to the camera person explaining things. If they've worked together before they'll be explaining things to each other. If they haven't and the director is inexperienced, he or she may simply be in a car biting nails over a clipboard.

So I identified Rob, Steve and Judith as I drove into the car-park even though they deviated from the basic stereotypes in some respects. They were standing by one large family-of-eight-plus-dog-carrying sort of car with Styrofoam cups of coffee. Rob was the one with the leather jacket, Steve didn't smoke and Judith looked neither more stylish nor more messy. Just more impractical: leopard-skin leggings, high spike-heeled boots, a wide gold belt over a black shirt. And of course a huge cascade of long honey-coloured hair. She did have the clipboard and was ticking things off on it as she talked to Rob, who was looking up at her as if she was speaking Serbo-Croat. Both of them kept glancing nervously at the sky, where the blue and the grey were still struggling for supremacy.

They weren't looking out for me. I parked, repaired the tear damage to my make-up and walked over the tarmac to introduce myself.

'Hello I'm Jess –' I very nearly said Harvey '– Wallace.' I was damned if even half of his name was going to get on telly because of me. I've always liked my own surname better than his anyway.

'Hello! I'm Judith Nunn, and this is Rob Strachan and Steve Rolands.' We all shook hands very solemnly. I like shaking hands – nice little bit of definite ritual to get you over those sticky first thirty seconds. Rob and Steve both made growling noises as they shook my hand and smiled uncertainly at me: suspicious that I might lengthen all their working days by doing everything in over sixteen takes. But then so was I.

'Thank you so much for agreeing to do this Jess, at such short notice,' beamed Judith. Close up she looked like a tall blonde mouse and sounded as if she'd had voice training from Jimmy Osmond. She was young, twenty-six maybe. Ex-PA I guessed, like David struggling up from the ranks. Her make-up was flawless but I have terrible unsisterly prejudices about such things, a gut-level reaction that tells me intelligence and false eyelashes can't be found on the same person. But I beamed back. This was after all TV.

'It's a pleasure.' Almost anything is for four hundred smackers a day.

'Can I get you a coffee?' A blonde mouse but great manners. This was definitely not the usual director stereotype.

'Thanks, I'd love one.' While Judith fetched coffees, Rob began to suss out their chances of knocking off work on schedule.

'Judith said you've done quite a bit of presenting before?' There's something disarming about a scouse voice. Scouses would make good interrogators: 'Aw, c'mon then, tell us who did it? You know you wanna.'

'A bit, but it was a long time ago.' No point trying to play it anything but straight. Pretend you know what you don't with a crew and they're like piranhas, 'To be honest Rob, I'm terrified.' Rob and Steve shared a millisecond long glance of 'Oh shit', but they knew their shortest route home was via boosting my confidence.

'Naw? You don' wanna be terrified. We look after yous. Won't we Steve?'

'Yeah. Falling off a log. It'll all come back to you the moment Judy says go.'

We were none of us convinced by that. The coffee arrived and we all got into the big car to travel to Janice's together.

I suppose the good thing about crying all the way to the RV is that I hadn't had the chance to get nervous. In the ten-minute drive to the Dog House I made up for lost time and arrived outside the tiny bungalow on the village edge hyperventilating and clammy.

'I think we'll just knock off the programme opening here,' said Judith. Nothing nervous about her. In fact she was disproving my exclusion rule about false eyelashes. Tough, capable and bright, even in spike heels and with terrible taste in automaton boyfriends.

Judith handed me a script with the opening written on it, and I paced about reading it, trying to get the words to stick to my brain whilst Rob and Steve set up the camera. My whole body seemed filled with white noise and a voice telling me most emphatically that this was impossible, that I was old, ugly and talentless, and that there was no way I could stand in front of a camera and talk.

'Ready when you are Jess,' called Judith. 'Just walk from where you are now and stop and talk when you get to the cherry tree.'

I tucked the script into the back of my jeans out of shot.

'I just need to blow my nose.' That could get me another, what twenty seconds or so, to calm down before she said turn over. I pulled out a tissue and buried my nose in it noisily. My heart was coming out of my mouth, my throat was dry, I was shaking.

I can't do this, I can't do this, went round in my head, a mantra at the volume of a pile driver.

'Are you okay?'

'Just give me a moment.'

What was I going to do? Leap into the car and drive off at speed? Tell Judith that it was all a terrible mistake and say I had to go home? Tell them I was too grief-stricken to work? Pretend to have a heart attack?

No. Because running around my skull in panic I hit a big brick wall. The same wall I hit after my parents died when I realised no one was going to make me hot toast and cocoa in bed ever again. No one was going to save me here. No one was going to sort out my life for me. If I walked away from my only potential employment, Martin wasn't there any more to pick up the tab. This work wasn't to try to keep some sort of self-respect in the face of Martin's huge success and my increasingly demanding career as nappy changer and milk machine. This work was to keep my kids in the house they loved, feed them, clothe them and fulfil my role as responsible parent. There weren't any choices. I had to do it. Nervousness was a childish luxury I couldn't afford any longer.

My heart beat slowly. My hands were steady. My head was almost uncomfortably clear.

'Sorry about that. I'm ready now.'

'Okay . . . in your own time then.'

I walked up the road. Relaxed. Natural. Smiling. I rewrote what I was going to say in my head to make it flow and be funny. I stopped at the cherry tree. I delivered my lines, word perfect. No fluffs. One take.

'Cut.'

'Dunno what you were worrying about,' said Rob. He patted me on the back. No reserve in their smiles now. I could see him and Steve thinking 'Home in time for tea in front of Brookie. Yess'.

Once Bono and Basil had decided that we weren't lunch, we got the interview done very quickly. The dogs behaved and Janice was a good talker. Judith wanted some shots of the dogs alone, so Janice and I were left to chat. Part of the job is nattering to contributors and keeping them happy.

'Have you always kept dogs Janice?'

'Yes. Not always Danes though. Dachshunds, that's what me and Les had. Our babies. Look.' She leaned across to the mantelpiece and took down a gilt-framed photo. There was Janice in the same mauve track suit with a small dark chap with thinning hair and a big nose. In their arms they each cuddled something like a giant frankfurter with ears.

'That's Les my husband, he left me.'

'No. When?' I couldn't help sounding shocked. The way she'd said it made it sound as if he'd just gone. Walked out the day before yesterday.

'Oh, six years ago.' She took out a hanky from her track-suit pocket and twisted it in her small fat fingers. 'Ran off with a girl from the office. He was a lorry driver for the quarry. She was in the office where they go to get their jobs for the day. Didn't come 'ome for his tea one night. Lamb chops it was. His favourite. They live in Kent now. I got a letter from there. Somewhere round there anyway.'

'What happened to the dachshunds?'

'Couldn't stand the sight of them after he'd gone. Had 'em put down.' I put the photo back in its place and Judith came in.

'That's it Janice, we've finished. We'll get out of your way.' Best thing to do if you meet a woman who has her babies murdered because their dad's eloped with another woman.

The llama people, the Mardy family, were just down the road. A new house tucked down the bottom of a long muddy track with all sorts of bits built on quite randomly and very likely without the benefit of any sort of planning permission. The garden consisted of a half-built swimming pool and a big field where the two llamas ran about like a pair of very skilled pantomime horses. They looked as though they were about to speak.

At first I thought we'd arrived by mistake at a huge family

reunion. There were children of all sizes and a surprising number of adults who seemed to treat each other as relatives. But it emerged that this was normal. Mr Mardy, Bob, was a solid red-faced chap and he'd built more house to accommodate more family. Including more wives. The llamas were bought for his first wife from whom he was now divorced.

'When did we get divorced Marge?'

'Oh, now. I never remember. Um was it '81 or '83? I know it was an odd number. Same year as Mother had her op.'

Marge still lived in the house and so did their three kids, plus their eldest boy's girlfriend and their baby. Marge and Bob still celebrated their wedding anniversary.

'Twenty-five year ago last August we were wed. I saw them llamas in the market at Gosmore, and I thought, that's it. That's what I have to get for Marge for our anniversary.'

Julie, Mrs Mardy number two, didn't mind.

'He got me a Marks skirt and a nice dwarf lop for our anniversary,' she said with some pride, 'although it doesn't fit me now,' and she patted her hugely pregnant belly. 'The skirt I mean, not the rabbit.' And the two women beamed and giggled at each other.

'More 'n you ever got out of me when we were married innit Julie love?' Julie's former husband and his twin baby boys by some other relationship were also Mardy residents.

I must admit we glossed over the complexities of the relationships for the programme. The Mardys didn't mind but I felt the Sunday newspapers wouldn't give them a moment's peace. So we emphasised the anniversary and didn't talk about the divorce. And anyway even after spending an hour taking tea with them all at Bob's absolute insistence, I still didn't quite understand who was who. What did get through was that Bob was keen on continuity. He'd been married to Marge and he wasn't going to lose out on all those shared years.

'I didn't want to get divorced you know. But I was determined not to lose her even if we did. It'd be a waste,' he said, 'if she moved away. I'll just build on a bit more when she gets hitched again.'

It made me feel much better about my suggestion of putting Martin and Dolores in the spare room.

There was one more story to do about a juggling Alsatian, but Judith wanted it to run without words as a music sequence, so they drove me back to the Little Chef to get my car. I could go home. It was half-past five, if I put my foot down I'd be back by seven. Get the kids from Kath's, home by seven-thirty – time to make them snacks, read a story and generally try to make them feel that they haven't been left tied to the table with a tin of beans and a can opener.

The moment we parked I was out of the car, saying goodbye as fast as basic etiquette would allow. Judith got out and walked across the car-park with me.

'David told me about your situation,' she whispered feelingly and put a hand on my arm.

'Don't give me sympathy Judith, I'll only cry all over you.'

'I just wanted to tell you, it will be all right. You will get over it.' Her conviction irritated me. What could a blonde mouse with false eyelashes know about what I felt?

'Clairvoyant are you Judith?' I hissed and pulled my arm away. That ought to shut her up.

But it didn't. She just put her hair behind her ears a few times, and started talking again. She was determined to have her say.

'My husband was violent. And when he started hitting my kids, I left. We had to climb over the garden fence at two in the morning while he was asleep. Marcus and Ellen were big enough to climb but I had to have Lucy on my back. We had nothing but a carrier bag of clothes. He fought for custody for a year, and after he lost he used to sit in his car opposite our house and shout abuse. He attacked me one night as I came home and that's when we got the court order. We don't have any trouble now.'

'Judith. I'm sorry. It's just that you don't look old enough for much to have happened to you.' A husband walking out in tears on a sunny summer morning seemed like two weeks on a beach in Cyprus compared with what Judith had been through. I felt myself blushing.

'I started early. I was pregnant at fifteen. Marcus is in secondary school now. I left my husband five years ago, it seems much longer. The first year was hell. I wanted to die. But I'm fine now and you will be too.' She looked right at me, out from under the Max Factor and the eye furniture, strong, sensible and determined. The leggings were camouflage for the blue stockings underneath.

All the way home it went round in my head like the tiger at the bottom of Sambo's tree, 'so fast it turned into butter'. All the sadness from all those lives. Janice driving to the vet's with the doomed dachshunds, Bob Mardy at the builders merchants buying the bricks for Marge's extension, Judith and her children fishing their clean undies from the one poly bag. And then Martin. Martin endlessly driving down the lane to our house. How many times did he stop at the top of the hill and almost turn back I wondered? Just how slowly did he drive those last few miles? Much as he might hate The Bangles, their corny lyrics were true for him too. What good was being strong, being the perfect dad and the perfect husband. What was the point if all he wanted was the person he couldn't have? Dolores.

I didn't cry on the way home. It was all too sad and way too ordinary. Just little humans all muddling along.

Thank God the kids had had a lovely time at Kath's. When I arrived they were still outside in a den of bamboo canes and old sacks. The remains of two vast pizzas were strewn on the grass being gobbled by Sal, their dog, and Dog, who'd spent the day there. The afternoon here had been warm and bright, and the evening seemed like proper summer, with light the colour of a good pudding wine. Kath was still in work, some conference do at the Court, Gerry was trimming the hedge, and swearing at the clippers in a good-natured sort of way.

'Can't stop luv,' he said, 'that Kaff she's a stickler. She'll 'ave me bits on a stick if I 'aven't done this 'edge tonight.'

'Thanks for having the kids.'

'No probs.' He stopped clipping and turned on the ladder. ''Ow was today then? Must say you're lookin' much better.'

'It was fine Ger. I can still do it, thank God. So my bacon is saved for a while.'

'Great. Oh, I just thought of somink. Kaff said d'you want a lodger . . . might help wiv the mortgage and that? She's got some chap startin' at the Court, chef or somink. I dunno. Talk to 'er.'

'Me with a lodger? You must be kidding! I'd have to give up walking round with no clothes on.'

'No! You just charge extra for that.'

'I'll call her later.'

I piled the kids into the car and drove home. Looking at them in the rear-view mirror I saw that the afternoon of playing had smoothed out all the little wrinkles of care, the evening sunshine gilded them with ordinary childhood.

They chattered about their afternoon like a couple of sparrows. I heard how they'd built the den, about the water fight, about Dog trying to mate with Sal ('My Dog is a Lesbian' says presenter of *Pets and Their People*).

We coasted down the last hill with the engine off, a little secret homage to my father who always did the same down big hills, an act of mini subversion that made him giggle with delight every time. Irritated the hell out of me whilst he was alive, so I do it now as penance, and I've come to like it. We cruised quietly to a halt in the yard.

I felt terrifically lightened, like a balloon when you let go of the string, or the space opening up between uncoupled carriages. I could work, I could earn to keep the children. I could go on wanting Martin, but practically, I didn't have to go on needing him. He could be free to go. Or to come back.

'They've cut the field Mummy come and look.' Dan and Frankie were wriggling over the stile in excitement, 'Can we go and play on the bales?'

The deep waves and billows of grass submerging the field opposite our house had been drained, shaved down to the white stalks. The ocean of plants had been all parcelled away, rolled up into great round monoliths of swirling green and jade. We walked over the spiky stubble between the towering giant bales.

The kids didn't want to climb them then, but wandered between them dreamily. The bales had a Stonehengeish sort of grandeur that invaded us and made us quiet. I put my face close to the coiled end of one of them, and looked at the stalks of colour riven through it: every shade of leaf and sea imaginable and a sweet spicy smell.

Dan found a black feather. The rooks had been here too, to the bottom of the grass sea, to pick up the stranded life left behind as the green tide rolled away.

Frankie found two, and soon there was a little rivalry between them. For a moment it threatened to curdle the other-worldly atmosphere, the sense of being outside our lives for a moment, away from all the crying. But then Dan gave a feather to Frankie to even up the numbers, and then she gave him all three feathers she found next.

'Time to go in.' And they did. As she climbed the stile in front of me, Frankie put her face close to mine and held a black feather between us, under my nose.

'Smell, Mummy. It smells of flying!'

It did. The dry musky smell of a hot bird's body flounced in the sun and the blue air.

She turned from the stile and ran in after her brother, and I stood and closed my eyes. Just for a moment I let go the pain, another string, another balloon, and I sent Martin a clean thought of a still summer evening and the sweet sad smell of new-mown hay.

Chapter Nine

By the end of the eight days' filming it was getting ridiculous. I mean it's only supposed to be one marriage in four that ends in divorce, but all the people we interviewed for the series had at least one divorce each. Sometimes two. There must have been about fifty marriages between the thirty or so people besotted enough about their pets to feature in the programme. Maybe that says something about how marriage partners respond to animals, or maybe it says something about how people respond to divorce. Probably both: you marry someone whose obsession with pigeons is so great they've converted half their house to pigeon loft, and divorce them when they won't take up golf instead. You start breeding setters because there's no one left to nag about dirtying the furniture now he's run off with his secretary. You keep eight Persians because you're afraid that otherwise no living thing will share your bed again.

In the space of a few days I was given a guided tour of divorce: from amicable to belligerent, from winners to losers, from the first day to forty years on. It was sobering. When a marriage crashes, nobody walks away without injury, usually the loss of limbs and other major body parts. Some people are still dripping blood twenty years afterwards. But what everybody does is to make a life, not the same, but just as complex as the one that existed before.

At the moment I can't imagine that for myself. My life after Martin seems flat and simple, like those rainforests built on sand after they've been logged. There's nothing in the soil, no capital. All liquid assets. Everything is in the living bodies of the plants and animals, instantly recycled into new ones when they die.

Cut down this forest and nothing will regrow, beyond a bit of weed cover with a few beetles in it. Maybe the occasional bird. They don't regain diversity.

But just because I can't imagine it, it doesn't mean it won't happen. I'm not unique. I'm not special. So there's no reason why I shouldn't recover just like other people do.

Maybe I'll suddenly discover a burning passion to breed black hamsters and teach myself lace-making and join a choir and take my children canoeing in Cornwall. Or I'll find I have a talent with tortoises and through breeding them I'll make friends with other tortoise fanciers and we'll go on tortoise viewing holidays in Greece. Or I'll find fulfilment through rescuing stray dogs and I'll fill my house with canine delinquents and spend all my life smelling of dog shit.

It's none of it as good as raising your children with their father, who is the man you love. But it could be something. It could be a life. Just not what I'd planned.

That's been my little internal mantra this week: 'It isn't what I planned'. Maybe I should just designate it now as my epitaph. Nothing on any scale seems to be how I'd planned it at the moment.

It certainly wasn't on Friday. Our last filming day. The day when we had to do all the links, all the little stupid bits of chat that join a programme together. Links are pointless, I mean when you read a magazine, you don't have links, you just turn the page. There isn't a bit at the end of an article about making cranberry ice-cream telling you how it is strangely linked to the bit on the next page about oral sex. Although, of course, there could be a fairly obvious link there. So links are redundant, but TV people love them, and cling to them and generally behave as if their lives depended on them. This is especially true at my end of the TV market, i.e. the bottom end, where programmes are thrown together in an afternoon, and the only way to make them even remotely coherent is to have some twit like me making spurious and bantering verbal connections between items that are completely unrelated.

So on our last filming day we had to shoot at least thirty-six links. More, because Judith wasn't sure if she was putting juggling Alsatians into programme one or two, or if the interior designer with the tree frog obsession (and the third husband) should go next to the policeman with a giant python in his cellar (wife left six weeks ago) or the postman (split from his boyfriend last year) with six cats in his van.

Judith had arranged to film the links in a large animal hospital, run on the Pets' NHS and 'free at the point of delivery'. I think she imagined that we'd be filming cutesy kittens with maybe one rather fetching little bandage round a paw, and seeing loving owners reunited with their beloved and beautiful pets.

But this hospital was in the toughest quarter of a tough town. Its bleak concrete walls rose out of a street knee-deep in needles and empty beer cans, lined with the dead eyes of empty shop fronts. This wasn't the place for little Tibbies with a thorn in their ikkle pink pawses. This was where Conan and Slag the Rottweilers came to be patched up when some opponent in the street fight had tried a Hannibal Lecter on them.

When we arrived the harassed and worn-down chief vet (who had the broken and bewildered look of a man who's sold his soul for a mess of potage) showed us the animals that we could use for filming: a kitten with no fur and a nice toasting of red scabs, a pit bull with its ears ripped off and an eye missing, and a hamster the size of Barry White.

We couldn't do all the links with an obese hamster, but at least we could make a start. It was too wet to film outside and anyway impossible to get a shot without the remains of some-one's last fix in it. Rob and Steve gloomily set up in one of the treatment rooms, muttering mutinously, whilst Judith twitched and fussed and crossed things off on her lists in pink marker.

I chatted to John, the vet. It was a slack morning he said. Fridays usually were. Sundays were their busiest days, people got drunk at weekends, he said, and got 'careless' about their pets. Last week he'd had to treat a Jack Russell that had been wrapped in foil and put in the oven. He never minded coming in on a Sunday, and even before he said it I knew why, 'no one at home since the wife left'. Wasn't there anyone left in the world happily married? Still it's an ill wind, so I covertly gave him the once-over: right age, intelligent, compassionate, but solving a hair-loss problem with a Brylcreemed low parting is a terminally bad idea, and forty a day is no good for your skin colour or the condition of your teeth. Nope. No good.

At last the treatment room was lit well enough to keep Rob's professional feathers unruffled. John got the hamster and I settled down ready to reel off a few pointless corny constructions with an inane grin on the end.

It's not easy holding a hamster. It feels like a small sack full of animated worry beads. Hold it too tight and it goes limp forever, not tight enough and it's under the table and behind the telly. Hammy kept wriggling out of shot, up my sleeves, on to the floor, or simply struggling so hard that our viewers would be compelled to phone the RSPCA. At last I got him to sit still, face popping with rage, but at least looking at the camera. But it must have been the worst of all possible hamster holds. At the end of just two links he bit me. And rodent teeth are substantial, they eat bark and wood, so going through a nice squishy finger and straight to the bone was a breeze. I'm not good with any sort of pain, least of all sudden and unexpected, and I snatched my hand away with a reflex reaction Damon Hill would have been proud of. I was so quick that Hammy didn't have time to let go. If he hadn't let go at all he would have been fine. A bit of an ache in the jaw, but nothing a little lie-in and a slice of carrot couldn't soothe. But he let go just as my hand reached the zenith of its arched pulling away, and went shooting across the room and into the wall at speed.

I'm sure he didn't suffer. It must have been instantaneous. So I don't feel so bad that we stopped filming and laughed solidly for ten minutes. There wasn't a window in the treatment room, so there were no witnesses.

At last I picked him off the floor, limp as a beanbag, but otherwise perfect. There wasn't a mark on him and his eyes were closed peacefully.

'Looks like it's sleeping,' said Rob.

'I don't think anyone could tell,' said Steve.

'If you hold it with just its little face and paws showing,' said Judith, '. . . mmm, that's it. Lovely. Ready Rob? Okay Turn Over. Action.'

We did ten links with a dead hamster. Then I sneaked out and popped him back into his cage in the middle of a ball of straw.

It was the perfect crime, but we still had a lot to do and no animals to do it with. We were about to cut our losses, borrow a bunny from a pet shop and take it to a park, when a fat man with ten years of jam stains on his jersey arrived with a huge cardboard box.

'You're in luck,' John told us, 'this is Jim, one of our regulars. Brings us all sorts.'

We stood off at a respectful distance as John and Jim talked. At ten feet with my impaired sense of smell I could scent Jim, a rich marinade of booze and old urine, and his box, a smell that had time-travelled straight from the open sewers of sixteenth-century London. Jim's voice was so thick with booze and jam that even though John's conversation with him was almost shouted I couldn't understand a word. It concluded when Jim shuffled off leaving his box, and John, beaming, brought the box over to us.

'Hedgehog,' he said. 'Bit concussed by the looks of things, but otherwise untouched. It might even stay uncurled so you could get a shot of its face.'

'Gread!' said Judith, holding her nose.

'I know the smell's a bit bad,' John apologised, 'touch of the runs I think.'

I opened the box and picked out the hedgehog. Its spines were uncomfortable to hold, but not painful. It was a slightly irregular sphere, uniformly spiked. Underneath it had uncurled a little and its small elfin pointy face protruded. Its eyes were shut tight as if tensed for some new indignity. Its front paws were invisible, inside the drawstring edge of the prickly mantle, but the back paws were just outside, folded like a Yogi's up next to its face. Clutched in one was a long pink sausage of flesh.

At first I thought it was the hedgehog's tail. But as I held it for the camera to see and did my link, it dawned on me that it was its penis. Traumatised and shocked, the poor little thing was clutching its most precious asset.

I didn't point it out. The indignity of appearing on national TV with dead rodents and masturbating hedgehogs appealed to me.

In the end we did our last remaining links with the cat from the washing machine. We found a way of shooting the hairless kitty wrapped in a fluffy blanket, so that it looked okay. At least not scabby and suppurating, so by the time the centre closed at eight p.m. we had at last done everything we needed to do.

There wasn't time for an end-of-shoot drink, hardly even a decent goodbye. It felt unsafe out amongst the spent syringes, and we had overrun by two hours. I'd promised the kids I'd be back at seven. I leaped into my car and just drove without anything in my head beyond safely jumping another set of lights.

I was half-way back before I thought of Martin. I'd had a whole day not thinking of him. A whole day without crying. A whole day of remission.

The kids were with Jo. I've given up resisting the fact that Jo and I have a lot in common since she peeled me off my car door one morning last week. I was leaning against it and sobbing, after dropping the kids off in school, suddenly overcome with a wave of loss and missing.

'Have you got people to talk to?'

'Yes, a bit.'

'I know we don't know each other, but our kids are sticking together. Helping each other – I think we could do the same.'

All I could do was nod, incoherent with weeping. 'Thank you.'

'I don't work Fridays. Why don't you let me have the kids after school? Then you can come and pick them up and stay for supper.'

'That would be lovely.'

'Next Friday?'

'Okay.'

'See you then. Chin up.'

I watched her walk away: a tiny, peroxide blonde in a suit like an air hostess and a pair of white high heels, a copy of the *Mirror* sticking out of her shoulder bag. I felt as if my big sister had just rescued my teddy from the pond, and yet another one of my class prejudices bit the dust.

I got to Jo's just after nine. She answered the door in a candlewick dressing gown and fluffy slippers.

'Stop saying sorry. They've been as good as gold. But they were so tired. They're all asleep. Pick them up in the morning.'

'But Martin's due to pick them up in the morning.'

'Well he can pick them up from here. That way you don't have to see him.'

'I don't think it's fair, to drag you into it all. Don't you mind?'

'You're not dragging me into anything. I don't know him. Only ever spoken to him once or twice.'

'Okay then. If you're sure.' I was still standing at the open door, shifting from foot to foot in miserable awkwardness. Guilt at letting someone I hardly knew take responsibility for my kids.

'Jess, come inside. Sit down and have a drink.'

'Well, okay.'

We sat down at her kitchen table with a bottle of wine and twenty Silk Cut.

'I don't smoke,' she said, 'normally. But nothing's normal these days.'

'Neither do I. Normally.'

Jo poured almost half a bottle into a huge glass. 'Right, drink that, then tell me all about you and Martin.'

I couldn't resist an approach so direct. I took two big gulps and began.

We were extremely purposeful after that. We drank. We smoked. We talked. We swapped our stories. We took it in turns to cry, to hand out the tissues and light the next fag.

'I see them almost every day,' she said, 'he's even got one of those name strips for his car – Mike and Melanie. I can't describe what Andrew's face is like when we pass that on the way home from school.'

What would I feel if I had to see Martin and Dolores every day? I'd have borrowed James's shotgun and done for the lot of us at the end of the first week. No wonder Jo was still looking like death a year down the road.

'Why do you still want him back?'

'I dunno. He's been such a prat, dancing on the bar in the Prince with a girl half his age. I came back from my mother's one night and I saw them in the car headlights, at it in the bus shelter.' Jo shook her head. 'But I can't stop loving the man he was. I can't believe I won't get my Mike back.'

'I hadn't the heart to tell her that an eighteen-stone man who wears a red satin flamenco shirt undone to the beer gut is so lost that no one is ever going to find him. But her hope is no more ill-founded than my own: no one has the heart to tell me that as he has the choice between a wife in wellies with two rowdy kids, and a lover in a basque with no encumbrances beyond a cubic metre of red hair, Martin would be out of his mind to come back.

The complete self-deluding misery of our continuing hope made me start to cry again. 'I'm just like you Jo,' I wailed, 'I can't give him up.'

She took one of my hands between hers. Neat narrow hands, smooth. Dainty rings on every finger. The complete Samuel's selection. The sort of delicate femininity that a man like Mike would adore. Dipstick.

'You don't have to give him up,' she said. 'Think of it as temporary. Just for now you can't be together. Just for now. That's how I manage.'

For all these weeks whilst I've been drowning in grief, my friends have been throwing all sorts into the water to help me – snapshots, high-velocity rifles, knives, bits of coloured ribbon, children's shoes. But 'just for now' was the first lifebelt. Small, but with enough buoyancy to keep my head above the water.

I sat for a few minutes just breathing, enjoying getting air into my lungs rather than waves, telling myself over and over, 'just for now, just for now.'

'Here. Dry your eyes and light another fag. I tell you. You can get through anything if you think it's temporary.' Jo let go of my hand and shook out her hair with a coquettish little toss. 'Even going without sex for eighteen months.'

'Eighteen months! Jo that's terrible.'

'Well that's how long it's been since he walked out,' she took a long drag on her cigarette and leaned back in the chair, 'and God knows the one thing Mike was ever any good at was sex. I suppose that's what little Melanie sees in him. Girl that age would think she'd died and gone to heaven. I know I did.' Hard to equate Mike's belly, the size of a full-term triplet pregnancy, and selection of chins with the notion of him as a sexual Adonis, but all sorts of weird stuff happens behind bedroom doors. Looking at me in my jeans and my garden sun-hat you'd never guess what Martin and I used to do in the greenhouse.

'I worry that I'll never have sex again and it's only been six weeks.' I worry that I'll get so desperate that I'll simply jump on the plumber when he comes to service the boiler, or that I'll make a pass at one of my friends' husbands. I know I've started noticing that Gerry has a great mouth, and wondering if Alex's bum is as nice out of jeans as in them, and if Chris's hour might soon be at hand.

'Don't be daft. Of course you will. Men are always up for it. You just got to choose one.'

'So why haven't you then?'

'Because Mike's the one I'd choose. I don't really want it with anyone else.' Jo stubbed out her cigarette. 'But it's amazing what you can do with a good imagination though,' she said. 'Virtual sex. I may not have had Mike for more than a year, but I've had everyone else I ever wanted. In here,' she tapped her forehead. 'I never knew I could be so dirty,' she giggled.

'Who then? Anybody we know?' Jo blushed. 'Not Martin. You haven't imagined Martin have you?'

'Oh no.' Jo looked as if I'd suggested public mud-wrestling as a nice way to pass a Saturday afternoon. Her response could not be faked: she didn't find Martin attractive! Not in the least. 'I mean, don't get me wrong. I'm sure he's a nice bloke and all, just. Not my type.' In fact Jo's face betrayed that she found Martin almost repulsive.

I was astonished.

'You're not offended are you? That I don't fancy him?'

'No. I'm delighted. I always thought he was so handsome everybody must fancy him. I always thought he could have whoever he wanted. That I was lucky that he chose someone as plain as me. Him being handsome and fanciable made me plainer somehow. It's great to find out someone thinks he's a bit of a dog.' I could see Jo didn't really follow. I'm not sure I did, but I was lighter inside, floating a little higher on the water. 'Okay then if you didn't have Martin who did you have?'

'Oh y'know. Film stars. Tom Cruise.'

'Too short.'

'Not in a Jacuzzi he isn't. Quite long actually.'

'Jo!'

'Well if you're going to have somebody you got to think of all the details.'

'Who else?'

'That bloke off *Between the Lines* on telly. You know.'

'Oh yeah. He's all right. Bit porky.'

'Oh I like a man with meat on his bones.' Yeah. So I gathered. 'I had 'im tied up. Strapped him to a big brass bed.'

'That's only two. Who else?'

'Well, you know the petrol station on the back road into town. There's a boy in there. At weekends. Ever so young he is. Seventeen maybe. Blond. Skinny.'

'I thought you said you liked meat on their bones.'

'Yeah. But this boy's eyes. Big blue eyes. And long legs. He looks so innocent you know . . .'

'And you imagined teaching him everything he needs to know?'

We hunched over our fags, spluttering. When Jo had stopped laughing and coughing she asked. 'So what about you then? Who do you fantasise about?'

'Nobody. I don't dare.'

'Whatcha mean you don't dare?'

'Whenever I try and think about sex with someone, it just turns into Martin. And I don't want to think about fucking Martin. So I try not to think about it at all.'

'Maybe you need to start with the real thing then, to give your imagination something to work on. Go and get filled up at that garage this weekend.'

Of course I wasn't exactly motorist quality material by the time we'd got through a second bottle. I would have curled up on the floor fully dressed, but Jo is a congenital carer and made me a proper bed on the sofa with sheets and a blanket and found me a nightie – all rosebuds and lace, very clean, full of the smell of an unfamiliar brand of washing powder. It was the big sister and the teddy feeling again.

I woke at nine with a steel bandana round my head and maggots crawling under my skin. Martin would be on his way, ready to collect the children from home at nine-thirty. He might already be standing at the back door. Pacing, a storm of disapproval and censure gathered under the blond curls like salmonella breeding in an innocent egg roll.

As I dialled his number my hands shook with the thought of his disapproval. What was he going to say about having to fetch the children from a house he'd never been to before? About such a very last-minute change of arrangements? I wasn't simply nervous or embarrassed about being caught out too pissed to drive home. I was actually frightened. Physically afraid as if he were some knuckle-duster thug with left and right tattooed on his fingers.

I put the phone down before it even rang. I wasn't sure I could manage to speak anyway. The kids were awake upstairs, I could hear the first sleepy murmurs and tiptoed floorboard creaks. I drew the curtains and let the light in. A sunny day, white and washed from the rain. Ten past nine. I had to ring him. The later I left it the more furious he was likely to be.

I braced my hands on either side of the window frame to stop the trembling. What the hell was I scared of? What did I think Martin was going to do? Turn up with a twelve bore? Slap me around in front of the children? Not his style. So what could he say? Nothing could hurt more than the words 'I'm leaving'.

A quarter past nine. It really was time to ring, now my hands were steady. I reached for the phone just as Dan thundered down the stairs and into the room.

'Daddy's picking us up here in ten minutes. I phoned him from Jo's bedroom.'

'Was he cross?'

'Cross? No. Why should he be cross?'

'Oh I dunno really.'

'Did you bring any spare socks for me Mum?'

'Sorry. I haven't been home.'

'What? Not even to let Dog out?'

'Oh God. I forgot.'

'Oh Mum!'

'I'd better go right now. Say thanks to Jo for me. Tell Frankie what's happened. Give Daddy my love. Bye sweetie.'

'Bye.'

I was definitely losing it. Paranoia. No clean socks and Dog dying of thirst and crossed legs in a locked kitchen.

There was a note on the door.

'Friday night. Called in on the way back from work (late YUK). Where are you? Hope everything's okay. Took Dog. She was barking, we'll drop her back tomorrow. Put your post on the piano. Dog has chewed one letter. Love Kath.'

On the kitchen table there was a pot of perfect strawberry jam, small perfect fruits suspended in a translucent blush of jelly. 'We're off to Sussex for the weekend,' said the note stuck on the side of the jar, 'meant to give you this last week. XX M'. Clever Mary. She'd left me a welcome into my own house just when I needed it so that the rooms seemed less empty, not so devoid of a family.

Chris had left a message on the ansaphone

'Get some country bumpkins round. I'm coming down on Saturday night to see you and I shall bring a great deal of food and drink. Just got a new contract. Lots of money. So you'll have to marry me now.'

I must have been St Francis or Mother Teresa in a former life to deserve my friends.

The steel bandana and maggot effect was easing off. I took a cup of coffee outside with my semi-chewed mail. A slightly whining letter from the bank together with a grudging approval for my solo bank account. And a wedding invitation, from sweet

Rubenesque Josie, with the feather-bolster bosom and the ever-escaping hair, our PA on *Mr Bounce*. It came with a note attached written on a little square of bright pink paper, 'So much for the PA bit . . . lost your address and only just found it. Hope you can come at this short notice. Love J.' Typical Josie, organised, but only at the last minute. She was marrying some chap with an embarrassingly naff name in an idyllic little country church with a reception in a big tent in one of her parent's fields. It was an invitation just for me. No mention of Martin. The grapevine's a great thing sometimes. But just seeing the word 'wedding' turned my stomach, it's not a natural choice of venue for the soon-to-be-divorced. But everyone knows that weddings are where you meet Spare Men. Hugh Grants a-go-go. In droves. If I could just grit my teeth and get through the ceremony it would be okay. Potentially a lot more than okay. Glorious even. I'd see old friends. Have a chance to dress up. I should go. In the interests of preventing myself from jumping on the plumber.

I put the letters aside and closed my eyes to feel the sun, warm on my lids. I'd been too frantic getting to work in time to look at Great Danes' backsides and home again in time to be grumped at by the children to arrange anything for this weekend. I was alone and apparently purposeless inside two whole days of empty house and garden. But it felt good, like stretching after a long cramped journey. Good to have the novelty of choice, to be entirely free of imperatives. I could just be with my plants. Wrestle with the mower, swear at the nettles.

I wandered down to let the chooks out. Relieved to be fed they followed me across the garden chuntering to themselves, and to me, mildly chiding me for being so late on such a lovely morning.

The garden was wet and green, ravishing, even though the border was entering its in-between time, looking a little sad, and the grass in want of a haircut. Out here it had always just been me. Not Martin. Out here was my room. Me and my garden, we were just the same together.

I got a good spot of mower-wrestling and then some quiet husbandry of my favourite delphiniums, cutting back their dead spikes in the hope of a second show. I clambered into the back of the border, got right down amongst the stems into the little secret world of knotty greenery where beetles run up and down the stalks with exaggerated purpose. I teased weeds from flowers and performed the necessary surgery of separation, pulling roots away from the soil in a delicious slow moment of murder. I was getting nicely mesmerised with bee hum and sap smell when Kath arrived.

She came tumbling over the lawn behind a wave of kids tangled in noise and dog leads. Living symbol of all I'd escaped from for the weekend.

The boys got to me first, standing on the edge of the border as if it were the bank of a stream. They're well trained about gardens. It's the death penalty at Kath's house for any football kicked into a flower.

'Look Jess. Dad's done us with the number two clippers. He says we look well hard,' announced Louis, swaggering. Macho I guess for a six-year-old. He and Joe had their high summer haircuts of black fuzz, like the coats of new black lambs. With their mum's huge black eyes they looked as well hard as seal pups on the ice.

'Why are you kneeling down?' asked Joe.

'I'm praying to the God of ladybirds to come and eat all the greenfly.'

'Oh.' This was the kind of explanation that Joe accepted without question.

'We're going to the show. Are you coming?' Louis leans back slightly when he speaks, like a portly councillor tucking his thumbs into a weskit over an ample belly. It looks funny on a skinny kid.

'I dunno. D'you want me to?' Without Dan and Frankie to be a parent for I felt a new role coming on with these kids. This is what I'd been like before I had my own children to feed, wash and nag. Direct and friendly, attractively anarchic.

'Yea-eh!' they said together.

'Okay. I'll come. Just let me get my wellies off.'

Breathless and newly freed from dog-lead bondage, Kath greeted me. 'How are you?'

'Pretty okay. I'm going to a wedding in a fortnight!'

'Is that a good idea?'

'Yes. Who knows I might get laid?'

'What's get laid?' said Joe

'It's what eggs do Joe. Why don't you and Louis go and see if there are any. Eggs.'

'Yeah cool.' Kath doesn't have chooks so mine have a certain cachet with her kids.

'Who will you go with?'

'Myself. Got to get used to it Kath haven't I?'

'Oh Jess.'

'Don't start, it'll only set me off.'

'Okay. Look, Gerry's working, we're going to the Hallerton Show. It's supposed to be a really good one this year. D'you want to come?' She saw me looking longingly at my border and then played her trump card. 'They've got a really big poultry section this year I hear.'

'Okay. I'm coming. But only if you and Gerry come round tonight for food and booze. Chris is coming down with both he said.'

'Lovely. We've nothing else booked. Haven't seen Chris in ages.'

'I'll just ring Jo and get her to come too, and Alex and Sarah. Then we can go to the show. I quite fancy looking at a few prize pigs.'

Big county shows are full of corporate hospitality tents, double-glazing sale rooms and stalls selling novelty chopping devices. The farm animals are relegated to some small white tent behind the Portaloos. They are full of urban people getting drunk, in a surrogate city.

At shows like the Hallerton, the animals are the main attraction, and the biggest concession to anything even remotely corporate is a bouncy castle, policed by some solid ten-year-old whose mother was a professional wrester. Hallerton is attended by people who think dog leads are too swanky and who wouldn't dream of keeping their collies on anything other than a bit of baler twine.

Kath and I go to these little shows to look at animals and to long for the day when we can have a small herd of sheep and a little sty of pigs and perhaps a house cow. Every year we choose our dream animals, and every year our kids nearly persuade us to buy something cute and unreasonable that would eat our gardens down to the mud if we were actually foolish enough to give in.

Louis and Joe found the first dream animals. A little pen of Shetland sheep. Neat and lithe, wild-looking without that lumpen top-heaviness that big breeds have. They pushed their Bournville plain noses into our hands, warm velvet wool covering their snouts.

'Feels like your heads boys,' said Kath.

'Dan would like this one,' said Joe.

'Yes, I think you're right.' Dan would. And Frankie. They were missing this ritual of summer that they so adored.

'Where are they?' said Louis.

'Oh Louis,' Kath hissed. She had clearly primed them not to mention the whole topic of Dan and Frankie's absence.

'Wot?' said Louis 'I just asked . . .'

'It's okay Louis, they're with their dad. With Martin.'

'Oh yeah. Sorry.' Joe kicked Louis in the leg without looking up from his sheep-caressing and Louis didn't even try to retaliate. I suddenly felt bereft. Miserable with loneliness, a hanger-on to someone else's family when mine had fallen apart.

I stuck it out through the pig judging, and took bets with Joe about which pigs would win best pair in show: the middle whites with their alarmingly sized genitalia, the sandy and blacks with their coarse ginger hair like a thinning bank manager, or the glossy black ones whose breed name we couldn't remember.

But I'd lost my joy in the whole thing. I could only see in snapshots of what Dan and Frankie were missing, and the shared experiences we had lost.

Kath guessed it wasn't going well when I suggested the bouncy castle instead of the poultry tent. Kath and I stood by with the other adults as the children threw themselves about on a giant blue-and-yellow dragon.

'Why didn't you want to go and see the chickens? You love that bit.'

'I can't hack all this without the kids. I keep thinking that they're missing it.'

'There'll be other shows we can go to this summer and take them.'

'I know. Don't take any notice, I'm just wallowing.'

'We'll go home after this. The dogs'll be over-heating in the car anyway.'

'Right. Good idea.'

We sang 'Oh you'll never get to heaven' all the way home.

> Oh you'll never get to heaven
> Oh you'll never get to heaven
> In a jumbo jet
> In a jumbo jet
> Cos the Lord ain't got
> No runways yet.

That and all the other mildly naughty verses that each generation of primary school kids thinks they've invented. Including the verse about Playtex bras which always reduces Frankie to helpless giggles.

I wanted to cry.

Kath dropped me at home. 'I'm going to call by the site and see how Gerry's doing. We'll be back about seven-thirty, if that's still okay. I don't have to bring the kids you know?'

'No bring them. Alex and Sarah are bringing Rosie and there'll be Jo's two as well. I'll make them pizza or something. I've got to get used to it. I'm going to be childless a lot now if Martin goes on wanting to see them.'

I went back to weeding for a while, but the patch I chose was full of nettles, tiny plants with vicious stings. The stems and leaves caught at my clothes, and the whole border seemed chaotic and hostile. I gave up and went indoors. But even there the space to stretch had become an emptiness.

I made myself busy. Cleaning, tidying, cooking. Making a place that other people could come and fill for me.

By the time Kath and Gerry arrived with the boys, and Sarah and Alex with Rosie, the house looked lovely. Full of flowers and fresh baking, wine chilling, glasses polished, a tall jug of pink squash ready mixed for the kids, the smell of sweet peas and home cooking covering the bitter undertone of desperation and longing.

I smiled and joked. Fussed. And drank fairly resolutely. It nearly always makes me feel better.

When Chris arrived he was almost entirely obscured by the flowers he carried. A florist's bucket stuffed with huge spikes of gladioli in every shade of pink from shell to screaming neon. Just like Chris to remember I'd painted my bedroom a new colour.

'Oh Chris they're fabulous. I'm going to put them all on my bedroom windowsill.' He pulsed with pure delight and I could sense the little germ of hope springing to life inside him again. He held me just a moment too long when I hugged him. Just a little too pressed to his pelvis.

'You look wonderful,' he breathed into my ear. His breath on my neck. Maybe it was time for Chris to get a little payback. Time for more than a fingertip on a jersey sleeve. He released me and turned to greet everyone else, and received their praise for the huge bunch of flowers. Chris doesn't visit me here often but he makes a big splash. Everyone remembers him.

'I've got a little man at Covent Garden who fixes me up.' How did he manage to make it sound as if this was someone who gave him blow-jobs rather than cut-price gladdies? 'I ring him at five in the morning and say, what have you got that's really good. Look: shall we all go and sit in the garden? It's become such a delightful evening?'

It had and we did. Chris was on top form. Full of optimism about a new contract for some German mag. Full of stories from Planet Fashion where everything is the opposite to life, like weird mirror writing. After the story about the little man at the flower market, the level of camp seemed to drop too.

He was flush. He'd brought four bottles of Moët with him, a side of smoked salmon and a bag of assorted loaves from Harrods. This was Chris at his best, kind, generous and performing for an audience.

We moved the benches out on to the lawn to catch the evening sun and spread all of Chris's lovely food out ready to eat. I sat on the bench next to him looking at the high cheekbones, the curving Roman nose, the dark glossy hair touched with grey. Really very pleasing indeed. And really not so short when he was sitting down.

We were just cracking the champagne when Jo arrived. She drifted across the lawn, her straight hair loose over her shoulders, in a long blue skirt. She looked lovely. Girlish. Tiny and perfect as a doll.

I'd completely forgotten about her and her kids so there was a sticky five minutes as Kath and I integrated Andrew and Angela into the complex pecking order of the tent. But they seemed to graft into the game quite well, and we left them to it.

Back at the benches the champagne was poured. Alex and Gerry were deep into a conversation about guitars, which consisted mostly of Gerry giving Alex a list of reasons to spend more than he'd planned. Gerry is great at spending other people's money.

Chris and Jo, however, looked as if they were exchanging life stories, head to head over a bottle and two glasses.

Well, I thought. Well, well.

I just spectated for a while after that. Passing food under people's noses, refilling glasses. Kath and Sarah were sharing the stupidities of their respective bosses and management structures, so I wasn't required as part of anyone's conversation.

Okay, I thought, not what I planned. But okay.

Things didn't become communal again until the children tore up from the tent in huge excitement, with Dog and Sal barking as if the last trump for doggies had just sounded.

'The cows have got through the bottom fence. They're in the garden.'

I don't know what we all thought we were going to do but everyone jumped up and ran down the garden.

In the twilight already gathering under the tall hedge, the black-and-white of twelve Friesians stood out luminously. They'd pushed through the unkempt hawthorn, probably by mistake given that Friesians don't have enough brain power to do anything on purpose, and now they didn't know what to do. They were lumbering around in serious danger of trampling the tent and crashing through my greenhouse. They looked un-comfortable and worryingly unpredictable.

The kids and most of the grown-ups were shouting at them, making a selection of whooping noises gleaned from old cowboy movies of the 'round 'em up, move 'em out' variety. The dogs were just as clueless, the basic instinct to herd large animals seems to have been replaced in Sal and Dog with a gene for biting human ankles when alarmed. The cows were getting panicky and banging into each other. One stumbled against the greenhouse door and it shattered. After so much champagne, none of the human adults was thinking very well.

Except for Jo.

'They can't see where they've come from. They're just getting scared,' she yelled above the barking and random

High Chaparral sound effects. 'Everybody go and sit down, I'll sort this out. Get the dogs out of the way.' Relieved, as we were all getting bored of whooping to no avail, we retreated. Jo hitched up her long cotton skirt and tied it in a loop so she could move through the long grass. Her legs were very brown. 'Chris,' she called, 'I need you to help.'

Half an hour later, Chris and Jo came back up to the benches, muddied and a bit grass-covered. Rather pink-looking I thought. But then that's what chasing cows does for you. It's why milkmaids were so sought after.

'They've made a mess of that bottom lawn,' said Chris.

'Your neighbour should mend his fences,' said Jo.

'Yes,' added Chris, watching Jo readjust her skirt, 'took us ages to get the gap closed up.'

Chris and I sat at the kitchen table over huge mugs of tea with a good shot of brandy after they'd all gone, relatively early in the interests of children getting at least some sleep.

'She's gorgeous Jess,' Chris said, 'but I know she won't look at me.'

'You must be blind Chris. She'd have been all over you like a rash if we hadn't been here. And what did you two get up to "mending the fence"?'

'I kissed her, that's all.'

'Well I think that constitutes a bit more than looking at.'

'Yes. All right. Maybe.'

'So,' I said, 'my fall-back position's gone then. Missed the bus haven't I?'

'What do you mean?' Yes, what did I mean? *I don't really fancy you Chris but I might have shagged you now I'm desperate?* That was what I meant. But you can't tell people things like that. Especially not old friends who bring you flowers and champagne. Why did I open my big mouth?

'Well, I've known you for a long time, and I really like you. And . . .' Chris had that awful hope-springs-eternal look about him. In a moment he'd forgotten all about Jo. What had I done?

'You mean. I might have a chance with you?'

'NO, I mean yes. I mean, I wouldn't want to spoil things for you and Jo.' Not for the sake of me getting a one-night stand anyway. But I'd said too much. Already it was too late. He had pushed aside his mug and climbed over the table quicker than you could say 'testosterone'.

'There's nothing to spoil. Not compared with what I feel for you Jess. I've loved you from the first day we met.'

Oh shit! That warm breath on my neck again. Martin could reduce me to helpless jelly by breathing on my neck.

And, surprise surprise, Chris proved to be a really very nice kisser. And to have a delicious warmth in his skin and his fingertips that seeped through my clothes instantly. He was out of practice and sweetly hesitant, but he got good at sex a long time ago and technique like that is like aged wine. Once it's the right temperature it just tastes better. For a few rocket-fuel-in-the-veins moments it felt entirely possible to have this one night with Chris, just for the sake of plumber protection. But I thought of Jo, sitting and crying at her kitchen table. Tears falling between the rings on her delicate little fingers. She and Chris might have a real chance, but not if I gave Chris the concrete hope of going to bed with me. Not if he thought I might be in love with him. He'd have wasted a real opportunity for the sake of me getting laid. And Chris was my friend – he deserved better than a lie. I'd just have to get a vibrator in a plain brown package.

He'd put me on the table by this time and stood between by legs, kissing me. Undoing the buttons on my shirt. His lips on my throat. Jeezuz.

I grasped his shoulders and gently lifted him away from me. 'Chris. Chris.'

'What's the matter?'

'At this moment I want you to make love to me very very very much. But tomorrow I'll be sorry.'

'I know that. I don't care. I've wanted you for so long.'

'And tomorrow you'll be sorry. If I was your lover now Chris, I couldn't say I was being your friend.'

He just looked at me like a kicked spaniel.

'Jo and you could be a good idea. Me and you is not a good idea.'

'Why?'

'Chris. It's just not. It's just not. Go for it with Jo. See what happens.'

Chris sat down and ran his hand through his hair. 'So now what do we do?'

'We go to bed. We sleep. We wake up. I make you breakfast. Well a cup of tea anyway. You pop round to see Jo. Take her some flowers. I'll cut you some from the border.'

'Okay Jess.'

'Goodnight Chris.'

'Goodnight Jess.'

What did I say? Not what I planned. Not even what I expected.

Chapter Ten

I lost my nerve twice in the last forty-eight hours. Once about divorcing Martin and once about going to the wedding.

Yesterday was the day when he was due to get the letter from Bertie saying 'I, Jessica Elizabeth Wallace, divorce thee, Martin David Harvey, for going and bonking somebody else'. Except it wouldn't be 'I' and 'thee', it'd be one step removed from that, 'our client' this and 'our client' the other.

Actually the truth was I'd no idea about the details of the legalese he'd get. All I knew was that it would be formal and impersonal and wouldn't say anything that I really wanted him to know.

Like the fact that I don't want to divorce him at all.

So when I got back from dropping the kids at school I paced. It was raining again and too dark and miserable to pace outside. So I did my usual circuit round and round the kitchen table. I must have worn a little path in the lino.

I was on about the fiftieth lap and almost deciding to ring Bertie and call the whole thing off, when Sarah rang from work.

She's taken to doing this a lot. I've become part of her technicolour dreamcoat of guilt, part of the cloth of tasks that she must do in life to become a better person. She can't see me very often, because her biggest task is work and achievement, so she phones instead. And although I know it's born out of her particular neurosis, I like it. I like to hear her concern.

'How are you?'

'I'm pacing.'

'Are you crying?'

'No. Not just now. I don't do it all the time now.'

'Have you eaten anything today?'

'It's only ten-thirty.'

'That's not a valid answer Jess.'

'Why am I going to divorce Martin, Sarah?'

'Is this a trick question? I dunno Jess. But I know why I'd be divorcing him if I were you. He's behaved like a total bastard. I wouldn't want to be married to someone who did that to me.'

'I don't care what he did. I just want him to come back.'

'Jess. You're crying now aren't you? Jess, listen. Okay. Look. Maybe he will come back. But the marriage you had is over. You may have another one. But this one is done. He has to understand that. And so do you.'

'D'you think we could get married again?'

'People do. It's not common Jess. Don't count on it.'

I remembered what Jo said, 'It's just for now. Just now you can't be together.' So I have to do things to survive, like a bulb hiding in the soil over winter. It's not forever.

'Okay, okay. I'm all right now. I know why I'm divorcing him. It's for me to survive. That's all.'

'I've got to go Jess. Eat something will you. You'll end up looking like Nancy Reagan if you lose any more weight.'

'Bye.'

Re-resolved, I sat down to write to Martin. To give him a little background to the 'my client requests the pleasure of your company at the divorce of . . .' To try to convey the divorce as survival strategy. To try to convey that it was because I love him. To try to convey that we're not on a one-way street.

I faxed him at Dolores's. She has a machine that does both things, ansaphone and fax, so I heard her voice. Irresistible. A voice out of male fantasy. Low, melodic with a slight catch so that you think she might still be in bed, warm and tousled, just awake. Available. Undressed maybe. And complete with the remnants of a brogue. You could hear the green eyes, the long red hair, the skin like Jersey milk.

'If you want to send a fax, just press yurr button now.' She made it such a sweet invitation. I thought of how many times Martin had rung that number. Clung to that voice. Left who knows what messages. Telephone sex with a voice like that would be so good it would make you want to be away just so that you could phone home.

The paper with my pathetic pleadings on it carrying the squeak and scratch of my own voice trundled through and out again.

I stood there feeling like an ugly first-former writing sickly love letters to the best looking sixth-form prefect in school via his girlfriend, who happens to be a model.

Wanting to be dead.

There wasn't much I could do to redeem the day after that. I'd lost it completely. No point in even trying to stop crying. But that doesn't matter so much now. I can do almost anything and not have to interrupt whatever little weeping project I happen to have on the go at the time. So I bathed Dog, to her enormous and enduring disgust. Even after six doggy choc drops she wouldn't speak to me. I made chocolate fairy cakes with buttercream icing and Smarties, in the hope that this might curry favour with Dan and Frankie, still busy sulking almost a fortnight after the filming was finished. I baked bread. I rearranged furniture and moved pictures. I tidied under Frankie's bed. I dusted Dan's collection of footballing figures.

And every five minutes I ran to the fax machine to see if Martin had sent me some reply. Nothing. He'd be out at work anyway. He wouldn't get my fax or Bertie's letter until he got home. Maybe Dolores would read my fax first, and she'd put her perfectly manicured hand on his shoulder to prepare him for the ordeal of reading it. Probably not an ordeal so much as a storm of irritation.

Just as I was about to leave home to collect the kids from school, I heard the fax machine bleep and do that clunking thing it does before it prints out a message.

I sprinted from the back door and waited trembling by the machine as it to and froed along the lines until the message was all written out.

It wasn't from Martin. It was a hand-scrawled note on David Herring's fax header.

'Can you make a meeting here, Friday 11.30? Urgent reply.'

I wrote 'yes' on the bottom and faxed it straight back.

He was going to have the decency to tell me to my face that they were giving the series back to Monica Mostar. Seemed a bit of a waste to go all that way just to be told you weren't getting a job, but at least it would prevent another day like today. Give me something else to worry about. Something good and concrete, like what are we going to live on and what am I going to do with the rest of my life?

The fairy cakes with Smarties did the trick. I made them an indoor picnic because it was raining too hard for an outside one, tiny sandwiches, slivers of carrot, stars of cucumber, raisins, biscuits, all distributed in a ridiculously inefficient number of little glass bowls and old cups, the crockery refugees from the Great Smashing. Afterwards we curled up and watched *Babe* together and I cried at the place I always do, when Babe says 'Can I call you Mom?' to the sheepdog bitch.

They consented to a huge bubble bath together, and I sat on the edge with my feet in the water whilst they did the stuff they used to do two or three years ago – making beards and hairstyles with the foam. They went to bed without a tear and were both asleep before I'd gone downstairs again.

Nights like that have always been rare. Now they seem like a gift from heaven. Getting Dan and Frankie to sleep, calmly and happily is as good as it was watching them fall asleep at my nipple, with a little trail of milk at the corner of their mouths, and signs in their eyes saying 'Full up'.

I went downstairs and looked at the fax. Nothing. Maybe he had nothing to say to me. There was nothing I wanted to hear apart from 'I'm coming home'.

I do sleep now, some nights. Really sleep. I have dreams too, not like the dreams I used to have before. Those were like dreams everyone has about turning up at the supermarket in pink spotty PJs, or about endlessly taking your GCSEs. Now my dreams are Directed, like movies. I have Quentin Tarantino dreams where Martin stars in a black suit and a gun, and blows my brains out so that I can see my own blood splashed over the walls, or the inside of the car. I have David Lynch dreams, with Martin and Dolores dressed in cowboy gear driving a Cadillac with me locked in the boot, and their baby, like a mini Elton John at the wheel. Something really unpleasant is always about to happen or happens to me at Martin's hands in these dreams. I'd prefer a change of director, some John Ford dreams perhaps. Dolores would make a great Maureen O'Hara I'm sure, and I'd be prepared to be a leprechaun if I could just get through a night without injury, torture or death.

It was a David Lynch dream last night. A severely aesthetically and vertically challenged version of Martin was about to do something very nasty to me in an inadequately lit room, so I was grateful when the *bang, whirr* of the fax woke me up.

It was four a.m. Just getting light. Birds doing preliminary tootling. Our smallest and most pugnacious cockerel clearing his throat set to crow.

I went downstairs and stood like a condemned person waiting for sentence as the fax finished its business and churned out the completed message.

The headed notepaper was from a hotel in New York. Interesting in itself as Martin was supposed to be picking the children up for the weekend in about fourteen hours' time.

'Jess,' it said, in Martin's spider-leg scrawl. 'Got the letter from Ms Taylor and your fax, sent on tonight from London.' So Dolores did read it all first. They were close enough for her to be opening all his mail. 'Surprised you want to get a divorce already, but glad. Best thing all round.'

Best thing all round? What? He sounded like some misogynist surgeon offering a hysterectomy: 'Just take it all away. All that nasty women's business. Best thing all round.'

'Can't have the kids this weekend. Delayed here until Monday at least. Martin.'

He was probably talking to someone else as he wrote it. As significant in his life as ordering a taxi. Just another little bump to smooth out, for him to run rails over without a whisper of inconvenience.

I went back upstairs and lay down. Weighted, pinned down as if someone were sitting on my chest. The evil dwarf from my Lynch-movie dream had escaped into life and done unspeakable things to me, in a dark room where there were no witnesses.

Definitely no heart for the wedding now. Even if someone will take the kids off my hands.

What with Martin the evil alien Martian, and being awake since four and having to tell the kids that Daddy loved them, but wasn't going to be home from New York in time for the weekend, I washed up on David Herring's doorstep like a bit of broken plastic shoe on a storm beach.

I had a feeling that even if this meeting was arranged to tell me of Monica Mostar's success as future friend to pets, I could perhaps get something out of it. After all, there were struggling freelancers who would kill their own first-born to get five minutes' pitching time with David Herring. For the sake of another batch of mortgage payments I had to try a bit.

I'd found some clothes that approximated to black-wear media uniform, my own black jeans and a black shirt of Martin's that he'd rejected due to its content of man-made fibres. I found a pair of old John Belushi sunglasses of Martin's (discarded in favour of real RayBans). The bags under my eyes were substantial enough for a two-year expedition to the Antarctic so these were essential. I wore the brightest lipstick I could find on the grounds that my lips were the only part of my face that looked even remotely presentable.

The blinds were up in David's office and the windows open. Light flooded in on to the grey grainy top of his huge desk. Too bright to take my shades off. Good.

A tray with a tall silver coffee pot and three white cups sat centre stage, and sitting around with David was a dark thin man, in a baggy suit and discreetly shiny watch. They seemed to be waiting, and jumped to their feet as I walked in.

Sometimes being miserable is an asset. I was too miserable this morning to smile much. This looks like poise to media folk. I was also too miserable to be nervous about the impression I would create, or even what this thin TV snake had to say.

'Thanks so much for coming Jess.' David had the charm switch turned to Max.

'That's all right David. I just hope it'll be to my advantage.' Might as well make him uncomfortable if he was giving the whole series to Monica.

He laughed. Nervously I thought. How strange for David Herring, fearless TV mogul, Mr look-you-in-the-eyes-and-sack-you-without-flinching to be nervous. What was going on? A little flicker of hope and ambition, wavered for a moment in my guts.

'Jess I'd like you to meet Derek Marchant from Channel 5. He's here today to discuss a number of projects we're collaborating on. *Pets and Their People* is one of them.'

'Nice to meet you Derek. What exactly do you do at Channel 5? I'm afraid I don't make a habit of reading the industry comic so I've no idea who you are.'

'Oh, I'm commissioning editor for factual programming, everything from knitting Aran sweaters to Scud missiles.'

'And which end of your output have you come to discuss today? I can't really see David being interested in knitting, can you? Shall we sit down and have some coffee? I'll pour if you like.' For a moment the two men seemed a little lost, Derek caught up first.

'Lovely. Lovely. White, one sugar please.'

'And you David?'

'Black, two sugars please.' It's funny how wielding a coffee pot can make you feel powerful.

'So, what have you two gentlemen got to say to me?' I sat back and stirred my coffee. I didn't know how I was going to keep this up in the face of David telling me that *Pets and Their People* was crap and that it wasn't even going to be transmitted. But I didn't really think that's what he had to say. In fact reviewing all our little interviews in my mind, keeping it clear of the 'self-destruct' sections of my frontal lobes, I thought it must be really rather good.

'We're very very pleased with *Pets and Their People*. You got some marvellous material out of your interviewees. Very funny. Very moving. In fact we'd like to see that side of the show expanded a little. Give more space to the stories behind the pets.'

'Thank you David. Does this mean that you have commissioned the series Derek?'

'Oh yes. Absolutely. In fact we're going to give it a much better, more high-profile slot.'

'Well that's very nice for you David but as you plan to give Monica Mostar the presenting on it, I really don't see why I'm here.'

'Um. We've reconsidered the choice of Monica as presenter. Obviously she has a big name. But we feel that . . . well . . . that you gave the show a unique slant, its personality . . . so . . .' David has always had a problem with coming out with some statement of commitment. (Poor Judith must have a terrible time with him. 'Well I could see my way to coming out with you tonight . . . but there may be one or two things we should discuss first . . .') He just hates having nothing up his sleeve.

'What David is trying to say,' said Derek leaning over the table earnestly, 'is that we'd like you to present the series.'

Misery helped out again. It helped me not to jump up, hug them both and dance on the table. Instead I managed a deferential little smile.

'That's very kind,' I said, 'and of course I'd love to do it but, in my present circumstances I have to be very certain that I get the maximum benefit from any career move, before I can make any decision.'

'Of course,' said Derek. David was quiet, with no chips left to bargain with he was already bored. It was, after all, going to be Channel 5 money, so Derek was my man.

'So let's talk about practicalities. If you can come up with the right money and the right timing of filming, then I'm sure I'd be delighted to do the series for you.' I smiled benevolently. More coffee before we discuss business?' If only Martin could have seen me, I think he might even have been a little proud.

I couldn't quite believe I'd pulled it off. Fifty days work, in four-day weeks for £400 a day. Enough money to gag the whining bank manager, and let Martin stay in New York until Christmas. New Year even.

I stopped at a petrol station on the way home and rang Kath at work and told her the news.

'Wow! Well done. Now you can go off to the wedding and really celebrate.'

'I don't know. Anyway I can't. Martin's in New York. He faxed me last night.'

'So? We'll have the kids. I'm not working this weekend. Stay overnight so you can go to the do after the reception.'

'Frankie will be foul.'

'Yeah. At first. But we'll put the tent up in the garden. She'll have a great time.'

'Oh I don't know. Seems mean to say "Oh your dad can't have you and neither can I".'

'Don't be stupid. You have to get out. Get yourself on the market. Go to the wedding.'

'Okay. I will. I'm going to get myself a pair of shoes and a hat.'

'Atta girl.'

The marvellously old-fashioned ladies outfitting department of the last big department store in town was an appropriately grand setting I felt for the writing of my first solo cheque. Miss J. E. Wallace. Not strictly true. But hey, showbiz people always use their maiden titles.

'That will be one hundred and forty pounds exactly madam, for all the items together.'

I didn't buy the special suede protector, which was probably a false economy, but paying seventy pounds for one pair of shoes was as much as I could cope with.

'I must say the colour match is perfect. The suede and the straw are exactly the same shade. Extraordinary.' Yeah. Especially when you see the shade of blue I'll be wearing them with.

It was also appropriate that the first items I should buy with my very own money should be so frivolous, so gloriously out of character as a pair of purple suede high heels and a big purple hat. My first definite marketing ploys. My new uniform to relaunch myself into the ranks of the sexually available, and possibly even desirable. And after all, a new hat and shoes for a wedding is almost traditional.

New lingerie in satin and lace, however, is not.

Chapter Eleven

Josie's wedding guests seemed to have soaked up every hotel room in town. In the end the only place I could find was a cut-price cancellation. It was in a posh country hotel, practically a Michelin three-star job – a rival of the Court's apparently, or so Kath told me when I gave her my contact details as I dropped off the children. They were remarkably sparkly. The thought of me in a big hat and high heels entertained them enough to let me go without complaint. Frankie even made me a card with a picture of me in my hat and dress on it 'Have a lovely Partee mummy' written in red crayon down the side.

The sun shone. My new-found earning power warmed my insides and the radio played all my favourite songs on the drive to the hotel.

The gravelled sweep in front of The Lodge Country House Hotel was obscured by a selection of Mercs, BMWs and Saabs all in tasteful shining livery. A muddied and battered country car with sweet wrappers in the back and an old curtain over the driver's seat didn't quite fit in. But I was high enough today to revel in the contrast and in the slightly dubious looks from the reception staff.

'Just the one night wasn't it Mrs Wallace?'

'Miss Wallace.'

'And it's a single occupancy?'

'Sadly yes.'

It seemed a bit premature to say 'maybe not'.

I'd arrived with just enough time to sweep into my glorious light-flooded room, get ready very carefully and sweep out again to the wedding. I unpacked my clothes, hung my dress in the bathroom, and prepared to prepare. The sound of a slow game of tennis drifted in through the window with the twitterings of house martins swooping over the roof. It was the perfect peaceful atmosphere. Martin and I could have made quiet gentle love on a bed like this in this sort of sunlight. I felt the wave of elation ebb without cresting. Seep away like a night tide.

I looked at myself in the long mirror from across the room. Sad. Face dragged downwards by all these weeks of crying, all my upward smile muscles have simply atrophied. Hair rather too coloured with that purply desperate look that says 'I'm old and I'm panicking about it'. Skin yellowish with that little tell-tale papery puckering where the underarm meets the shoulder. Even this skinny, the place under my ribs still wrinkles loosely eight years after there was a baby in there.

Sad. But not irredeemable. I had the room. The dress. The shoes. The opportunity. No matter how sad I felt, this was an investment in the future. In feeling better sometime somehow.

'Be positive' I said out loud. 'At least I can look at myself in the mirror now.'

And it's true, when Martin was around it was impossible. All I ever felt when looking at myself was the awful disparity in the standard of our looks: he, an eight out of ten without trying, and ten on a day when he felt good and hadn't been drinking. Me, a four if I put on make-up and struck it lucky with the hair dryer, minus two to minus six most of the time. But without Martin as a standard to fail against for the first time I can look at my good bits: there aren't many, so it's not a time-consuming activity, but I can decide to make the best of them.

So I put on the radio. Tasteless disposable pop. Not so loud as to disturb the tennis players, but loud enough to take the stillness from the room for the transformation ritual. No crying allowed for the next two hours at least. No negative thoughts about orange-peel skin, or under-eye wrinkles, or varicose veins. No fantasising about Martin's mouth, the backs of his legs, his solid forearms. No thinking about sex in the past. Only the possibility of sex in the future. Hopefully the very near future.

I laid out everything in order, from the new lipstick and disposable razor, to the hat, the stockings and the fragile blue lace underwear. I shook my dress just to hear the *shirr-shirr* sound of the silk, and put my divine and marvellous new shoes ready beneath it. I didn't take them out of their box. I left them, nestling inside the smooth cool cardboard, their colour muted inside their tissue-paper nests. They were the final anointment to be saved and savoured. The last magical ingredient to add to myself and send me out potent and irresistible into the wide world.

At least that's the old mystic guff I was giving myself as I ran the bath and spread something like green peanut butter over my face.

Anyway, the positive thinking worked. I don't remember enjoying 'dressing up' like that since I was about sixteen when me and my mate Christine would spend all of Saturday afternoon getting ready for a party. Conditioning hair, and trying to lie still, without giggling, for half an hour to let the zit control face-pack take effect. Applying the latest in lurid tan spot concealer, three shades of eyeshadow and stroking mascara on to each eyelash individually. All for the sake of being given a tonsillectomy by a boy so pumped up with cheap lager and pubescent testosterone that what we were wearing or even what species we were could hardly have mattered.

I timed things very carefully so as not to have a lot of time standing in front of the mirror and picking holes in myself before I had to leave for the church.

After years of dressing to go out in ten minutes whilst browning fish fingers and giving the babysitter counselling on her A-levels/latest boyfriend/new haircut, making myself do things slowly and thoroughly is still the hardest task.

Next, to the major suspension of disbelief in myself that I had to manage. The suppression of the little voice threatening 'who are you trying to kid?' as I put on the bright cerise lipstick and swept a hint of pink blusher over my cheekbones.

Five minutes before scheduled departure my make-up was complete, my underwear on, my hair dry. All I had to do was slip into my dress, hat and Divine Shoes. This was of course a high-risk strategy. Any zip failure at this stage would prove fatal. In Martin Days the stress levels induced by such a situation would have made me put my fingers through my stockings and my foot through the flimsy silk of the dress. The sheer charge of my anxiety would have made the nylon of the zip melt.

But the disciplined ritual of preparation had made me cool. With a minute to spare I slipped my feet into the shoes, and they hugged themselves round my soles and popped me upwards into a new stratosphere. I gave myself one last spray of perfume and smiled back at the glamorous woman in the mirror.

I stepped out into the sunshine.

I hadn't bargained for how exposed I was going to feel, as if there were a chill little breeze whistling cold down the side of me where Martin should have been. Somebody was sure to come up to me and challenge my right to wear high heels and silk frocks like a real girly: the ugly sisters catching Cinderella at the ball and sending her home before the Prince got to dance with her.

I walked rather too carefully across the churchyard. Walking in high heels takes practice which I haven't had. You have to do that bum wiggling thing to swing your legs from the hip. I know it's the easiest way to walk in heels. But I somehow feel I haven't the right to do it. You have to have confidence in the quality of your bottom to sway it around like that and in your status as a proper grown-up girl. So I just teetered, imagining myself with a heel trapped between flagstones and having to be extracted by the fire brigade.

People were already going into the church, so I filed in behind, wanting and not wanting to see anyone I knew.

At the back of the church was a pew full of people I hadn't seen for five years and more, since I stopped molesting teddy bears for money on national TV: my old producer Julia with her husband Charles, looking the picture of staid refinement in a Jaeger linen suit, camouflaging her ability to make farting noises with her armpits and do perfect Frankie Howerd impersonations. Trudy and Kate, Julia's assistant producers, in vestal virgin diaphanous frocks so that you'd never know that they specialised in shagging all the male PAs, vision mixers and production trainees under twenty-four. Josh, our floor manager, looking every inch the wicked wastrel rogue that he is, a heart disease candidate at thirty through his dissipated habits. His wife Rachel, gorgeous overblown English rose with a drinking pattern likely to send her to an only slightly later grave than her spouse. Peter. Dear gorgeous hopeless delightful Peter who has never held down a relationship for more than twenty-five minutes, my co-presenter and secret heart-throb. Dark and balding now, thin, fearsomely clever and so funny my face would ache with smiling after a day in the studio with him.

I was overcome with a flood of affection for all those old times, and all the stupid things we used to do to try and maintain our sanity and self-respect in the face of making programmes for an audience with a smaller vocabulary than Washoe the chimp: awarding prizes for the greatest number of *double entendres* fitted into a single script, leaving soft toys and puppets on the set in dubious sexual couplings, singing our lines to the tune of 'Bohemian Rhapsody' or Bach's 'Toccata and Fugue'.

We did a volume-controlled version of the screeched and rather hysterical 'luvvy' greeting ceremony, and I scrunched into the end of the pew, just as Josie, 'ex-PA *Mr Bounce*' arrived in a huge white frock, like something spun from sugar by a chef on LSD. Having been bending and twisting to reach me from mid pew, the luvvies all stood up straight, ready to be solemn witnesses to Josie's big moment. And then I saw who was sitting at the far end of the pew. Peter's younger brother Stewart. I didn't actually see Stewart. I saw his eyes. Neon blue, blazing out of the dimness of the church.

I remembered Stewart. He'd spent a summer vacation from Oxford working as dogsbody on *Mr Bounce*, and had every woman in the building drooling. He wasn't a hunk, more of a sort of well-made muscly waif like his brother. A kind of greyhound with Rottweiler touches. But he could charm snakes with his smile, and his voice could melt ice cubes at a hundred and twenty paces. I was pretty smitten with Peter at the time, my little crush on the side, but even *I* found myself blushing one day when Stewart pulled his T-shirt off with his jersey by mistake in rehearsals.

I looked at the blue eyes at the end of the pew and remembered that moment now. In a flash of realisation I understood why fat old business men always employ women for looks rather than talent. I'd have given Stewart an executive producership on the strength of that one blissful mistake. The face around the eyes smiled and mouthed 'Remember me?' Oh no. Hardly at all. At least not with any part of my brain.

I didn't notice the wedding march. I was swimming in a sea of lust. And gratitude. Even if the chances of bonking Stewart were possibly smaller than those of getting up-close and personal with my husband again, I was glad to feel desire for someone who wasn't Martin, and was fairer game than Chris. Stewart, of course, could only be a fantasy. How old was he? Twenty-five? possibly twenty-six? At least thirteen years younger than me. Born in the seventies when I was taking my GCSEs and A-levels, and getting very drunk for the first time. And meeting Martin.

By the time I came out of my sinful little reverie about Stewart's eyes, tummy-revealing T-shirt and other only imagined regions, Josie and her big butch hunk, who I'd never met before, were doing their vows. Even from the back of the church I could see that they were looking at each other with the kind of intensity you only usually get between the characters in *Star Trek*. Even Josie's chap's name didn't break the solemnity of the moment.

'I, Josie Louise, take thee, Wayne Jarred, to be my lawfully wedded husband.'

The church was full of stillness so that the atmosphere of the sweet blue summer's day washed through it. A single swallow had flown in and was scooping up the space under the arched nave. Back and forth it flew like a mantra of motion blessing these two people, busy below making outrageously romantic and unrealistic promises to each other.

'To have and to hold, in sickness and in health, for richer for poorer, from this day forward as long as we both shall live.'

Okay, well maybe. At least they were off to a rather better start than I had been. I got married to Martin in a registry office in the middle of town, round the back of all the big shops. The ceremony, which was pathetically brief, was almost drowned by the bleep bleep bleeping of lorries delivering the next load of nylon knickers to Marks and Spencer. It was as romantic as a Ford production line. If it had been summer we'd have needed gas masks for the smell because all the photos taken outside afterwards feature the overflowing metal dustbins of the adjacent Chinese takeaway. But it was winter, cold and bright and we smiled blissfully into the camera without turning to notice what was stacked up behind us.

As I looked at Josie in her ridiculous confection of white gauze and taffeta, with her lumpen bear of a partner, I couldn't help remembering that day. And all the other days since, when I'd sloppily squeezed Martin's hand, standing as I was now at the back of a church at someone else's wedding. What had he felt on our wedding day? Trapped? Had he just spent all those years waiting for a chance to escape?

I began to cry. Quietly and discreetly at first. Tears oozing out of the corners of my eyes. Quite acceptable at a wedding. But then I felt the sobs gathering up, irresistible as a bad dose of hiccups. And my nose began to run with an ocean of snot. If I had stayed in my seat I'd have been keening in a sea of mucus inside five minutes. Doing the sort of thing that would be considered over the top even over the coffin at an Italian funeral. So I braved the high-profile click of the purple shoes and walked out.

At the far end of the churchyard out of sight of the main door was a little garden, a couple of beds and a seat tucked against a stone wall. Here I was out of earshot, so I let rip for a while. Until Peter came and sat beside me.

'You didn't think to bring tissues did you?' he said, 'I fetched a box from the car. Here.'

'Fanks,' I said, in a kind of strangled cough. I used up quite a lot of the box of tissues before taking a final sniff and reaching for my bag to find some cosmetic Polyfilla to paste over the blotches.

'Okay now?'

'Yeah.'

'You haven't told me anything Jess. All your note said was that Martin had left you. What happened?'

'He left me. Found someone else and left me. Nothing else to say. Not really.'

'How are you? I mean how are you managing?'

'Like this is how I'm managing. Falling apart on a regular basis and wondering if I'll ever get to bed with anything apart from a good book ever again.'

Peter looked lost. Out of his depth with big grown-up emotions, and vaguely worried that he might have to go to bed with me again as an act of human kindness. Things could be worse, I thought, I could be Peter.

'I'm fine,' I said. 'Look, I'm putting on bright pink lipstick and you and I are going to go and be in the photos and I'm going to flirt with your brother.'

'He could do with it. He doesn't tell me, but I think his love life is quiet just now.'

Oh yes. Indeed. Things could be a lot worse.

By the time we arrived at the reception in the grounds of Josie's parents' farm, it was clear that Josie's TV mates were the unofficial cabaret. We'd been given a table to ourselves in the marquee, centrally placed to afford all the other tables a clear view.

We didn't disappoint. After five years' separation and a bucketful of Pimms on being reunited, we were ready for all sorts of misbehaviour. Or rather Josh and Rachel, Trudy and Kate were ready to create it. The rest of us were, as usual, merely happy to join in.

We started with loud and ribald conversation, progressed to embarrassing reminiscence and complex drinking games and then to eating strawberries in pairs with no hands. Each couple tried to outdo the rest in lasciviousness. I hadn't been quite decisive enough in my choice of seat, so Stewart was two people away. Peter was next to me and, with our history of professional collaboration, my natural partner. A good thing. I'd have dribbled too much with Stewart.

Peter and I were pretty good, having spent so many hours of waiting in studios talking about the detailed minutiae of sex — that was far more important than the one rather disappointing night of not-very-passion we'd spent together. But it was Julia and Charles who showed all the younger people what real sensuality was about.

I watched Stewart and Trudy with great interest. But Trudy giggled too much and the whole thing was over in two clean bites. Disappointing.

There was lots to drink and the more I had the more possible Stewart as goal became. I told my reflection in the Portaloos, 'No you can't . . . he's thirteen years younger than you,' and my reflection just leered back 'Yes you can'.

Eventually, by the time we'd got to cake and speeches, our table had deteriorated into a session of very physical musical chairs, with the men being the chairs and Julia and Charles providing the music in the form of very accurately rendered hums of soul classics. I landed on Stewart's lap, with just a little manipulation of events, as the speeches began. There seemed no reason to move as I was sitting down. So I didn't. And as Jarred went through his jokes and Josie's dad read his bit of doggerel, Stewart's arms wound a little tighter around my waist, his face came a little closer to my body. 'Oh yes I can.'

After the speeches, we all danced. The TV team with each other in a big heap like puppies. With various elderly relatives and rhythmless five-year-olds. We danced round the now very drunk Josie as if she were a handbag.

In between dancing we sat around our table and talked. More and more I talked to Stewart. I heard about Oxford, about travelling in India, about his ambitions to be in telly, but more successful than Peter, about his new job at the BBC. I sat close. I put my feet on his chair. I began to breathe him in. Behind him at the other side of the table, Josh and Rachel grinned at me, waggled their fingers, and mouthed 'Naughty'.

We danced some more, this time in twos. I danced with Stewart, and every time I looked up from my purple shoes I found his eyes.

Inevitably, after playing so much I liked, the disco hit a patch of stuff I loathed, starting with James Brown's 'Sex Machine'. I left Stewart and Josh doing something embarrassing to the music and went for a little stroll to the edge of the lawn where a gate stood between the garden and a mown field. I leaned against the wood, and watched the moths tangling in the grass and listened to the music blur and change in the background. Tired, drunk and gratefully blank inside for a while.

Stewart walked up to me, I hadn't heard him. As I turned from the moths he was standing unnecessarily close. Curved over me so that when I looked up his face was directly above mine, in his own shadow.

'This can't be a watch,' he said lifting my wrist and looking at the teeny little gold watch the size of a five-pence piece.

I used to be very bad at spotting this kind of chemistry. Boys used to come and visit me in my college room and sit and talk for hours and hours, perched on my desk, or sprawled on the bed. I used to wonder why they stayed. Didn't they have essays to write? But age, desperation and three months without sex had made me super sensitive. His touch on my arm was so magnified by my nervous system that I probably could have drawn every whorl of his fingertips.

Yes. Yes. It was possible. If I didn't do anything stupid. If I could just stop shaking as he touched me I'd actually get this delightful man into bed.

'No it's not actually. It's a radio transmitter. I can summon the assistance of my colleagues from other planets at any time. If you listen you can hear the transmissions.' I took the watch off my wrist. He didn't move, just kept leaning slightly over me with that smile always on the verge of a laugh. I lifted it up and held it to his ear so that my whole hand lay along the line of his jaw bone. I could feel the slight roughness and wondered if anyone had ever thought of telling the time by men's beard growth. But then I suppose it varies with testosterone levels. Some men's chins would be telling you it was home-time before coffee. They'd all have to be individually calibrated.

But by anyone's facial hair it was late. Dark blue beyond the lights of the marquee. On the dance floor, ties loosened all around, and mascara smudged.

'I can't tell what they're saying. Can you translate? You listen.'

He bent his head next to mine and held the watch to my right ear. The ends of his fingers moving slightly into my hair. Breathe. Remember to breathe, only nice and slowly. Panting would be such a giveaway.

'Mmm. I can translate but it's really bad news. We have only a very short time before the earth is picked up by a giant spaceship for use in a game of multi-galactic billiards.'

'Would it be possible to see the approach of the spaceship?'

'Well yes, but not from here. We'd have to move further from the lights. In the total dark.'

'Would the field next to my tent do?'

'A field would be a good place.'

'Should we take anything?'

'A bottle of champagne . . . the optical properties of the glass in the base are extraordinary. Better than the top astronomical telescopes.'

He fetched a half-empty bottle from the marquee and we climbed over the gate. I took off my shoes and walked barefoot. The ground was stony under the grass and I stumbled. Nothing to do with the Pimms.

'Ouch!'

'Lean on me, I've got sensible shoes. Are you okay?' His arm went protectively around my shoulders. More self-advice not to pant.

'Oh yes, I mean this could be my last night on earth, so what's a little bruise on the feet?'

'Shall we sit down?'

'Yes.'

'You know what you said about the optical properties of champagne bottles?'

'Mmm.'

'Don't they need to be empty?'

'Yes . . . but this one's almost empty. I mean if you drank some and then I did it would be.'

'No, you first.'

I swigged as if it were pop. He drained the bottle.

'Where in the sky should we look?'

'Oh directly upwards.'

'Then maybe we should just lie down. We can lie on this.' He spread his jacket on the grass.

'Won't it spoil?'

'It's the last night of my life. I won't be wearing a suit again.'

We lay down side by side looking upwards. Rather chastely just touching arms and sides.

Hmm, I thought, rather too much like a remake of *Gregory's Girl*. He may be young but he's not that young.

'Should we look through the bottle yet?'

'It's really not worth it until they're a bit closer. I'll need to listen to my transmitter again.'

'I think you're lying on it. It's in my pocket.'

I'd led him along so far and he hadn't made a move so I was almost shocked when he rolled on to me and reached under the small of my back into the jacket pocket.

'Got it,' he said, his face very close, 'aren't you scared of the end of the world?'

'Of course.'

With the weight of a man on top of my body for the first time in what felt like three and a half million years, telling myself not to pant was really a waste of time. He was so close now I couldn't have focused even if there had been more light and less alcohol.

'I can feel your heart beating against my shirt.'

'Because I'm so scared.'

'Don't be.'

I've always been keen on kissing. It should be taught in schools. If people really got the hang of proper kissing there would be fewer unwanted pregnancies and far less venereal disease, AIDS could be stopped in its tracks. With the right sort of kissing, teenagers wouldn't get as far as undoing their flies.

Now, after so many weeks of feeling stretched and wracked, of being without desire, two abandoned minutes with Chris aside, to be kissed was a shock: what a cactus must feel like when it's slopped with the first cold rain in twenty-five years.

And this was high-quality kissing. Not Martin, but still good. Stewart knew about transferring everything that might be happening in his underwear into the skin of his lips.

'We can go into my tent, if you'd like.'

'Good place to hide from spacecraft.'

We got up rather uncertainly and wobbled across the field.

A rogue beam of light escaped from the marquee as someone else slipped out the back way. It fell on the ridge of Stewart's under-canvas accommodation. Not so much a tent as a bivvy bag. The ridge was hardly more than knee-high off the ground at its highest, and had a ski-jump of a sag in the middle. We were neither of us in a condition to care. Any dark and reasonably private space where we could remove each other's clothes as quickly as possible would have done the job. You know that bit in *The English Patient* where Ralph Fiennes is bonking Kristin Scott Thomas up against a wall, just round a corner from where the expat Rotary Club are having cucumber sandwiches? Well I never found it convincing, until that moment outside Stewart's tent. I'd have had him in a sleeping bag in the middle of the dance floor at that point.

He knelt and undid the tent's little front door and the zipping sound was almost unbearably erotic. He peered inside and immediately recoiled. For a moment I thought some other rampant couple must have beaten us to it.

'Oh shit!' he sounded as though he'd hit his thumb with a jackhammer or caught something vital on a tent peg.

I knelt down beside him and looked into the dark space under the fly sheet. Standing there still and solemn, with a kind of silent dignity you don't normally associate with their kind, was a sheep. It had been inside the tent quietly and calmly for who knows how long. No, we both knew how long: since bloody Josh Barton had put it there, that's how long.

'Barton, I'll have your balls on a stick if it's the last thing I do.'

'I'll help you thread them.'

Hell hath no fury like a couple whose passion has just been thwarted. In livid and simmering silence we coaxed the sheep out of the tent, across the field and through the gate back to its mates. This took some time, as it didn't have any kind of guiding device like a collar or a halter so we just had to bury our hands in its wool and steer by force. In the sheep's defence, I think it found the whole episode rather distasteful and embarrassing.

Back at the tent we found that the creature must have been undercover for some time and evidence suggested that it hadn't always been as calm as when we found it. We threw all the bedding out on to the grass along with all the currants we could find by feel. Then, chilled in the night air, and fabulously sober considering the amount we had both drunk, we sat down on the doorstep of Stewart's little bivouac with two feet of cooling sward separating us. All passion apparently spent in shepherding.

I hugged my knees in misery. Perhaps my only chance of making love to anyone ever ever again had just evaporated along with the alcohol boiled from our blood by anger and frustration.

'I don't think we're safe out here,' Stewart moved closer, 'you know with the killer sheep and the spacecraft. I mean, I know it's not much protection but it might be safer inside the tent . . .' He snaked his fingers around the back of my neck and I suddenly thought of those gas adverts, you know, where the flame jumps up at the touch of a finger.

The eroticism of the sound of the tent undoing half an hour before was nothing to the sound of it closing behind us. Camping will never be the same again now that canvas-zipping and the smell of sheep droppings have a new meaning. God help me, after one fuck in a field I've acquired the sexual responses of a Welsh agricultural student.

Inside it was too cramped to do anything but lie down. Not that we wanted to sit around and play cards. There wasn't a light of any sort, but after the best part of an hour's adaptation our eyes were good in the dark. I could see Stewart's shirt quite well enough to undo the buttons.

'If you ever have a job interview with anyone female, or gay of course, just make sure you wear a white shirt with the top three buttons undone.'

'Hard to do that with a jacket and tie.'

'Stuff the jacket and tie. You do the business with the buttons and you'll get the job, no matter who else applies.'

Seduction has never been on my list of accomplishments. I've never 'pulled', so the sensation of delight and triumph as I gained access to Stewart's body was completely new.

'Will this dress come off over your head?' he asked.

'No.'

'Ah, I see.'

He undressed me with the excitement and efficiency of a schoolboy unwrapping a favourite sweetie. Two twists at the coloured cellophane and a scrunch of foil and I was as naked as sherbet fruit. And about the same consistency on the inside.

He rolled me on top of him. I think I probably moaned. Which was kind of bad form for so early in the proceedings. Then he froze. Suddenly rigid in all the wrong places.

'Jesus!' he said, with the air of someone who has just realised on the plane to Bali that they've left the roast beef in the oven, 'what do we do about contraception?'

Earlier, I had given a single brief thought to condoms, comparing the immediate risk of ruining possibly the last fuck of my life with the nebulous and distant risk of pregnancy. So the answer to Stewart's question was: we play Russian roulette.

'Don't worry, I'm still on the pill,' I lied easily, smoothly. I was not going to be deprived at the eleven and seven-eighths hour. Twenty years ago that was enough to keep any boy quiet. No one had heard of AIDS then.

'But I don't know who you've slept with.'

Me? I wish. I sat up astride him, scraping a ridge pole at both ends. HIV hadn't impinged on my consciousness during the condom thought, because I began my sexual career when the biggest worry was genital herpes. So I did the sort of analysis done by people who end up with five obscure forms of pneumonia and a prescription list the size of a Dostoevsky novel: 'My prospective sexual partner cannot possibly be promiscuous or a drug user, they look healthy and nice. And anyway, bad stuff happens to other people.' In short, a kind of microcosm of human stupidity — I-want-it-now-and-sod-the-consequences.

'I've only slept with Martin, for the best part of your lifetime,' I said. Pretty true. Apart from one drunken end of series night with Peter.

'But who has Martin slept with?' God whoever said that the AIDS propaganda didn't work?

'Dolores.'

'Yeah. And who has Dolores slept with?'

'The entire population of inner fucking London for all I know. Look, I'm safe. Martin and I always used condoms.'

'Why, if you're on the pill?'

'Because I wasn't on the pill when I was with Martin. It's a gynaecological thing, to regulate my periods after the shock.' That surely was going to shut him up. I wriggled a little and lay down on him.

'I'll go and find a condom if you really want,' I said, sitting again and making a little more significant contact. This time Stewart did a little bad-form moaning.

'No. No. That's okay. Sorry.'

He unfroze. The instant gas flame jumped inside us again.

'How sorry?'

'As sorry. Ahh. As you want me to be.' There, now, condoms were finally irrelevant.

The last thing I remember actually thinking with a verbally orientated bit of my brain was that Stewart was not so sweetly inexperienced as his age and eyes might suggest. Or rather sweet. But not inexperienced. Yet not recently active I guessed: he seemed to enjoy my body so much. He kept saying ridiculously flattering things to me. So I suppose he can't have had much for a while if he can tell a thirty-nine-year-old that she has 'the body of a teenager'. It was strange to be doing things I'd learned with Martin with another man. Things I'd done and enjoyed so many times. The familiarity, the practice and of course the water-in-the-desert pleasure of it kept me from worrying about the crêpiness of my skin or the flabbiness of my bottom. It was dark enough not to think about crow's feet and rubbed in mascara.

Through all the sameness of the mechanics of what we did, it felt different. I felt different. Another person.

We both lasted a long time thanks to all the interruptions. Long enough to stop, pass a bottle of water between our joined bodies, drink, change position, continue, a lot of times. We'd emptied a two-litre bottle of Evian by the time we were completely finished and lying shell-shocked side by side and gazing upwards once more.

It was cold, and the surface under the ground sheet was sharp and lumpy. We were both going to be covered with bruises. Stewart pulled our bits of wedding clothing over us to make some sort of bedding. We clung close for warmth and soon he was asleep. But I don't have the necessary Yogic skills to sleep on a bed of nails no matter how nice the chest I have available is to lean on. Gently I deprived Stewart of some of his coverings, wriggled into my clothes and out of the tent. Somewhere in the knee-high dawn mist covering the field was a pair of purple high heels.

'A young gentleman called in earlier Miss Wallace,' said the Barbie doll on reception as I checked out, 'he left these for you.' She pulled the purple shoes out from under the counter, and risked a grin. At least it was shoes and not knickers.

Shoved inside one shoe was a crumpled order of service from the wedding with a note written on the back.

'Thanks!!!!! I'll get your number from Pete. Thought you might need the magic slippers back if the UFOs didn't get you. Love Stewart.' Not exactly a declaration of undying devotion but at least some intent to contact me again.

'I hope you enjoyed your stay,' said the receptionist, looking me straight in the eye.

'Mmm,' I said, 'it was very good indeed. Amazing actually.'

Yeah that's right darlin'. I had him, that really very nice-looking young man with those blue eyes that you didn't fail to notice. An old lag like me.

I picked up my shoes as though they were a trophy and walked to my car.

Chapter Twelve

Sarah stretched her legs out on the grass and kicked off her shoes. It's the holidays, the students are long gone, she can allow herself a little freedom. 'You do realise that this Stewart of yours is the same age as some of my third years?'

'Yes I do thank you very much Sarah and it isn't a source of delight to me. Just shows how bloody impossible the whole thing is.'

'Not at all, I know loads of women who have successful relationships with men much younger than them.'

'Yeah? Who?'

'Mercedes. Her boyfriend is twenty-three and she's nearly forty. They're blissful. He worships her.'

'He must have lost his mother before she breast fed him. Anyway, she's in Madrid half the year. He probably shags sixteen-year-olds while she's away.'

'Stop it Jess, don't be cynical,' Kath was genuinely reproachful. 'There're plenty of people with younger partners. Look at me and Gerry.'

'Kath, that's the right way round. People think it's okay for a man to be older than a woman.'

'But that's nonsense.'

'I know it is, you know it is, but the receptionist at the hotel where we go for our first dirty weekend won't, and being looked at like a child molester or some desperate old bag paying for it isn't my idea of fun.'

'For God's sake Jess. He's twenty-five. Not underage. The receptionist will be jealous. He sounds gorgeous. How come all my male students are unwashed and spotty with glasses like the bottom of milk bottles with less dress sense than a slug?'

'Just as well. Think of the temptation. It's terrible, believe me. We had a sous-chef at The Court two years ago. Twenty-two he was. Colombian. I had to open the windows every time he came in my office to cool myself down. I was so glad when he left. Another month and I'd have been wearing suspenders and no knickers to work every day.'

'Anyway. It's all a bit premature. It's been ages and Stewart hasn't called. He knows how old I am. He sobered up and did the maths. Simple as that.'

'If he didn't want to bother he wouldn't have left the note in the shoes.'

'Kath's right. Think about it. Young man, lays gorgeous older woman at a wedding reception. It's pure male fantasy. He's probably too nervous to ring you. You should ring him.'

'There's one fatal flaw in that argument. The word gorgeous.'

They both groaned. Kath struggled to her feet and brushed off the grass clippings.

'Okay. I'm going home to get these kids fed.'

'Me too,' said Sarah. 'If bonking some man fifteen years your junior isn't enough to give you confidence, then there's nothing we can say to help.'

I didn't blame them for being fed up. I had been behaving like a fourteen-year-old after her first snog in the darkened corner of a school disco. So really they'd been pretty long-suffering. They'd put up with the soupy fantasising, the umpteenth description of the exact shade of Stewart's eyes and the endless angst-ridden enumeration of all the things that were happening in 1972 that I can remember but Stewart of course, being nought years old that year, could not. They tolerated it out of relief, I guess, that since my uncomfortable night in a tent full of sheep shit I appear to be in remission. I've stopped crying all the time. I sleep better. I've even eaten. I smile. I don't wake up with my heart racing and my sweat glands going for some sort of world record. I've begun to enjoy my kids again. Since they broke up for the holidays we've had outings . . . zoos, seaside, surfing, they've slept in my bed every night. We've done things Martin didn't enjoy, breakfast and telly in bed, cuppa and videos in bed, wet afternoon stories in bed. I've got back my parental gravity, I feel I might have enough pull to hold the three of us together.

At first I didn't want to think too hard about what this meant. The fact that the grief at losing a man I love deeply seemed assuaged by a single bonk with a total stranger. It might indicate that I'm terminally shallow. So I simply tried to accept it at face value – my only living proof that I could get up off the scrap heap where Martin had thrown me, and walk.

Even in the face of another delightful communication from Martin. A fax from the same hotel in New York.

'Jess, I hear on the grapevine that you've got work. [What grapevine goes from me to New York? The one that runs in two directions, from the kids saying 'Mummy's got a job' and back from Martin ringing all his TV contacts to find out who gave it me and for how much.] So you won't need my financial contribution for a while. [Just you wait until my lawyer gets her hands round your wallet.] I'm delayed here in the US for some time. I have to go to LA in a week. I don't expect to be back until September. [Okay. So I earn enough for three people to live on whilst also handling all of the child care.] I will write separately to the children. Obviously I don't want this long period of absence to affect our relationship. [Obviously I don't want my shit to smell.] Martin.'

It came late at night after I'd spent an evening being the punchbag for the children's anger: me feeling better was the catalyst for a while for them to feel worse.

The glow I gave out for the few days after the wedding seemed their signal-light to let out some more of the feelings they'd been too scared to express in earnest. Too frightened by my fragility to feel they could do their own screaming and crying, they began to do some catching up the moment I seemed strong enough to take it. So I had Dan throwing his whole weight bodily at me, fists flying, telling me I was the worst mother in the world, in response to being asked for the second time to wash his hair. I had Frankie slamming her door and doing target practice by hurling Barbies at my head when I suggested she might do a little more violin practice. The concluding tableau was the two of them lying on top of me on the landing sobbing apologies into my arms. Of course by the time we got to that stage we'd had two hours of shouting, slamming, hitting, abusing and despairing all round and were all as wrung out as a set of holey dishcloths.

I put them in my bed in the end, with three pillows down the middle to prevent territorial disputes. Then, lying balanced on the pillow wall, I talked and stroked them both to sleep. I wished there were someone to do the same for me. Even in my wildest imaginings I couldn't see Stewart smoothing my tearful brow until I fell into a dreamless slumber.

I came downstairs to find Martin's fax was still warm in the machine. Not hand-scribbled this time but direct from his modem, dashed off with all the other end-of-office-time messages before he dressed for dinner. I was feeling insubstantial, blown away in parts like a scarecrow in Hurricane Betsy or after a bad night with the mice. So I wasn't ready to withstand the screaming force ten of anger that hit me when I read it. I sat down on the floor and felt hot waves of murder throb through me. I spluttered internally with all the 'how does he expects?', and 'it's all right for hims'. What all of it boiled down to was fuck me and fuck the children, he'd got what he wanted: freedom to pursue his career and his penis.

Anger and disgust throbbed through me for an hour. I sat by the lavatory physically wretching with it. When the throbbing stopped, instead of leaving me crying, it left me cold. The sort of cold and sober you get the morning after a night spent parting company with some duff prawns. I could see Martin's behaviour very clearly and it made me ashamed for him. Astonished and ashamed. Not a word he'd said in twenty years was left unshaken by that chill of the most profound and poignant disappointment

A great fat umbilical chord of wanting snipped through, cutting another of the bonds that held me to him, but leaving another bleeding end.

Beside that, what I felt about Stewart was meaningless, just fevered adolescent fantasies about a person I didn't know. He was not a dude on a white horse ready to change my life and straighten everything out with one blow of his lance.

But the event was significant. My job, my stupid shoes, my one-night stand were symbols that some sort of new start was possible. But not yet. Not this full of tears and enough high-quality violence to make a Roman beast show shrink. And not with someone who's too young to remember Mott The Hoople and the Arthur Ashe Wimbledon final.

So when Stewart phoned the next night, he and Martin together had made it easy for me. He bounced down the phone, breathy and enthusiastic. Slightly nervous. Painfully young. With nothing like enough history to begin to understand.

'Hi. It's Stewart. How are you?' Every day since the wedding my heart had doubled time at every phone ring in case it had been Stewart. Now it beat slow and boring as ever.

'I'm fine. You?'

'Busy. Loads of work. They've given me a contract until Christmas, and there's a possibility of a three-year extension.' A sweet and decent boy. Full of excitement about his future. Worried that I was somehow a nail on which his progress could catch. But worried too that he had hurt me. I felt like an ancient aunt.

'Well done. That's great.'

'I was, um, going to come and see you this weekend.'

'Really? That's sweet of you.'

'But y' know I'm really, um, busy. And moving into my new flat and stuff.'

'Don't worry Stewart. We'll have lunch in town one day perhaps.'

'I'd love that.' He couldn't believe his luck. Reprieved. No retribution for his drunken mistake.

'Okay then. Call me in a couple of months. I won't be so busy maybe. Look, I have to go Stewart. I had a lovely time with you on Saturday.'

'Thank you. I did too.'

'Keep in touch. Bye.'

'Bye Jess. Bye.'

It didn't hurt at all. I'd let him go believing I was some sort of *femme fatale*, so we could both hang on to our little memory and smile when we smelled a sheep.

So. Miss Jess Termite had stripped off her wings. No husband. No lover. No overnight solutions to anything. Least of all bloody child care for the kids. Filming for pets started in just over ten days now and was due to run on until almost Christmas. For four days a week I'd be gone before eight and sometimes not back until ten or midnight. I needed a surrogate parent for when I was not around. Someone who could drive, and who had their own car and was prepared to work irregular, unpredictable but also part-time hours. All for not much money.

Such a person does not exist. I placed ads in every local paper from here to Devizes plus one in the *Lady*. I had three replies. One from a Knightsbridge nanny who fancied a little country interlude but who couldn't do without her own bathroom suite and sitting room. One from a man who wanted to know what colour underwear I was wearing. And one from a lady who'd been a cyclist she said for fifty-five years and was sure she could collect the children from school and get them to run the four miles beside her bike.

Relying on friends to do my child care for me was no good either. Kath and Sarah live from hand to mouth with their own. Jo's mother takes her kids after school, I was pretty sure she wouldn't welcome another couple of kids to mind. And there were Dan and Frankie's feelings to be taken into account. Up to now they'd always been pretty relaxed about going to friends' houses for a night or so, to let me whiz to London to see Martin, happy to disappear off into someone else's garden for a day in the holidays. But Martin has destabilised their world, so they'd become as territorial as homing pigeons.

'I don't want to go to someone else's house all the time. I want to be at home.'

'I don't want to be with a load of boys all the time.'

'Rosie's not a boy.'

'No. She's a baby. I don't want to be with boys or babies.'

'Why can't you take care of us Mummy? Oh why can't you?'

I bit my tongue. I didn't say, 'Because your father has signed a secret no responsibility clause to cover his whole life.' I told them calmly that it will only be for a few months, and that I have to work so we can keep the house and eat at the same time. Yet still, the whole issue of where they are going to be whilst I work had become so loaded that I could hardly mention it without someone beginning to whine. And by last week it was usually me, imagining six-hour filming-day drives with Dan and Frankie in the back reading comics and throwing up from car sickness. I had one week left to organise something before I took the children away on holiday as I'd promised I would. To France. And the day after we were due back I was booked to be in Swindon with a person who breeds prize-winning chinchillas.

I lay in bed seething with worry and anger, imagining the children in car crashes, mashed to pieces on the way home from a shoot, or mauled by Great Danes, or on the psychiatrist's couch describing the terrible sense of loss and displacement they felt every time their mum went off to work. And I imagined Martin, on the phone, fixing another job, flying to another city, with nothing more difficult to organise than a clean pair of his own socks.

I was doing some night-time pacing over it all, allowing it to expand like a genie, let out of a dark bottle, when Kath rang.

'How are you?'

'Fine. But panicking about filming and what I'm going to do with the kids.'

'I can help once term starts again but Joe and Louis are going to Mum's for the rest of the hols. I'm headless in work then and Gerry's got a huge job on.'

'It's all right Kath. It's not a problem you have to solve for me!'

'Well this might help it a bit. Maybe.'

'What?'

'I've been meaning and meaning to ask you about this. And I've forgotten so much it may be too short notice. I need a favour Jess. But you'd get something out of it too . . .'

'Kath. Slow down. What are you on about?'

'Sorry. I'm just embarrassed because I've been so inefficient. 'We've got this gardens guy coming to The Court. He's a specialist in organic gardens and garden design. He's Dutch and he's coming for a couple of months, p'raps a bit more, to redesign the gardens here. He needs a place to stay, and there's no spare staff accommodation, so he asked me to find him a family who'd put him up. We can't have him because of building the extension. The money's quite good, it's part of his deal with The Court. I mean, I know you don't need it so much now, but at least it might help pay for child care . . . I think Gerry might have mentioned it to you a while ago,' she finished lamely.

'I'm not going to be here to cook for a lodger every night. I can't cater for my own kids at the moment let alone some complete stranger.'

'He's not a complete stranger. I mean, I know him. He's called Pieter. He came here in the winter. He's sweet. Really nice. He stayed with Gerry and me and he cooked for us. He's terribly domesticated. But he'll have his meals up at The Court except for breakfast. He'll even babysit.'

'How come I never met this paragon whilst he was with you?'

'You had laryngitis. Martin was in Africa. You weren't in the best of moods.'

'When is he arriving?'

'Um. Quite soon. I'm not sure. He said in the next couple of days sometime. Please Jess, say yes.'

'Okay. After all you and Gerry have done this summer I owe you. Send him round. I'll get him a key cut. At least he'll have the place to himself for a week. He can feed the chooks whilst we're away.'

'He'll probably have Dog for you too.'

'Nobody is that angelic.'

'We'll have her then.'

'Wow . . . if you have Dog whilst we're away I'll have a whole fleet of gardeners.'

It's a measure of things that've changed since Martin's departure. Having a lodger before would have been impossible – I'd have spent all the time trying to make everything domestically perfect, shushing the kids, gagging the cockerels, disinfecting the fridge. Now I just don't care any more. The night that Kath persuaded me, I looked at the spare room, I moved two broken chairs off the bed, turned the photo montage of our wedding to the wall and picked up some bits of Lego from the window sill. Fine, that'll do, I thought.

By the time Pieter actually arrived I'd forgotten about him. Partly due to the my-husband-left-me-and-now-I-don't-clean-my-fridge syndrome, and partly due to the fact that we were celebrating.

Especially me. Mary had solved my child panic. I'd taken the kids over to say hello, enjoying the indiscipline of no school to go to and no work to rush for. But I was in a yet deeper circle of hair-tearing having rung another nanny agency who couldn't help. Mary was out in her garden with the dogs surging round her ankles like a mobile carpet.

'James mended the old tree-house at the weekend,' she told Dan and Frankie, 'why don't you go and inspect it?' They tore off into the huge complicated maze of Mary's garden in delight with the mobile carpet, Dog now ruining the pattern, in disarrayed pursuit.

'All set for your holiday Jess?'

'Me? Mary! I haven't even found my passport.'

'Well, strictly speaking that is all you need. Any joy with your nanny enquiries?'

'No, the score is still the same. One Sloane, one loony and a rapist. None of the agencies even wants to speak to you unless you can offer a three-bedroomed nanny annexe with built-in pony accommodation.'

'Why don't you let them come here? There's only a week more of the holidays left after you come home from France, and then after school, well it's just a matter of a few hours.'

'No Mary, that's too much to ask of you.'

'You didn't ask. I offered. Make it more business-like if you want. In a week's time Georgina will be back from Greece. She's at a loose end and I'm sure she'd like to earn some money. She won't be going back to college until October. So you pay her and between us we'll do the job until then. What do you say?'

I didn't say anything. I burst into tears and flung my arms around Mary's pearls and twinset.

'I take it that is Jess-code for "yes please".'

'Yes please.'

The kids turned cartwheels all the way home with delight. There's something about Mary's formality and the old-fashioned garden with potting sheds and shady corners that they love. They met Georgina only once, last Christmas, but she made an absolutely indelible impression by giving them each a high-speed ride on the back of her scrambling motorbike round

James's woods. They came back only recognisable by the smiles showing through the two-inch layer of all-over mud.

A picnic by the sea and a spot of mackerel fishing was what we needed to celebrate. That and some very loud music. I put on my Michael Bolton CD, now permanently out of my knicker drawer, and we had 'Love is A Wonderful Thing' at full volume several times. And as it played, we got the picnic ready, plastic plates, cheese, rug. I threw the plates one by one in time to the music to Dan, who's a good catcher and snatched from the air stylishly on the off-beat. Then he threw them to Frankie, and did a twirl after each one. And Frankie put them into the basket with a bottom wiggle that Marilyn would have been proud of, and we all joined in with the backing singers oo eee oooo. We repeated the whole thing with every item we needed to take, adding dance steps, twists, hand jiving, using the kitchen chairs as partners. Tom Cruise in *Cocktail* couldn't have had better use of props or timing.

And after the third repeat of the track we were all packed and ready to go, breathless, giggling. Dog, wild with infected joy, was racing round and round the table chasing imaginary flies. I turned to hit the stop button on the CD and saw a man standing in the open doorway, leaning comfortably on the frame as though he had been there for some time. He was long. Long body, long arms, long legs, folded in angles. The only part of him that was short was his hair, a dark grizzled stubble all over a very round head. He was smiling with a long mouth in a deeply tanned face and looked oddly ageless. He could have been thirty or fifty. He stood up straight and made his face a little more serious.

'Hello. I am Kath's friend Pieter.' His voice was slow, finding its way around the English words precisely but not without a little thought and effort.

'Hello. I'm Jess. This is Dan and Frankie, my children. Um, we don't normally do . . . this.'

'Oh. I was hoping that you did.'

'I'm terribly sorry, I wasn't sure when to expect you.'

Dan and Frankie had turned their backs on Pieter and were making frantic what-about-our-picnic faces at me.

'I can go away, come back later. I can go up to The Court. Not a problem.'

Dan and Frankie nodded furiously. Why do children believe that if they can't see you, you can't see them?

'No,' I said, ignoring my children's disgusting display of inhospitableness. 'We're going to the seaside. Would you like to come?' It seemed as good a way as any of starting to get to know someone who was about to live in my house.

'Is it far?'

'No, about forty minutes. Less than an hour.'

'That would be very nice,' he said, with a serious and deferential nod, the polite acceptance of a well-trained guest, then without giving me even a hint of that adult-to-adult complicity he said, 'if that's okay with you kids. Do you mind if I come?'

Disarmed by this they turned round, and stood studying their own feet, and mumblingly acquiesced.

It didn't take them long to work through acquiescence to curiosity. From there it was a short step to hero worship. Once Pieter had told them that back home he had a house on stilts by an estuary so you could fish from the bedroom window, he attained the status of a deity. If he had started pulling salmon out of the glove compartment of the car the children would have been unsurprised. So, by the time we were out on the boat, they were openly competing for his attention.

'Pieter look, look, I've got a big one!'

'Pieter, I've got my line tangled.'

Good-naturedly he went from one child to the other apparently taking huge pleasure in fixing their hooks and hauling in the blue and silver tigered fish.

I need not have been there at all.

It's an institution that the mackerel boat at our nearest beach takes you round the bay with a load of baited hand lines for a couple of quid. But I never normally get to appreciate the simple pleasure of this little bit of summer. Normally I'm the one baiting hooks, offsetting discouragement. Today I could fish. Quietly off the back, throwing my own line into the water, blue-green and so clear it felt like flying to float on it. The children and the lodger were occupying each other, leaving me free to look dreamily into the sea, and back at the big red-brown cliffs, crumbly and moist, giant slices of chocolate sponge.

Back on the little jetty we stood with our six mackerel strung through the gills, turgid and still bright with recently departed life.

'We'll take them home and cook them for supper,' I said, taking control, responsibility back again, being the polite and slightly distant host. The English Woman and her Foreign Guest. But Pieter hadn't been playing that role. He'd come with us because he'd wanted to. Not because it was polite. And now I had suggested something he didn't want to do.

'Why?' Pieter asked, as if I'd suggested something mad.

'Don't you like fish?'

'Of course. But why take them home? Is it permitted to make a burning on the shore?'

'A fire? Yes. I think so.'

'Good.' He smiled at me with his long mouth. 'Then I cook for you these fishes.' He took the fish from my hands without asking, and strode off along the beach. Completely relaxed, completely at home. Doing what he wanted, and knowing we'd like it too.

He cooked for us these fishes, on a driftwood fire, skewered on sticks, gutted in the sea with his penknife. We ate all six and sucked the bones. I ate too. A whole fish, charred skin and all. They were sweet and chalky, nothing like mackerel from a shop more than a day from the water and oily with age.

I didn't talk much as we cooked and ate the fish. Idle polite chitchat was obviously a waste of time with someone like this. I wondered how I was going to share a house with someone who just didn't acknowledge any kind of social mask.

Eating finished, the kids ran off along the beach to paddle and throw sticks for Dog, always trying to get her to swim. She never does more than wet her toes and bark in frantic defiance at the waves. Pieter threw his last fish bone on the fire and lay back on the shingle, eyes closed, long hands behind his head.

'Very good fish,' he said.

'They were. Thank you for cooking them.'

'You have cooked them on the beach before?'

'Yes. Once. With Martin, my husband.'

Pieter rolled over, propped his head on an elbow and looked at me very intently, like a paediatrician examining a small child for a rash.

'Yes. Martin. Kath told me about Martin. I'm very sorry for you.'

'Don't be, I'm quite sorry enough for myself.'

'I don't understand.'

'I mean you don't need to be sorry, because I'm . . . oh never mind.'

'You love him?' Well I supposed Dutch is nearly Nordic and they're all very direct aren't they?

'Yes. But I've got to stop.'

'No. You can love things you can't have. You can't have the sea. But you love the sea don't you?'

'Yes I do. Does it show so much?'

'You look at the water like it was a handsome movie star.' He sat up and made a face of hopeless adoration with slightly crossed eyes and we laughed together for a long time.

The kids fell asleep in the car on the way home. I drove and did none of the stuff I normally do with new people: nervously and even obsessively pointing out nice views or giving a running commentary on the scenery. I just drove and looked at the sky.

'I would like some music. Would you like some music too?' asked Pieter.

'Yes. Just choose something.'

Pieter rifled comfortably through my tapes, and I didn't worry about his opinion of my frivolous tastes. Especially not when he chose a tape labelled 'Top Hits'.

Spice Girls, Hot Chocolate, The Drifters, Chumbawumba, Village People, Madness.

He rewound 'Baggy Trousers', laughing.

'I love this band. I learned English from these lyrics, when I was at school.'

He sang along, word perfect and melody terrible to the whole song. I joined in the chorus, and discovered that for all these years I'd been getting the lyrics completely wrong.

At school when Madness were making the top ten would make him what? Thirty-three or so. Much younger perhaps. He didn't say secondary school after all. But why was I calculating? Long and strange, practically scalped with that haircut, he was consistent with my new Queen Termite theory . . . no more wings, just digging and child-rearing.

All the same, something benign and calming settled in the house on Friday night with my new lodger's presence, so when I woke at two, the sound of Pieter snoring for Europe in the spare room was a comfort. I rolled in my duvet and, smiling, went back to sleep.

Chapter Thirteen

Lawrence of Arabia or Redmond O'Hanlon couldn't have felt themselves to be more touched with the dusty glamour of adventure and travel than I did, drinking black coffee at the Brittany Ferries' terminal at six in the morning. I was out into the world alone, sole leader of my little expeditionary force, which was currently stuffing greasy croissants in the back seat of an overloaded estate.

The smell of rotting seaweed and diesel, the towering other-worldly bulk of the ferry and the sea beyond, shiny, like smoothed clingfilm, filled me with an inflated sense of potential. I could run away across the wide globe with my two babies and never come back.

All quite ridiculous since we barely managed to get to the port without the bikes coming off the rack or Frankie throwing up in a lay-by. Nothing to do with travel sickness – she's just her father's daughter and Martin finds early starts virtually impossible. Bit of a handicap when dawn light is so great for photographs.

We got on the boat, and all around were Mr and Mrs Cardigan and their kids, Sweatshirt and Track Suit, so that everything in our surroundings screamed normality, ordinariness: taking a ferry is no more special than a bus into town from the gas works on Station Road, everything said. But still I felt intrepid. Clever as Moriarty to have organised a cabin. Original as Einstein to be going to France. Courageous as Cavel to be a parent alone, taking two children to a country where I couldn't even ask for an Elastoplast, let alone explain that my child was showing the symptoms of meningitis or that I thought my clutch had gone.

I felt big, three-dimensional, not small and flattened, nor temporarily inflated, but solid, round, and potent.

All a reaction to the eleventh-hour cold-feet of my friends, trying to convince me that taking a tent to Cornwall was a better idea.

I had been feeling quite laid-back about our holiday. All arranged rather serendipitously because one of James's friends was lending us a half-converted gîte for free and the ferry company had some cheap deal going on cancellations. But everyone else seemed to be worried about it at the last minute. Sarah came over yesterday whilst I was trying to be ruthless about the number of clothes the kids might need.

'Are you certain this is a good idea?'

'What, taking two pairs of shorts not three?'

'No. Going to France alone.'

'I'm not going alone.'

'Jess don't be stupid. You know what I mean. You know if you get very, well, *down* there, there won't be anyone to turn to. No distractions.'

'Apart from the cheap booze, the lovely beaches, the glorious countryside, no nothing really.'

'Supposing you start crying all the time again?'

'I'll just go round one of their nice supermarkets and I'll instantly feel better.'

'What about doing all that driving alone. Suppose you get ill?'

'Bloody hell Sarah, it's less than fifty miles from the ferry to the gîte. Listen to yourself!'

'Oh all right. I'm sorry. I'm just worried. That's all. So is Kath.'

*

Then Chris called.

'Jess. I've got something terribly important to tell you.'

'Mmm?'

'I'm in love. I've been ringing Jo all week and we've really advanced things. I'm coming to see her. Midweek before I go off to Aberdeen.'

'Aberdeen?'

'Good place to shoot winter fashion. It's always cold and somewhat brutal. Anyway. Can I pop in?'

'Well, you can. You can meet Pieter my lodger. But we'll be in France.'

'That's marvellous darling. Who are you going with?'

'Nobody Just me and the kids.'

'Jess. You're mad. You can't go alone. You must take someone with you.'

'Chris, I'm going to France, not a war zone in the Sudan. It's not even as far from here as Aberdeen.'

'Take my mobile number with you. Ring me if you need me.'

'I'll be fine. I'm going on holiday for God's sake. I wish someone would be pleased.'

Flic was pleased, but like everyone else it seemed only until I told her it was just me and the kids.

'I think it's pretty obviously fucking silly really,' she said. 'You'll be in the middle of France with two children playing merry hell, ready to do murder and suicide and there'll be nobody.'

'There will be phones you know. It's not like time travel.'

'Well don't call me in tears. I shall just say I told you so.'

'Thanks Flic.'

'You're welcome. Why do you have to go to France? Why can't you go to somewhere sensible like Cornwall or the Norfolk Broads or somewhere?'

'Oh yeah, you'd go there wouldn't you? Where was it last time, Costa Rica or Cuba?'

'That's different, I'm not travelling with two kids.'

'France is hardly uncharted territory and if I can't give my kids happy families at least I can give them a little adventure.'

'Yeah. A suicidal mother is a real adventure.'

I didn't let them rattle me. Well only a bit. And by the time Dan and Frankie were leaning over the side and marvelling at the blue of the water and pointing out all the little boats in St Malo harbour I was sure it was going to be fine. I felt happy. Not wanting anything more than that moment: the turquoise sea, the kids' excitement and France stretching out like an unrolling carpet in front of us.

Of course the one little detail I had conveniently managed not to think about was driving on the other side of the road. I'd only driven once in France: on holiday with Martin when Dan and Frankie were almost sub-talking. Martin had stiffened and tutted around every bend. Sighed. Put his hand over his eyes. Hit the floor with his braking foot. I burst into tears after half an hour and gave him the wheel. Driving on the right was something beyond me. Too much of a right-brain skill for me to manage. Something Leonardo could have done. Or some RAF jet pilot, but not me.

But seeing a fair proportion of Mrs Cardigans at the wheel as they trundled stiffly off the ferry gave me courage. If a gal with Crimplene hair and stirrup trousers could do it, then so could I. After all, deaf, dumb and virtually blind French peasants and probably their goats can manage right-hand driving so . . .

I still crawled round the first few roundabouts, terrified of forgetting and going clockwise head-on into a Norbert Dentressangle lorry carrying twenty-five tonnes of French lamb to the coast.

But I didn't forget. I took to everything happening in mirror-image as easily as Alice. It all seemed quite normal and by the time I hit the big dual carriageway I was even overtaking. Dan and Frankie cheered.

'Clever Mummy.'

'You can do it!'

I felt great. The whole of the European continent beneath my wheels. I almost wished we were driving to the Pyrenees not just eighty kilometres down the road to James's mate's gîte-in-the-making.

I had the key with me, so there was no negotiating with ancient concierge-type bods in my almost non-existent French. It was half of a farmhouse, the retired farmer and his wife, I'd been told, still kept the other side of the building, beyond the clipped box hedge. The gîte had its original door, straight out of *Madame Bovary*, heavy, thick with wrought-iron work and clogged with French blue paint. The key was enormous, something from a fairy-tale chest. But it worked and the door creaked open. Inside the whole space had been gutted, every wall removed, and half the upstairs floor gone. part of the ceiling was still hanging with broken boards and strips of mouldy lino from upstairs. But the downstairs floor was newly tiled in expensive terracotta, and all the windows newly repaired and neatly shuttered. James's friend was a developer. Every time he sited another Tesco's he did a bit more to his gîte. We took down the shutters and the light flooded in from three sides. It was marvellous to be in so sparse and light a space. So long as you didn't glance upwards.

In one corner up on a kind of little dais was a shower unit, and beside it a lavatory, behind a little folding screen. In the opposite corner was an ancient fridge and a table with a camping-gas stove. Against the shared wall a pile of mattresses. In the middle of the room where a major dividing wall had once been, a marvellous state-of-the-art open fire stood, with its newly pointed brick chimney snaking to the roof. A pile of logs had fallen over beside it and spread like an obstacle course across the floor.

The whole place was going to be gorgeous when it was done. I wondered idly if James's friend was single, or if he might need someone to stay and supervise the building work.

The kids were keen to nest in this new temporary space. So we got the bags and the box of food in from the car, started up the fridge, which whirred and jolted like Sparky the talking piano. We put the mattresses in a ring around the fire and laid out the sleeping bags.

It was still hot at four, so we drove the little way to the beach and ran down the sands to the sea. A few French families lolled stylishly beside picnic baskets, but the yellow strand was largely free and empty, and the sea too blue to look at straight.

We jumped waves. Wrote our names big in the sand. Chased the idling seagulls. Played tag.

I felt ten years old again. Light. Free in a way I'd never felt with Martin. These two companions could, for at least a year or two, be counted on to welcome me, to want my presence. I never felt so sure with Martin. He always looked the other way. At the horizon, at something just out of shot. Running down the sunny beach with my two children I felt a contented happiness, sufficient to itself. Not uneasy and wondering, the way I always did with Martin. I knew now what that feeling was, it was the fear of what might happen. And now that worst thing had happened and the tension of all the years of waiting under the hanging sword was gone.

We bought bread and wine on the way home. And *moules* from a lovely fat lady in a black dress. We cooked them on the camping stove with lots of garlic and butter. The kids ate as they haven't in weeks and got through two baguettes. Then we lit the big fire and I told them stories as we lay in our sleeping bags in the firelight.

After they were asleep I sat in the fire's glow and sang sad songs to myself and cried a little bit, but only tears without salt or acidity, that washed, but didn't burn.

It was my best twelve hours in about fifteen years.

It didn't last of course. Or rather, it lasted a bit. Two days, in which we cycled and swam, built sandcastles and picked flowers. The kids learned how to buy bread and cheese in French, and behaved as if they had learned some magic charm, as if '*du pain*' and '*du fromage*' were abracadabra or open sesame.

Then, on the third morning, we cycled to a nunnery just down the road a few kilometres. Open for visitors with a lovely garden and nun-made honey for sale. I'd planned it badly. We'd started too late to catch the coolness for the whole journey there and back. Even by the end of the outward leg we were hot, a little tetchy – overly grateful for the cool inside the stone chapel, enclosing green light between its pale cream walls. Whether it was physiological gratitude, or the fact that the whole place was designer religion . . . buff-coloured stone, nuns with natty cream habits and designer skinny wrists . . . I don't know, but even the kids were instantly affected by it. They went quiet, tiptoed round like grannies viewing a stately home when they know the Earl is currently in residence.

I give lip service to atheism, but really I subscribe to any old spiritual presence I feel might know more than me. Anything from fortune cookies to Christmas carols. I have this odd belief that there is an answer. That there really is a right and wrong written down somewhere. That two names are scribbled in a heart on the sandy beach in front of Old Pappa Time's condo. I just want to know whose two names they are, that's all.

So I did something I hadn't done since I spent two terms at a Catholic school by mistake, I lit a candle and said a Hail Mary for Martin. For Martin and me to be the two names on the sand. I hadn't said the words in twenty-five years, but something about Sister Mary Ignatia's terrifying presence must have lodged it deep enough in my brain not to fall out.

> Hail Mary, full of grace
> The Lord is with thee
> Blessed art thou amongst women
> And blessed is the fruit of thy womb.

I always found the womb part embarrassing as a child. Oddly inappropriate somehow for nuns to be so enthusiastic about wombs. Anyway, I'd said it now without a blush and set the candle on the shelf with all the other little wavering wishes for life, and deliverance, for babies, for passing exams.

But wishing is such a passive thing. It put me back in the hands of fate, back in the passenger seat beside Martin on that French lane so long ago, instead of out on the Route Nationale driving. So I came out of the chapel snivelling. The kids snivelled too, affected by the solemn sadness of the place and seeing their mother reduced to wishing on candles to get her life in shape.

Miserably we bought some honey, and some nun-made candles in the little dark shop and sat under the trees against an old wall to eat our bread and fruit in silence. Tense and distant from each other.

We should have waited for it to be cool again, but there was nothing else to do but pray in that place, so we set off. The lanes were open to the sun with no trees for cover. By the fourth hill, I was cycling back and forth between children, encouraging, jollying and chiding them to get to the top. It didn't help that the lid had come off the water bottle and it had lost its contents. At the top they huddled in a little pool of shade under a pathetically stunted hawthorn.

'You should have checked it,' said Dan, pink and angry with heat, shaking the empty bottle at me.

'Now I'll get dehydrated,' said Frankie petulantly, ready for a little dramatic weeping.

They lasted another two hills. By which time Frankie was crying all the time and Dan was becoming incandescent.

'You're so stupid. Why did you make us do this? You should go and get the car right now.' He was getting hysterical.

'I can't get the car. I can't leave you, it's not safe.'

'Get the car Mummy!' wailed Frankie.

'Just go and get the car!' Dan shouted.

Then it got to me: the chapel's empty promise of knowing. Martin leaving me here in the middle of nowhere to take two kids on holiday with leaky water bottles and no shade. In the middle of my life, too far along to turn back, too loaded down to change direction. How could I make something new? Who was going to take on tantrums in the middle of a French D road, wrinkles and cellulite?

'I can't,' I exploded at them with venom meant for Martin, a dose of poison in my voice big enough to fell a grown man. An overdose of massive proportions for two little kids. 'I just can't. Okay, understand? It is just not safe to leave you. Or are you so dim you can't understand that?'

'Great. Insult us now. Call us names. Great.' The defiance crumbled and Dan burst into tears. Sobbing, he threw down his bike and stomped up the verge. 'Great. I hate my life. I hate my life.'

'And I hate you,' Frankie screeched and ran to join him.

I turned my back on them and pedalled away as fiercely as I could. Slamming my feet down, wanting to tear muscles and pop ligaments. In that second I was cycling away forever to leave them, to leave everything.

It took me just five minutes to reach home and get the car. I don't know why I hadn't left them at the nunnery and done that in the first place. I met them as they were cycling down the last hill, faces hot and streaked with tears. Frightened because they'd seen the intent in my first hundred metres flee from them.

I got the bikes on the back and drove to the gîte. Frankie wouldn't get out of the car. Dan ran in and buried himself at the bottom of his sleeping bag for the rest of the afternoon. There wasn't anything I could do or say that would make any difference.

So I went and sat at the rickety picnic table by the *Madame Bovary* front door and watched the shadows track across the garden, lengthen and merge.

By dusk Frankie was asleep in the car, Dan too had cried himself into temporary oblivion. I had reached the bottom of nine francs and eighty centimes of Corbières, and was ready to reach for as many more bottles as it would take to lay me out cold, when a little face poked over the top of the dense green hedge, key-lit by the last of the sun. Round, ruddy and wrinkled as a winter-stored apple, topped with a flat cap. It was my temporary neighbour the retired farmer. Like most English kids who did O-level French, I can barely speak a word, so I didn't understand the first burbling he did at me. I didn't need to trot out my word perfect '*je ne parle pas Français*', he saw immediately I didn't understand a syllable. Holding up a straight fat finger he said '*Moment*', and disappeared.

Behind the hedge I heard a high-intensity whispered conversation between him and presumably his wife. Then footsteps. Then a cork being pulled. The sound of glasses. Then two people appeared round the hedge, carrying a bottle of wine and three glasses between them on a tin tray. I was immediately reminded of the dwarves from 'Yellow Brick Road', there was something bustling and pixie-esque about these two. And they were both pretty small, shorter even than me, their perfectly rotund little bodies encased in the same blue track suits. Only the tops of their heads seemed to distinguish them from each other. He wore the cap, she wore the luxuriant blue-black wig of shiny curls. Smiling and chattering they sat at the table, set down the tray and poured out the wine.

'Yourr gude helt,' said the man and raised his glass encouragingly to me.

'Bottoms up,' I said.

He inclined his head, 'Again?'

'Bottoms up.'

'*Ah bon*,' they chorused merrily. 'Buttums urp!'

We did several 'buttums urps' before they introduced themselves by pointing to the middle of their padded chests and saying their names with exaggerated care and volume.

'François. Fran . . . çois. François.'

'Bonjour François.'

'Marie. Mar . . . ie. Marie. Marie.'

'Bonjour Marie. Je m'appelle Jess.' They nodded enthusiastically and we shook hands with much smiling and pulling of arms up and down. Then François poured some more wine.

'You arrr eere alone?' he asked.

'Yes. I mean no. I have my children. *Mon fils et ma fille.*' It's amazing what you remember after lots of alcohol. Marie and François nodded and smiled encouragement at the sound of my attempting French. I felt much bolder.

'*J'ai un mari,*' I said, '*mais il a depart.*' I made what I imagined to be a suitably French gesture to signify him sweeping off. Warming up now, I began to remember all sorts of things.

'*Il a trouvé une femme qui a les cheveux rouge. Et les jambes très longues. Elle est plus jolie que moi. Et plus jeune. Elle n'a pas les enfants. Elle et libre.*' By the looks of deep concentration on their little apple faces I wasn't sure that my school-girl constructions were actually making any sense. But now I'd started . . .

'*J'aime mon mari. Beaucoups. Beaucoups. Mon coeur est cassé, totalement. Cassé. Je suis desolée.*'

There were tears in Marie's eyes. Either she understood or she was reacting the same way my French teacher used to at my accent. She pulled a tissue from her blue track-suit sleeve and dabbed at herself. Then patted my hand.

'Where ees yur 'usband?' asked François sadly.

'In London. With, *avec sa fille nouvelle.*'

'Verree sad. *Triste,*' he added. Marie patted my hand again. She was now crying quite a lot. I was rather afraid I'd said something that I hadn't meant to, and sorry that I'd upset them.

François put his arm around Marie to comfort her.

Then, quite suddenly, they both got up.

'Good nyette,' said François.

'*Bonsoir,*' snivelled Marie, still holding her soggy tissue to her face.

Then they picked up the tray between them and reversed around the end of the hedge as if someone had played a film backwards.

'Why was she crying? What did you say to them?' asked Dan, stepping out from the shadows by the door frame, where he must have been standing for some time.

209

'I'm not sure. I know what I thought I said. Maybe my accent was so awful it upset her.' He didn't notice the joke.

'Can I have something to eat?'

'Yes of course. Let's get Frankie out of the car first.'

We didn't need to, she'd already got out and was picking her way barefoot up the darkened stony path.

'Who were they? They looked like gnomes or something.'

Marie and François's mysterious visit and departure gave us a distraction, allowed us to redeem the day a little. We cooked potatoes on the ashes and told stories in the dark. I lined up the mattresses and bags so that I could have an arm round each of the children as they fell asleep.

'I'm so sorry about today,' I said.

'We thought you'd left us alone,' said Frankie, instantly tearful at the memory.

'Oh sweetie, I'm so sorry. I didn't want to frighten you. I would never really leave you.'

'It was just too hot,' said Dan, 'I don't want to talk about any of it any more.'

The holiday was broken from then on like weather after a September storm. It didn't help that we saw François and Marie each morning as we left the gîte and every time, Marie burst into tears and ran inside at the sight of us, closely followed by a worried François.

We went to the beach, but everywhere there were elegant French families, handsome men, beautiful women and perfectly happy children, reproaching me for the shameful loss of my man and my marriage. I sat reading in my ugly shorts and dirty T-shirt whilst Dan and Frankie squabbled and sulked their way through the days. When I could be bothered to stop reading, I snarled at them. I couldn't even tell you what I read. Blank pages.

I began to see Martin. I caught sight of him getting into a car at the supermarket after the beach that third day. He had a redhead next to him as they drove away. I ran after them, calling, across the car-park, and when I got back to our car the children were leaning against its doors crying. I knew, then, it couldn't have been Martin. But I kept seeing him. Once more that day, twice the next. Sometimes alone sometimes with her, always just out of reach. Disappearing into the crowd at a market, silhouetted against the bright surf.

The days acquired a nightmarish dislocated quality with whole sections of time moving about, peculiarly extended or suddenly obliterated, as if we'd all been dumped on some cartoon storyboard. Everything began to scrape on my senses. The tubs of red geraniums and blue lobelias I'd found so charming when we first arrived jumped out at me glaring and repetitive, throbbing like triffids. In the car the slightest rattle had me pulling over and ripping out the contents of door pockets and dashboard shelves to locate the tiniest loose object. At night I paced and the children slept and whimpered. In the day I drove them to the beach, to dinky historic little towns to wander like the undead amongst the living.

Driving back to the gîte on the fifth day, I found myself looking down the ravine at the side of the road and thinking it might be a nice rest to drive us to the bottom the quick way. The chorus of my friends saying 'I told you so' in several part harmony played at full hi-fi quality and volume in my head, took my foot off the accelerator, made me change down to round the hairpin bends.

I stopped at the next telephone box and phoned the ferry company. Yes, they had a space on the crossing to England that night, and it was no trouble to move my booking.

We drove off the ferry at Plymouth at seven a.m. into the muggy grumpiness of a slightly wet summer Friday at the dog end of the school hols. Instantly, familiarity cheered us. We stopped for awful sandwiches at a service station and rejoiced in their day-old sogginess. Immediately the kids began to serialise their holiday, instant reminiscence about *moules* and beaches and buying bread, about those sparkling first two days. By the time we were home, the past had been reinvented.

'That was one of the best holidays ever Mummy. Thank you,' said Dan as he climbed over the bags and out of the car.

'I'm glad we're home,' added Frankie very quietly.

'I am too Frankie,' I said.

Only standing safely back in my garden, looking at my border and the lawn spangled with daisies, did I know what a long way I'd been to France. Right up to the very edge and back again, right to the limits of the black and the white.

Chapter Fourteen

It was of course utterly inevitable that sometime during the course of making a series about pets somebody would be bitten by something. Steve would stick his microphone up some Rottweiler's nose, or Rob would put a tripod on a cat's tail.

We were 'penance pending' for the hamster incident anyway.

But the deity who presides over pet rodents must have powerful friends in the spirit world, or maybe that fat hamster was some kind of small mammal guru, because everything in this first filming week has been out to get us.

First, it was the chinchillas. I've never liked the look of them anyway. Combining stupidity with big incisors isn't a recipe for an ideal companion as far as I'm concerned. And there's the way they sit, hunched over, staring into the distance, just waiting for a chance.

The one that Marge, the chinchilla breeder, had chosen for me to handle was called Anthony, a young male with, she said 'impeccable manners'. Though what constitutes good manners in a big grey puffball with a face like Bill Gates I don't know. Although after Anthony, I could make a good guess.

It was a hot day, and Marge was anxious that Anthony shouldn't be heat-stressed, so she insisted we film him with me and her under the pergola. This, of course, put Rob in a sulk because of the high contrast stripes of light. He and Judith went off into a huddle of high-intensity whispers, the only part of which we heard was Rob suggesting that the whole thing would look like a pair of Parkhurst pyjamas. But Judith must have said she'd settle for that, because shortly afterwards we began filming.

Like all animals that aren't supposed to understand human language, chinchillas recognise one word, 'action', and they take it literally. Anthony's interpretation was to leap from Marge's lap and wedge himself behind the pots of hostas.

Marge coaxed him out again, but now the local parachute club was doing a low-level droning circuit to drop some of its novice membership from a not-so great height. Now it was Steve's turn to sulk. Steve was raised in Adelaide on a sheep station and I don't think Marge was used to the sort of language he used the fourth time we had to stop filming because of the deafening giant wasp sound of the plane.

By the time we had silence and chinchilla in the same place, Anthony had peaked and was well down the straight past-his-best-before bar code. When I leaned across to stroke him casually behind the ear, as we had arranged, he leaped on to my right shoulder and sank his teeth into my ear, neatly perforating the cartilage. I'd have liked to have ripped him from me and dashed his brainless little skull against the tasteful terracotta pots, only the fear that he might sever an artery in my wrist prevented me.

Practically hysterical, Marge, an economy-sized girl, leaped up and ripped off her beige cotton sweater and threw it over Anthony, who, being a chinchilla instantly assumed it was night and calmed down. In the process, she broke the cable linking the little microphone pinned to her jersey with its battery pack in her back trouser pocket. Steve's language instantly became world-class expletive production. Judith, suddenly transformed into mother-of-three mode, ordered him out into the street to cool off. I stood there bleeding, reassuring the indifferent chaos in front of me that I was all right. Then I fainted. Only Rob stayed uninvolved and in command of the situation.

'Cut,' he announced. 'I kept running Judith, gotta have something for the Christmas tape this year.'

We filmed Anthony and several of his little friends in their palatial cages, and once I'd stopped bleeding, Marge and I did the interview without animals and in the glorious sunlight in front of her hydrangeas.

'And did you find the chinchillas a comfort when your marriage failed Marge?'

So, with killer chinchillas in the morning, we were understandably nervous about the rabbits in the afternoon. The Marstons were a whole family of specialist rabbit breeders. But the breeding seemed to be a two-way business, because rabbits certainly bred Marstons. The brothers, twins, Geoff and Derek were the senior partners and each had ten children. But that was only by their first marriages, made in their young and fecund twenties. The Marston boys were now in their forties, and each had a new and nubile wife, with babies to match, four and three respectively.

Somehow Marston brothers wives and their twenty-seven children were accommodated in a teeny pair of semi-detached cottages. As I looked at the assembled clan lined up for the camera in their shared front garden I imagined them all stacked inside, like a human jigsaw puzzle. Or perhaps they were hollow, and fitted together like Russian dolls after hours becoming two super beings, with the faces and bloated bodies of the brothers on the outside.

In comparison the rabbits accommodation was palatial. No such overcrowding for the bunnies. Each little family had it's own spacious home with sleeping quarters and a run.

Four fifty-yard rows of hutches and runs all painted in a rainbow of off-beat colours, the sale bargains from the DIY shop where the eldest Marston girl was a leading retail light.

As if the Marstons couldn't supply enough cutesy child shots for any director, Judith had imported ten kids from the local primary school, to be filmed 'meeting the bunnies', and choosing their favourite from the twenty-five or so different shapes, colours and sizes that had sprung from the Marstons' productive hutches.

Geoff and Derek, assisted by sundry smaller Marstons of pre- and post-school-age, showed the schoolchildren round the runs enthusiastically, followed by Rob and Steve, sound and camera rolling. There were a few near misses with tangled cables, but mostly it looked good. Judith even stopped crossing things off on her clipboard and put her pink highlighter away.

The final shot was me and the schoolkids all holding their favourite bunnies and briefly telling the camera the reason for their choice. Rob and Judith lined up the shot and rehearsed it with children and sans bunnies. All fine.

Geoff and Derek loaded the children with their rabbit of choice. I got one small enough to have small teeth . . . just in case, black-and-white with brewer's droop type ears. It must have looked lovely, ten beamy kids each with an armful of extraordinary rabbit, long brown aristocratic ones, little grey fluffy ones, huge white ones, spotted ones, blotched ones, ears up, ears down. A glorious celebration of diversity.

But the moment Judith said 'action', the Rex and the Californian, the Dutch and the Giant Flemish, the Dwarf Lops, were transformed into werewolves. One by one they sank their substantial incisors into the sweet soft human flesh around them. In less than three minutes the orderly line of fluff-cuddling was reduced to a wailing straggle of bleeding infants. Rabbits dropped from arms hopped on to each other and did what rabbits do best. Fearful of the loss of genetic purity, Geoff and Derek set about pulling them apart with a zeal that seemed a little churlish in men who were clearly just as keen on procreation. The only rabbit that didn't bite was mine, but, traumatised by the situation, it had an attack of spontaneous and violent diarrhoea. How could something so small contain so much? Same principle as the Tardis and the Marstons' semis, I suppose.

At the end of the first day it was all pretty funny. But after the Pekes who took a chunk out of Steve's mike cover and bit Judith's ankle (owner Rodney divorced 1991, non-smoker, GSOH apparently, all reasonable offers clutched at); the shire horse that scrunched my thigh and left a bruise like a dinner plate (owners Jane and Mark happily married for fifteen years, hallelujah); the hooded rats that tried to bite everything within range (owner Louise serial heartbreaker, used boyfriends littered everywhere) and the tarantulas that flicked itching powder hairs over everybody (owner Marcus terminal BO, forty-seven and never been laid) – a failure of sense of humour was imminent.

When we arrived on the doorstep of a crumbling Georgian vicarage on Thursday morning we really weren't so ready to laugh. But we were there to film birds and at least they don't have teeth.

Judy, our designated interviewee, opened the door to us, and we sensed another difficult day stretching out to the horizon. She was in her sixties, tall, with a weft of long grey hair that sat on top of her head like a disused nest. She wore what must have been a tailor-made grey Donegal tweed suit, with a pencil skirt and stilettos caked in mud – as though she had walked out of a society lunch in 1956. I wondered if there was perhaps a rotting wedding feast somewhere in the building . . . The white pattern on each shoulder was made of bird dropping, deposited there as an epaulet of affection by one of the twenty or so free-flying parrots. They swooped above us in the hall, squawking as if they were about to be curried, and dive-bombing us. Just passing through, we knew how truly selected Judy was with her 'pips', our decorations were far more randomly distributed.

The hall was furnished in classic English country-house style, with the sort of furniture and big paintings that you only acquire from long-dead relatives with lots of money but no taste. The tall sash windows that flanked the door were hung with heavy curtains and pelmets with swags and ropes, all there from the first time those were the in thing, long predating the birth of *World of Interiors* mag. But everything had been given over to the birds, and birds have no respect for sixty-quid-a-metre damask and Great Uncle George's Jacobean chest. There was a crust of white on every slightly horizontal surface, thick enough to grace a modest Peruvian guano mine.

'Al-fie, Josephina, Paaaa-trickkk,' trilled Judy, looking up into the throng of wings with indulgent affection. 'They're such babies,' she said, lowering her eyelids and pouting the way she'd done forty years ago at her coming-out ball, 'but they'll come to like you. I've made us some refreshments. We'll take them on the veranda I think.'

Leaving one lot of birds shut inside we went into the garden. Just like Judy, it had been classically beautiful. The veranda was wide, Bath paving with stone pineapples and odd busts along the low enclosing wall. But all were cracked and fallen, and ragwort had sprung up between the flags. I had a pang of pity for the neglected borders that must once have burst with phlox and achillea, acanthus, day lilies and of course delphiniums. Nothing to see now but scrub, nettles and brambles clogging the feet of two huge cedars of Lebanon.

A red tin folding table with four little green stools stood in the middle, where some of the weeds had been trampled flat. On it was a jug of something greenish, and glasses.

'Home-made gooseberry cordial,' announced Judy proudly as we approached the table. All of us had a simultaneous vision of Judy's home-making facilities: a kitchen full of flying birds, where there was one ingredient common to all recipes.

Judith had her wits about her and asked if we could begin to film at once. Rob and Steve set up without a dissenting murmur, only I was going to get the benefit of the cordial.

I was saved, in a way, by the macaws. The moment Judy and I sat down they flew in from the cedars, with a single deep squawk and a rush of air, ready to demand an explanation for this invasion of their world. Two of them landed on the table, one on Judy's head and two more on the veranda wall. They were beautiful, deep petrol blue and butter gold, three feet long with beaks the size of Captain Hook's iron digit. But right from the start they had a brutish swagger about them. Like a gang of South American cocaine barons, packing a heavy whack of fist in a Versace suit. Petulantly, the first one bit through the glasses and threw aside each one in turn.

'Erol,' said Judy, mildly scandalised, 'that's really not very nice.'

The second stuck its head inside the jug, then tried to climb on to its rim, knocking it over and sending a wave of green splashing on to the stones. The gang on the wall sounded their approval, then flew to give the crew the once-over. The birds ignored the equipment, all the fascinating little shiny knobs and cables and went straight for the people. Intimidation tactics I guessed, but trying to talk to Judy I couldn't tell what was going on as the macaws milled around the crews' feet.

Until they tried their trick on me, coming close to the back of my ankle, one of them tweaked my Achilles tendon in its beak, hard enough to hurt, hard enough to tell you 'Snipping this is easy for me. I slice Brazil nuts with this piece of hardware. So don't step out of line.' It was easy to see how Judy had let the birds take over. She'd had no choice.

The bird on Judy's head had ambitions to be Vidal Sassoon and was vigorously rearranging her hair. I sat very still and asked my questions. Conducting the interview was like Joyce Grenfell doing her infant teacher sketch. All Judy's answers were interspersed with gently chiding remarks made in her perfect cut-glass accent. 'Eddie, no dear. I really think that's unacceptable.' 'Marilyn. Marilyn. Stop that at once.'

The finale came when one of the thugs, Eddie, or Marilyn, jumped on to my lap and in seconds removed the buttons all down the front of my shirt, snipping them off neat as a dressmaker. Having shown their strength, demonstrated the mayhem they could create if they wanted, they flew off. Back to the trees to beat the shit out of the thrushes for practice.

Judy was the birds' slave. We filmed where she incubated their eggs for them, fed their helpless babies, healed their wounds and cared for them in incontinent, bald and aggressive dotage. All the while, the Gang followed us around the outbuildings, never far from a door or window, ready to fly in and snip a tendon, gouge an eye if anyone transgressed.

By the time we left at the end of the afternoon, we could have been held at gunpoint by the Jackal himself we were so jumpy. At the last minute as we stepped through the front door again, I had a wild impulse to grab Judy, pull her into the car and drive away fast. But she'd have needed plastic surgery and a false passport to get away from that lot, and our programme budget barely ran to lunchtime sandwiches.

I'm grateful for such a week really, I mean it's hard to think of Martin and Dolores snogging on a tropical beach when you're having the rodent ear-piercing service in. I'm grateful for quite a lot at the moment, because after France everything feels like a reprieve.

'I think you may have turned a corner,' Mary told me when I picked up the kids the other night, 'you look much better.'

'Being attacked by things must suit me.'

'Perhaps you should keep bees.'

She's right. Not about the bees but about the corner. I'm round one, away from Martin, so that he's out of sight most of the time. It's true I have a new life of sorts: work and kids sorted, money not a trauma for a while. I sleep without dreaming and the horrible realisation feeling isn't always there when I wake up. Food tastes of something. The fact that it feels like I've swapped a Mercedes convertible for a Datsun pick-up is irrelevant. I still have a life to drive forward in.

And I'm getting really so bored of crying that I can see that soon I might stop. I'm even tired of talking about crying. When Chris rang late the other night I told him about France.

'It was brilliant. We had a wonderful time. As soon as I can afford it I'm going away with the kids again.'

'God Jess, you sound better.'

'I am. The kids have done me a star-chart for not crying. Every half-day I don't cry I get a star, and I've got two since last Saturday.'

'Like giving up smoking. Or booze.'

'Yes. I'm starting BA, Blubberers Anonymous. Hello, my name's Jess and I'm a cry baby.'

'One day at a time, sweet Jeezuz,' sang Chris.

'That's it.'

'Jo's an awful lot better too.'

'Yeah and we know why that is.'

'She's coming up to London this weekend. Her mum's having the kids.'

'Chris! Hey, do I need to get myself a hat for the big day yet?'

'Jess, you're incorrigible. Anyway I'm not marrying anyone unless you're my best man!'

Maybe this little patch of calm is just that, a patch, but I'm rolling around in it. On my first day off of the four-day week I blagged out of David Herring, the last Friday of the kids' holidays, I did no housework. Just gardening. I buried myself in the minutiae of removing dandelion seedlings from my creeping thyme, lovingly feeding all my flowers, picking sweet peas. I filled the tiny paddling pool for the kids and they spent lots of the day throwing themselves into it and filling it up again. I let them improvise their own meals and I didn't nag about nutritional content or mess. They went off at five for a picnic tea of honey sandwiches and cooking chocolate at the top of the hill, not believing their luck.

With the garden child-free I could really go at the brambles with a machete and the liberal use of expletives. Brambles are hateful. You chop them and they spring at you snarling and scratching. They twine and insinuate themselves into impregnable corners. Nothing breaks them and not even rhino hide can keep their spines from ripping your hands. They make me more angry even than nettles. So I was pretty absorbed and didn't hear the garden gate click open and shut again.

Pieter's voice came from just behind me. 'It looks nice, your border.'

Once again he was standing looking as though he'd been there for a while. He'd been late most evenings since we got back from France, and gone to his room. But a few times I'd arrived home with the children to hear him pottering about upstairs. We'd started, shyly, a little routine of cooking together. Talking about food and plants. He'd chat to the kids a bit. Play draughts with them. He's showed them games on his computer. But he's been a hit with them since the first day on the mackerel boat. They talk about him when he's not around. 'Pieter let us play this really neat game on his computer.' 'Pieter says I could keep a Venus Fly Trap on my windowsill.' 'Pieter had a dog as big as a horse when he was little.' 'Pieter says we can go and watch when they drain the pond at The Court and see them take the carp out. He says there are some as big as cats!'

But Pieter and I are still a little formal. Friendly, amiable, jokey even, but there's a kind of reserve that I can't put my finger on. I suppose he feels I'm his landlady. And he hasn't been here long.

No formalities between Pieter and Dog however. He'd done a good job of chook and Dog care whilst we were away. In fact Dog was completely besotted with him by the time we came back. He must have overfed her and thrown sticks. It's a short one-way street to Dog's heart. The first conversation I had with Pieter after we came back was around Dog. It had been early, six, one morning. Pieter sat drinking coffee in the kitchen and scrunching Dog's ears lovingly as she gazed into his eyes.

I was still sleepy or I wouldn't have risked a remark that could be misunderstood so easily, especially by someone whose first language isn't even English.

'She can never give you children you know,' I told him.

'I know,' he sighed. 'But we could share great walks.'

He didn't even look up. Neither of us laughed but it was a golden comic moment that I savoured all day. I was no end impressed with Pieter. My lodger was definitely a good thing.

But casting a real professional eye over my border, he made me nervous. 'Well, it's not very good at this time of year, and the brambles get rooted in the wall and try to take over all the time . . .' I tailed off apologetically.

'It looks good. But you need more for late summer. June you have flowers, but now almost nothing, *phhtt*.' We both looked sadly at the bloomless green mounds. There was an awkward silence.

'Jess, I wish to ask you a question.'

'Yes.'

'What is bollocks?'

'What?'

'Bollocks. You said it while you pulled things here. When I come through the gate. Two times. Three perhaps this word. Bollocks. I would like to learn what it is.'

I unfolded myself and carefully picked off the catching limbs of bramble. He seemed quite serious, his long mouth straight, his deep eyes quiet.

'Well. It's a swear word.'

'Oh yes, of course. Like fuck and bugger and arseholes. But what does it mean?'

'It means testicles.' Why the hell was I blushing? 'But it also means a load of rubbish, something that's nonsense.'

'So a noun, with meaning "testicles" also for something stupid.'

'Yes. But it can be a verb too. You can bollock somebody. I mean if I bollocked you, I'd be telling you off, shouting probably. You might bollock one of your gardeners if they put a wall in the wrong place or something.'

'Oh yes. I would like a lot to bollock my gardeners. But the noun I like better. Bollocks yes. Bollocks. Thank you Jess. You would like some wine? I bought bottle to share.' He didn't wait for an answer but walked off laughing to himself across the lawn, long legs folding and straightening, folding and straightening, as if walking were a new craze. 'Bollocks I like this word.' A moment later he waved the bottle through the kitchen window 'I need a screw? You have this?'

'In the drawer on the left of the sink.' Thank God Mrs E would be in her milking parlour at this time and out of earshot.

He's definitely part of this patch of calm, Pieter. Hearing his music coming under the spare-room door late at night, hearing the sound of him humming tunelessly as he shaves at his bedroom sink in the morning. A restful and undemanding presence. But he's still a mystery. Even now I know little more than the fact that he's a garden designer with a house on stilts and an interest in English vernacular speech.

'It's actually a corkscrew,' I told him once we were sitting out with the wine poured. 'This thing. It's a corkscrew. Not just a screw. A screw is a little thing like a nail. Metal that you hold things together with.'

'Oh yes. Of course I knew this.'

'But screw is something else too. I mean you might as well have the complete set of English rude words. Screw means the same as fuck, although not quite as rude.'

'You are blushing. I have embarrassed you. I'm sorry.'

'No. I've embarrassed me. I didn't have to explain the alternative meaning. It's just that if you lean out of windows shouting "I need a screw" it might get you into trouble.' We both giggled like six-year-olds mentioning poo-poos.

Pieter poured some more wine. 'I like your house very much.'

'I haven't been much of a host.'

'I have been a bad guest also. Out too late. We are both very bad. But now I am good again. I will cook for you a meal now. Tonight.'

'There's no need.'

'I like to cook you know. I picked fine vegetables from The Court garden.'

'Do you cook at home in Holland?' Or does somebody cook for you I wondered.

'All the time. You are in good hands. Drink the wine. I will be quick. A stir-fry?'

'That would be lovely. The soy sauce and spices are . . .'

'I learnt this while you are in France. Sit. Drink.'

Half-way through my sitting and drinking with sizzling smells coming through the kitchen door, Mary's daughter Georgie rang. 'Jess, the kids are here.'

'Oh Georgie I'm sorry you must be sick of the sight of them.'

'Actually no. Charles is here, my chap, and we wondered if you'd lend us the children for the night. He's got some new fiction he's been sent and he wants to try it out on the right audience. And I feel like making something messy and childish to eat for us all. Then we can all sleep in the tree-house.'

'Georgie, do you really want two kids with you when you're in the tree-house with your boyfriend?'

'Nonsense. It's good practice for when we have children.'

'Are you wearing your halo and wings, and if so where is the harp?'

'No halo or wings. We'll bring them back to you in the morning, overexcited and stuffed with chocolate and you'll hate me.'

'See you later. Thank you Georgie. Make them be polite. I think you're out of your mind.'

I picked up another bottle from Martin's wine rack, ten francs' worth from the *Supermarché*, and went back into the garden.

'Ah. Good timing. Carry the plates please,' said Pieter.

*

We got through two and a half bottles, and talked until one but I still didn't have much more ordinary information about Pieter. I didn't know if he had a girlfriend, where exactly he lives, if he sees his mother, how many brothers he might have. But I did know that he could grow cress before he could speak. I knew that his favourite shrub is philadelphus and his favourite flower *Lilium regale*, which is like Raymond Blanc saying what he really likes to eat is boiled egg with Marmite soldiers or prawn cocktail made with salad cream. I knew he can't get trousers the right length because his legs are too long, and that he can't eat lobster any more after he had food poisoning on a botanical expedition to Crete. I suspected he'd never done anything he didn't really want to do. I knew that he made me laugh. I suspected he'd chosen to have few lovers. I knew that he's not a ten, more like a sly seven when he catches the light right, which doesn't seem to be more than three or four times in an evening. How I knew all this I couldn't tell you. We talked for five hours, about what exactly and in what order I have no idea. But it was more comfortable than a warm bath and easier than eating coffee ice cream.

We both went to bed with our windows open and I fell asleep lulled by the faintly musical sound of his gentle snores.

I was slightly hung over the next day, not up to doing more than a little light laundry and tidying in the morning. Which is how I found the tickets shoved into my knicker drawer, where I'd put them the night I got home from Francis Weaton's fiftieth. *A Midsummer Night's Dream* in the grounds of Ettington Hall as part of the Festival. I'd forgotten all about fat DJ Morgan, the gay, probably, costume designer and his troupe of beautiful boys. Two tickets, I could probably plead that two children were one adult. It was outdoors so there'd be lots of room.

'Kids. D'you fancy a bit of culture?'

'What?' They were in their rooms, both shattered after a night of literary criticism and chocolate fondue in a tree-house, but they came running all the same.

'I've got tickets for an outdoor play.' Selling this to the kids could be tricky. 'It's about fairies and magic and um,' what was *A Midsummer Night's Dream* about? 'and there's lots of funny bits in it.'

'Sounds cissy,' said Frankie.

'Yeah, just for little kids.'

Ah, now I could play a winning card, 'No. It's for grown-ups. Very grown-up play actually. Kids aren't really supposed to go, but one of the people in it gave me tickets. I'll have to smuggle you in.'

'Woah. Cool Mum.'

Hah. Hook line and sinker.

It was the perfect evening for it. Clear, warm and still. We got there early as I wanted the kids to soak up the atmosphere. I bought food from the bar and brought it out on to the lawn in front of the hall to eat. Ettington Arts Festival is part performance, part workshop. It's the gathering of the middle-class peace, love and tie-dye brigade, people who would live in benders and play folk, fiddle or jazz guitar if only they didn't earn so much money as accountants, lecturers, doctors and bankers. Ettington is their one chance of escape in the year, and God love 'em, they take it.

As we sat eating our brown rice salad and Moroccan chicken, a group of madrigal singers were doing 'The White Swan' under a big beech tree, giving it the full forties newsreader pronunciation, maximum *Brideshead Revisited* welly. Beyond them, the African drummers were feeling the rhythm 'from deep in their pelvises', and whacking it out on huge instruments the size of municipal wheelybins. From the sound of what they were getting from their pelvises I think they could all have done with a spot of Ex-Lax. But what do I know? Two fat girls with tight bodices and blusher like Pocahontas were running up and down voice scales under the rose arches, and a stream of Morgan's beautiful boys and other actors in fantastical concoctions of lace, wire and velvet were legging it across the lawn to the amphitheatre. The kids eyes were boggling and their ears going round like detectors on a TV licensing van. They were so absorbed in their surroundings that Frankie ate the chickpeas in her salad and Dan didn't notice the raw tomatoes.

Not all Ettington festivalites are visitors. The Ettington Triangle has residents. The sort of people who only buy houses on ley lines. If you live in Ettington you can get your palm read, your aura healed, your feet acupunctured. You can get a basket-work wok carrier, a packet of organic non-dairy creamer, wholemeal filo pastry. But if you want a leaking pipe mended, or you need a pint of milk, then forget it.

Next to us on the lawn, just finishing a marinated tofu and kombu sea vegetable sauté, were a little group of locals, sharing some small scandal about somebody's homeopath husband who'd run off with a candle maker to Cork, or something.

One of the group, a woman, kept catching my eye as I chatted to Dan and Frankie. Every time I glanced up she was looking at me. I wondered if I had a huge bogie on my nose, but the kids are a pretty reliable checking system for that sort of thing.

She was extraordinary-looking, the way Titania herself might have looked after finally kicking Oberon out for being a waste of space, and setting up a Magic Collective with Peasblossom and Mustard Seed. After a while, when the kids were taking the plates back to the bar, she slipped across to me and sat down.

'I'm sorry to intrude,' she said very quietly, 'my name is Marcella. I'm a clairvoyant. Would it offend you if I told you something?'

'As long as it's nice I won't mind a bit.'

'I'm not sure what it will mean to you. But someone above your head has been saying it all the time I've been sitting near you. Martin is not sure of Dolores.'

I felt myself go white. Of course she was a charlatan because they all were. She must have heard me mention those names. Or seen me somewhere else. Or knew Martin. Or something. There was no point asking her how she knew the names. She wasn't about to give away trade secrets. So I just thanked her politely and said that the message was indeed very meaningful for me. I tried to behave as if spirit messages were always coming through to me. Heard one, you heard 'em all. But when the kids came back and it was time to take our places, I knew my walk was not steady.

There was no problem over the tickets. And as soon as the performance started and the kids were sucked into the words and action, the music and the costumes, I escaped inside my head to read that fax from the spirits over and over again. I knew it was a trick, but believed it wasn't. The message was pretty obviously true anyway. Nothing I didn't know or guess. But was there more to it? How unsure was Martin? Unsure enough to come back? And when? Now? Tonight? Would he be there when I got home?

By the end of act one I had concocted an entire fantasy world of Martin's repentant return, right down to therapy for the grieving Dolores and dinner parties a year hence for Martin and me, Dolores and her new partner. It's not the first time I've done it. I've constructed resurrections for Martin and me that would make raising Lazarus look like a cheesy card trick. All of them founded on chance remarks, tiny fragments of hope, or the cockeyed logic that operates at two a.m. Convincing myself of the unconvincing has become a bit of a speciality. But it doesn't last. Reality gets in there somehow and messes up the whole thing, like hot water on a snowman.

The entrance of reality this time was more revelatory than destructive. Just as I was, in my fantasy, going to bed with Martin on the night of his return, my arms wrapped around him, I heard snoring. Pieter asleep in the spare room. There were voices from the kitchen too, James and Mary, Kath and Gerry, Alex and Sarah, Chris and Jo . . . cooking something and calling me downstairs to join them. Before I could stop it, Martin had raged through the house and thrown everybody out. Then he kissed me goodbye on the doorstep and left for Timbuktu.

That's what it would really be like if Martin came back. Just the same. An empty house and a kiss goodbye on a cold doorstep. What would the spirits say over Martin's head now?

Dan and Frankie got through to the end of their first Shakespeare play without falling asleep more than once or twice and they managed to understand vaguely what it was all about. Which is probably better than the average for an RSC production.

They were still excited enough to be impressed when one of the actors led us to Morgan. Not only the costume designer apparently, but director of the company too. He was chatting to a group of fans as technical bods ran about him dismantling things, a great big spider in the middle of a web full of flies. In a dark suit and formal tie he looked less gross and less gay.

He smiled when he saw me as if I were a cream bun in a matzo factory. Maybe my hunch about his sexual orientation was wrong.

'You probably don't remember lending me this,' I said, pulling the torch from my bag, 'but I felt honour-bound to bring it back.'

'Well thank you.' He smiled again, a wide smile. 'I do remember as a matter of fact. Was the dress damaged?'

'No. Not at all. You did a great job.'

'Did you enjoy the play?' he asked Dan and Frankie.

'Ye-es!' they chorused with unfakeable junior enthusiasm.

'That's the best review we've had all season,' he laughed. 'And you, I'm sorry I don't know your name?'

'Jess Wallace.'

'Jess. Did you enjoy the performance?'

I almost said 'What performance?' I hadn't seen or heard a thing, being too busy with my internal discoveries. 'Yes, very much, it was marvellous.'

'Would you like to join me for a drink, I'm on my way to the bar right now?'

'I'd love to but I have to take these two home. They're very tired.'

'No we're not,' said Frankie, yawning behind her hand.

'Well perhaps another time? We're at The Court in a fortnight or so — our last performances of the summer. That's up your way isn't it, near Francis's place?'

'Yes, walking distance almost.'

'So. Do you ever go up there?'

'Bit out of my price bracket. But I have two friends who work there.'

'Oh really? Maybe we could meet for a cocktail after a performance, they're early. I'll be through at nine-thirty on both nights. Or maybe lunch.' He had the charm button set to maximum. Within the constraints of two child spectators and a production waiting to be dismantled, he was trying very hard.

'I'm not sure. Why don't you call me nearer the time.' I scribbled my number on a Tesco's receipt, unable to decide what I thought about a come-on from a trainee Robbie Coltrane in a sharp suit.

On the way back to the car, Dan and Frankie giggled and nudged each other as they walked behind me.

'He's nice Mummy,' said Dan.

'Quite good-looking,' said Frankie.

'But a bit fat,' said Dan.

'He could be a Bumper-sized Boyfriend,' said Frankie. That's the level of humour that brings down the house if you're eight. Sometimes it's good to be a grown-up.

Chapter Fifteen

It never does to relax in my experience. The moment you do, something bad happens. Glance up to admire the blue sky when you walk down the street and a dog turd will be just waiting to slither under your sole. After nearly two decades of knowing Martin, I'd thought I was safe. He's stuck me this long, I'd thought, so he must love me. I relaxed. And look what happened: I landed in a pile of doggy doos worthy of a pack of Irish wolfhounds.

I never learn either. I'd been slowly relaxing since Martin's last fax because with him busy in America there have been no other communications. Not to me anyway. Cards came for the kids, flopped on to the mat one Saturday morning the end of the first week of term. Posted in LA, artsy defocused photos of streets of neon. Probably some of Martin's, although I didn't look at the credits on the back.

Dan read his out to me: 'My Best Boy, I'm missing you madly. I'm sorry I haven't seen you in the summer hols. But I'll be back soon and we'll do something nice together. All my love Dad.

'Wow. That's brilliant. I'm going to put that up in my room.' He did, and I could hear him crying into his pillow from downstairs.

Frankie glanced at hers and ripped it in two.

'That's just stupid,' she said fiercely, 'he's stupid. "I miss you." Why isn't he here then if he misses me so much?' She threw the bits into the bin, and went to sit in with the chooks for an hour.

I didn't say anything. I stayed busy and left them to it. Scrubbed the kitchen floor, tidied the fridge. I didn't trust myself to go and comfort them. I knew the snarling in my heart would squeeze out somehow: 'Oh darling. Of course he misses you. Especially on days when he's got nothing exciting to do.' 'I'm so glad you put Daddy's card up. It'll help to remind you that he exists when you haven't seen him in so long.'

I have to give him positive press because I don't want to give him any opportunities for trying to get on moral high ground. Not even the slightest hillock. Not even an anthill. He's in a bunker and that's where I want him to stay.

But me, I've been saved from any of that scab-picking. With no forced reminders, I've been able to implement a policy of deliberate forgetting. If I think of Martin, I just run on the spot for five minutes or I start singing some silly song of the kids . . .

Kookaburra sits on the 'lectric wire
Jumpin' up and down
With his pants on fire.

Once you've sung that a couple of times, sentimentality becomes almost impossible. If I find a photo in a drawer I turn it over and put it back. I changed my route round the supermarket so I don't go down the aisles with his favourite biscuits or beer.

I did some more clearing out of clothes, not Martin's this time but mine.

'Will you take these to The Court tomorrow Pieter?' I said one night, struggling into the kitchen with a good few coat hangers loaded. 'See if any of the women staff want any of this.'

Pieter was deep in garden scheming, his long fingers spread over the fuzzy scalp, muttering things in Dutch. Scale plans and drawings, suppliers' catalogues strewn on the kitchen table, a half-finished bottle of wine that we had been sharing in the middle of it all.

'Why Jess? These clothes are nice. The leather jacket, very expensive, very beautiful.'

'Martin gave them to me,' I said, my practicality beginning to wobble. 'I don't want to see them any more.'

'Do you want to speak about this?'

'No.'

'Okay, I'll put them in my car now.'

He does a good line in unquestioning understanding does Pieter. He's helped with the voluntary amnesia a lot just recently, as we've been thrown together in the evenings. I've had two weeks of local filming days, lots of muddy farms and anodyne links, but it's got me home in time to cook tea for the kids. He's had a lot of construction work to supervise, and builders knock off at five sharp, so the kids and I have come in to a house already full of human presence, his papers covering the kitchen table, his music drifting down the stairs.

He calls out if he's upstairs, and runs down to say hello.

'Bitten by something today Jess? A little mouse eat you?'

'No, just lightly savaged by a cameraman. Rob had toothache and growled all day. I thought Judith was going to burst into tears.'

'Hey kids, I have a game on my computer. You want to try? Go and see.'

Almost every evening he's been doing this, letting the kids play on his laptop, balanced on the dressing table in his room. He needs a proper desk.

'I'm gasping for a cuppa. D'you want one?'

'No. It's six already. Alcohol time. Yes, yes. A glass of wine? I have a bottle.'

'You're always getting me wine.'

'So? I get a cheap deal with The Court. Come. Sit in the sun. It's September, the summer is almost gone.'

And we sit out and chat. His English is becoming brilliant. He tells me about his lazy builders, about The Court politics, the crazy chefs, and imperious hotel managers. About his plans for the new gardens, and how it will look in the spring, in summer. We don't talk about Life, or Philosophy, we don't talk in Big Canvases, we talk Little, like all those tiny paintings Sisley did, gardens full of fog and snow and blurry flowers. Sharing day-to-day with this stranger sometimes feels more like a family arrangement than marriage with Martin ever did.

The sound of intergalactic dogfights comes from upstairs, Pieter tells me about the scouse chef whose recreation is fighting in clubs. I concoct a meal from three tins and a packet of pasta. Amidst this new absorbing domesticity, thinking about Martin's legs, the sweep of his back, the sound of his voice, is difficult.

So I'd been lulled into enjoying simplicity again: sleeping, waking up, having someone to talk to. Thinking the worst was over. Thinking I could probably speak to Martin quite happily, imagining having lunch with him one day, catching up on his gossip, telling him about the God Of Fat Hamsters. Both of us sparkly and glamorous, still quite fancying each other the way old friends often do.

I'd been relaxing.

Until the day I had to go to the county court to get the petition for the Decree Nisi sworn.

Judith, of course, knew about the word Nisi so she arranged a slack morning to give me time to get it done. She kept asking if I'd be all right going alone. I couldn't understand why. The petition itself was upsetting, my marriage reduced to two lines of type and a bit of Martin's spider scrawl which I folded under out of sight. But inside its envelope it was harmless enough. I imagined the swearing process would be just a formal signature by some old guy in a wig and a black suit. Five minutes in and out. No problem. Right up until the moment I walked into the county court building I still thought it would be easy. Tedious but not painful, like those dental check-ups when the dentist just says 'fine', and adds your money to his yachting support fund.

But inside the building it was dark and polished, like a giant Victorian coffin, and in the space of three seconds I fell from 'okay' to 'snivelling'. Like a plane crash; one second you're swigging your courtesy plonk imagining yourself as Disco Queen in a Cephalonian nightclub, and the next minute the plane's dropped a thousand feet and you're wishing you'd told your mum you loved her on the phone last night.

The guy at the door was a corpse, and as such, indifferent to the trials of the living. He directed me along a corridor straight out of Kafka. I walked with echoing footsteps in the gloom and saw no one but a whey-faced clerk who scuttled past me and back into a Munch painting. At last I came to the right heavy mahogany door and pushed it open, expecting more Dickensian funereal trappings. But inside was the interior of a small town bank from the 1970s, complete with the glass counter and little trough to pass over documents.

I rapped on the window and out came a fat girl with her neck in a brace and a flesh-coloured jersey with an egg stain.

'Yes?'

'I've come to get my divorce petition sworn.'

'Right.' She sniffed hugely, shuffled off a few feet and back. I couldn't see her feet, but I knew she had grubby pink slippers on.

'Take this in your right hand and read the words on the card.'

She pushed a greasy Gideon Bible with a dog-eared piece of card through the trough.

I had to swear on the bible that the writing on the petition was indeed my husband's. So I had to get the paper out and look at Martin's thin black hand, insubstantial-looking, almost like an accidental mark on the page. I wondered if he had had to do the same with a paper with my writing. He'd probably taken Dolores and a bottle of champagne along to celebrate this ceremonial first stage in his release. He certainly hadn't stood in another office crying like this. Speechless with dull misery.

"Do you want to come back another time?'

I shook my head. 'I'll be a' righ'.'

This is what our marriage had amounted to. This was what all those years had led to . . . all the sex on Sunday mornings, toddlers in our bed, sandcastle building on the beach, getting drunk with friends, house hunting in the rain, meals out we couldn't afford, stripping woodwork, playing music and making plans, was just to get here. Inside the registry office was the delivery room where our children were born, inside that was our house and its garden and inside that, nothing but this dismal room and this sticky card and its words dredged from a dead culture.

'I swear by almighty God . . .'

The paper was stamped. I went back down the corridor and out. In six weeks I'd be single. This was the start of my new start. But it felt like another bit of the end. The last bit of road that you drive off before the rocks start and the axle breaks.

Pieter did more unquestioning understanding when I got home after work. Got me to talk about my favourite flowers, explained to me about apple root-stocks, gave me onions to chop. I cried gratefully.

He answered the phone for me and was almost apologetic when he said, 'It's a man.'

The thought of having to speak to Martin was like cystitis: you know you have to, but you know what it'll do to you. What a long long way I had to go before exchanging chitchat over a lunchdate!

'Hello?' I croaked.

'Jess? It's Morgan. Hi!'

'Oh Morgan.'

'What's the matter? Were you expecting another call?'

'Yes. Mr Hyde as in Dr Jekyll and.'

'Excuse me?'

'Don't worry Morgan. How's the tour?'

'Great. That's why I was ringing. I have a day off before we set up at The Court. Tomorrow actually. I was wondering if I could take you out for lunch?'

'That's lovely Morgan. But I'm working. I won't be finished until seven.'

'Oh. Well then. Dinner?'

'Um. Okay.'

'Shall I pick you up at seven-thirty?'

'Fine.'

'I'll see you then.'

If I hadn't been so busy hyperventilating with relief that it wasn't Martin I might have put him off. 'Dating' has always seemed pretty pointless to me. 'Going out' somewhere with a person you barely know, and then spending the evening patrolling around each other seeing if, downhill with a following wind, you might want to go to bed. But it's what single people do with their spare time. It's how they 'get to know' each other. The human equivalent of dogs smelling each other's bottoms. Bottom smelling is easy as a student, there are lots of opportunities to have a surreptitious sniff, you sit next to each other in lectures, you meet accidentally in the cinema queue. You don't need the artificial set-up of a date. But when you're a grown-up with a job and a house and kids and a life full of bills and washing machines, there are no bum-snuffling chances. So you have to make them. Even if initially the bums to sniff aren't perfect.

My worry as I put down the phone was how I was going to tell Pieter. Why did the thought of going out with a man feel like being unfaithful? Absurd. Pieter was a dear, but he was still just my lodger.

Yeah, and why did I feel slightly offended when Pieter calmly agreed to babysit?

'D'you mind the top down?' asked Morgan.

'If I start to freeze I'll tell you.' It was my first time in a real sports car, I wanted the full effect even if it meant hypothermia.

This guy was intriguing. The director of a small-scale theatre company doesn't make enough to run a Deux Chevaux let alone a Mercedes soft top. Maybe the connection with Francis was just money: they both had lots of it.

'Nice to see that dress again. I love the shoes.'

'They've got their own little history already. I nearly lost them in a field in Oxfordshire a little while ago.'

'Tell me more.'

'No. I'd need a lot to drink before I'd tell you that story.'

'Well I'll see what I can do. What time does your sitter need to leave?'

'He doesn't. He's my lodger.'

'Oh. Right. So I could keep you out all night?'

'Depends what you wanted to do?' Why do I respond to flirting in kind? Why can't I just let it lie. I might as well have said 'Let's pull into a lay-by and fuck on the way home'. Pretty safe from that though, Morgan was wearing his side of the car rather than sitting in it. The chances of him leaning gazelle-like over the gear lever to ravish me must have been about the same as Demis Roussos winning the downhill slalom.

'Well, I guess dinner. Then, dancing, but not quite what you may be used to.'

'What d'you mean?' For one ghastly moment I thought I might be in for an evening in a line with people in Stetsons.

'Do you waltz?'

'Yes. Badly, but I do. And tango and I can do the military two-step. My school was pretty hot on ballroom.'

'Great. Then I think I may have made the right choice of venue.' He glanced over his shoulder at me, charming, confident. Maybe only four stone overweight. And he is tall after all.

He took me to a 'Dinner Dance'. One of those events my parents went to with 'People From Work', and my mum would get her mink stole down from its tissue-paper nest at the top of her wardrobe, and her beaded bag, and her shiny frock too. Morgan's dinner dance was at a very swish hotel and had a quaint forties feel to it. It was a County Set charity do, so it had the same mix of people and styles that had been to Francis's party. I even thought I recognised some faces. But no one came and told me about their marital difficulties, and no one seemed to know Morgan either. We could be anonymous together.

We ate Dinner, and then we Danced. There had been enough Chablis to let my hindbrain remember what it had learned at eleven. Morgan was just as good at ballroom as he'd been prancing around behind the disco lights in his loud shirt. After the first few numbers I stopped worrying about my stilettos piercing his toe caps, and began to be able to talk and dance at the same time. The mixture of formal steps and physical closeness began to work on me: that's what they don't tell you when you're learning to waltz with Charlotte Williams in the second form, that dancing is sexy, hand to hand, eye to eye, hip to hip. Just like being in bed.

I'd never been courted before. Wooed. Flattered. Persuaded. All evening Morgan treated me with a brand of gallant politeness that I think only survives in American men from very good families. And he was from a very good family. From Alexandria in Virginia, where his parents had a big white house with pillars at the front. He grew up fishing in the creeks on his dad's land. Hunting deer in the winter. He'd come to England as a graduate student to Oxford and never gone home. He was a good abstracter, he put in just enough for my imagination to fill in exactly what it wanted in the way of detail.

By the time I climbed back into the Merc at midnight I was pretty well softened up. More than slightly drunk, full of stories of a childhood out of Huck Finn and hints of a romantically broken heart. Beginning to believe that I was as attractive and irresistible as Morgan told me I was. Beginning to believe that it would be cruel to deny him something he thought so marvellous. He'd sold me a vision of myself: the gorgeous object of desire of a man with a history. And I bought it, so when he took a detour on the way home I didn't say anything.

'Can you walk a little in those shoes? It's dirt but it's packed pretty hard.' He opened the door and helped me out of the car.

'Where is this?'

'It's an airfield. Pretty disused these days. I'm the only one who comes here. I wanna show you something.'

We walked across the grass runway, dry, bald of grass and showing pale in the moonlight, towards a huge hangar. Morgan loosed a padlock, slid back the door on a cool, cold blackness and beckoned me inside.

I could feel the space and the cold.

'Wait here.' He stepped out of the single line of light and disappeared. I heard his footsteps moving away into the dark and had a sudden vivid little waking nightmare about sliced female body parts in black bin-bags.

There was a snap, like breaking twigs, and the lights came on. Sitting in the middle of the hangar looking small and rather lonely was a Spitfire. I knew what it was because Martin still had his Airfix models hanging from the ceiling of his bedroom at home when I first met him. This Spitfire was in poorer condition, only half painted and with the little round insignia looking sad and faded.

'This is the real reason I don't go back to America. I can't afford to take her with me.'

I walked up to the fuselage, my heels making a ridiculously amplified sound in the echoing space.

'You wanna sit inside?'

'Yes.' What else do you say? 'No, I'm not interested in military memorabilia. Please take me home.' Morgan didn't realise how close he was to blowing it with me, undoing all the careful work of the evening. Collecting things, even just one thing, is a complete turn-off. Just get your anorak and leave by the nearest door mister. And I was sobering up by the second.

But I must have spent more Sunday afternoons than I

imagined watching B-rate war movies about the Battle of Britain. All that stuff about the dashing nineteen-year-old pilots, all handsome, all frightfully well educated, chasing about in these tiny planes, the last exemplars of one-to-one trial by combat in the modern world. So sitting in the worn seat, before the solid round little dials and switches, was another strangeness. Like the dancing, and the car and the flattery. Morgan was editing a kind of pop video in my head, hoping that the final image of us bonking frantically in an aircraft hangar would cut perfectly on to the end. I was being managed, manoeuvred, directed. But so what? I read novels. I go to films. This was just another kind of escapism. Another little holiday from pain. And since Martin left I've had the attention span of a grasshopper, so escaping into books and movies isn't an option, recreational romance is all there is left.

Morgan climbed the ladder bringing his face to my level, so close his breath was on my neck.

'What d'you think?' he said, his cheek almost brushing mine. He wasn't asking about the plane. But I wasn't ready to give Morgan his final edit yet. I sat back out of reach.

'I think the plane is extraordinary. I've seen these so many times in the movies. I'm not sure what I feel about sitting in one.'

'D'you wanna come down?'

'Yes. I'm getting cold.'

He'd kept up the gallantry as I'd gone up the ladder and studied his shoes. But as I climbed down he looked up at me quite openly.

'Not many women wear stockings these days.'

'Hold ups, not stockings. Lots of women do. You'd be surprised.'

'Just as good as stockings anyway.' He ran a hand up my thigh, under the dress to the edge of the stocking. I stood on the last rung of the ladder, turned towards him, looked at him in the eye. 'I don't have to make love to you because you took me to dinner. It's just a date.'

'You think I brought you here to seduce you?'

'Morgan. Don't piss about. You took me out to seduce me. The whole evening has been a great romantic fantasy. I don't mind. I'm reasonably willing to enjoy fantasy. You convinced me. Almost. But I also like a little honesty. So don't pretend you just thought of it.'

He looked at me and laughed quietly. Looked at his shiny shoes and up again.

'Okay. Okay. I confess. I'll be honest. The whole deal was seduction. But hey, I'm a fat bastard – I have to try real hard. Now can we fuck?'

'I haven't made up my mind.'

Morgan purred the car into the yard at four.

'I'll be through at nine-thirty. I'll pick you up at ten.'

'Where will we go?'

'I'll find somewhere. It's summery. We could go to the ocean from here.'

I was up at seven, ready for a day with a family of pot-bellied pigs and a flock of geese. Pieter was in the kitchen yawning and rubbing his round head. He didn't smile at me when I handed him a coffee.

'Did you have a nice time?' he asked, looking down at Dog.

'Okay.'

'Only okay? But you came home so late.'

'Did I wake you?'

'Yes.' Surely this couldn't be jealousy from Pieter? Who had so willingly offered to babysit for me.

'I'm sorry. I tried to be quiet.'

'I was awake. That's okay.' Pieter still looked at Dog. His voice dull without its usual underlying promise of humour.

'Didn't you sleep well?'

'No.'

'I'm going to be very late tonight. The kids will sleep at Mary's.'

Pieter got up as I spoke and reached for his car keys, he turned and looked at me intently, 'And where will you sleep?' he said, and closed the door behind him.

It could have been an accusation. It could have been a reproof. That's how I took it for twenty minutes after he had gone. I slammed around the kitchen, muttering about effing lodgers not being my effing blinding keeper. But I knew it was really a request, an invitation to think, and that Pieter was asking himself as much as he asked me.

'Lights on nobody 'ome' said Rob coming to sit on the bale beside me. Judith had given us a short break whilst she lined up the next piglet to film.

'Yeah. Sorry Rob I'm not really with it today. Knackered.' I scratched the piglet's back and it leaned against my leg and closed its eyes.

'You never do that for Steve and me.'

'You don't squeal the right way, or I would.'

'How come you're knackered then?'

'I snogged all night in an aircraft hangar with Robbie Coltrane.'

'Only snogged. C'mon!'

'Can I help it if you don't believe me?'

He got up, pulled my hair and walked off grinning.

It wasn't so much the tiredness that was keeping me quiet, and sticking strictly to my lines. I was going over and over the previous night with Morgan. I'd left him at four elated, in control. I'd proved myself a modern grown-up girl, able to take or leave my pleasures as I chose. But all set to notch up another lay on the wood of my empty Martinless bed. Morgan and I had parted in no doubt that we were starting an affair. Finding the time and the opportunities were the only constraints. That not fucking on our first date was just the promise of fucking on the second, the third, the fiftieth.

But half-way through a working day, stinking of pig and on only three hours sleep, the paint-work of shiny self-determining independence that I'd slapped all over my night with Morgan began to drop off in great big flakes. The car growling along the lanes in the moonlight, Morgan's perfect charm, our terribly grown-up exchange on the Spitfire ladder. It all seemed thin, a soiled chiffon jockstrap, over the sordid business of rolling around with a flubber mountain on a pile of mouldy tarpaulins. I was about to start a very grown-up, very sexual affair with someone I suspected of having as much depth as a paddling pool. Someone who couldn't stand at a shaving mirror and see their own feet. Someone whose charming veneer was as tough and as impenetrable as aircraft varnish. All because he made me believe that I was too fabulously sexy and attractive to be resisted. If I went through with it I'd be screwing my own ego.

In the middle of the afternoon between pigs and geese I borrowed Rob's mobile.

'Hello, Kath De Freya speaking.'

'Hi it's me. Are the theatre company there yet?'

'Yeah, they've been setting up all day.'

'Can you get a message to Morgan Lindsey, their director? Just say I can't make tonight.'

'Interesting bloke. How do you know him?'

'I met him at Francis Weaton's do. Anyway, can you tell him I won't be able to make it. He wanted a few contacts in Charlatan. I was going to chat to him over a drink.'

'Okay. I was talking to him at lunch. D'you know it turns out I was at college with his wife? Jess. Are you still there?'

'Sorry Kath, it's a mobile and the batteries are low. I'd better go.'

I didn't change the arrangement with Mary and Georgie. There were some other junior bits of James's family staying whose public-school term hadn't started. They were grateful for playmates, so I'd sanctioned a sleepover and a Friday off school. I didn't want to see anyone. Not even my own children. I felt sick.

I had told Morgan a little about Martin. That we'd been together for a long time. That he'd left me. But I'd never asked him if he was married. And he hadn't told me. Would I have known a lie?

I'd made myself into a Dolores, pretty much. I'd done to Morgan's wife what Martin and Dolores had done on their first night together. How had it been between them I wondered? Alone together for the first time in Martin's flat, awkward with the knowledge that with their first touch they would become lovers. Waiting for the moment, knowing it would come. How in a way it had already happened.

Had she been deceived? Had she simply not asked? Or had the knowledge of my existence made it better? Heightened their passion by being stolen and illicit?

I thought of Morgan's wife, like me probably at home folding little T-shirts and putting school socks into pairs, whilst her husband was being exciting and creative. And unfaithful. I tried to think of some way to make it better for her. To warn her, to tell her, to apologise.

'Hello. You don't know me but I'd just like to say sorry that I nearly fucked your husband.'

'Hello my name isn't important but I think you should know . . .'

'Hello. My name is Jess Wallace. I'd like to come and see you to talk about your husband and his infidelities.'

'Hello. I wonder could you tell me if your husband is habitually unfaithful to you or just once in a while?'

But if I had never known about Dolores, if Martin had kept his double life, I would still at least have my half of it, my children would still at least have the daddy they loved. There was nothing I could do, except feel sad and sorry and ashamed.

I sat drinking wine outside the kitchen door. When it got dark I fetched the duvet off the bed and wrapped it round myself. Dog came and snuggled in, but even her warmth left me feeling dead as a stone, cold and sad as clay.

At about midnight the phone rang. I thought it would be Morgan, I was ready for Morgan. I could have Bobbited him down a phone line.

But it was Martin, in good spirits, complete with the slight mid-Atlantic sloppiness which he always brought back from America.

'Hello Jess.'

'Hello Martin. Where are you calling from?'

'The seaside. I got back two days ago. Very successful trip. I'm here until Tuesday. In Tim's house on the coast.'

'I thought you weren't getting back until September.'

'It is September Jess,' the long-suffering tone of patronage again. Poor Martin having to tell his stupid wife what month it is.

'What do you want Martin?'

'I'd like to see my children this weekend. I'll come and pick them up on Saturday, quite early, then bring them down here. The weather seems set to hold.'

'Fine. If there's nothing else . . .'

'I want them to meet Dolores. I think it's appropriate that they should meet my new partner.'

'I suppose it's about time they met her.'

'I've no interest in your opinion about my children meeting Dolores. I thought I might mention it out of common courtesy.'

'Mentioning when you fell in love with her might have been common courtesy. Appropriate.'

'Well I can see you aren't ready to behave like an adult. I'll be picking them up at nine, and they will be staying with me and Dolores until Sunday night when I will return them.'

'Is she coming with you to pick them up?'

'No. She'll stay here.'

'Are you planning to see the children again soon? Because it's Dan's birthday in three weeks.'

'I can't discuss access arrangements for my children with you Jessica. It must all be done through my lawyer.'

'I'm just asking if you might be around for Dan's birthday.'

'I'm sorry Jess. I cannot discuss this. All access discussions must go through my lawyer.'

'We're talking about our son's birthday here. Not how much fucking maintenance you'll have to pay.'

'Jess you are hysterical. If you can't talk without becoming over-emotional we'll have to do everything through the lawyers.'

'All right then I won't talk about the children. I want to ask you about Dolores. There's something I want to know, if the kids are going to meet her.'

'I won't answer anything of a personal nature.'

'Did she know that you were married the first time you went to bed together?'

'For God's sake Jess. What can it possibly matter now?'

'Did she know?'

There was a long long silence. Then a sigh. I'll never understand why he answered me. It gave so much away. Perhaps it was the last piece of true communication we'll ever have. 'No. She didn't know.' Then he hung up.

So Dolores didn't know he was married until it was too late. He took her out. They talked, and his wife and children were so small a part of his world that it was easy simply to leave them out of the conversation for a long time. We were already something long ago and far away. Like childhood pets, Mum's fruitcake, a first crush, we were the sort of life detail that doesn't get exchanged until you've been to bed together enough times to want to watch telly or drink tea afterwards.

Handsome, charming, exciting Martin – how could she have failed to love him? And loving him, convince herself that losing him was too great a price to pay for the happiness of three people she didn't even know, and who Martin had almost forgotten about. If I had fallen in love with Morgan, I might have made the same choices as she did.

Standing in the dark sitting room, by the desk he had worked at, I remembered a day two summers' ago, when Martin came home from three weeks in Tanzania. He'd had a day in London seeing editors, so he was smart and linen-suited when we met him from the train. He swung Frankie high, his hands like a cage around her ribs. His brown fingers and their curled blond hairs against her white T-shirt. There was no wedding ring.

'You've lost your wedding ring,' I said, 'never mind. I'll buy you a new one sweetheart.'

'No need. I just put it in my pocket whilst I washed my hands on the train.'

But looking at that snapshot in my mind again, the little ribcage inside the white shirt, those marvellous hands around it, I saw there was no white line to show where the ring had shielded his finger from the sun. Martin hadn't worn his wedding ring while he was away. Perhaps longer. Perhaps he had a ritual of removing the ring as he got on the train to London. He was only married when he was at home. Away from me, he was another person. Single. Available. He wasn't lying to Dolores with his ringless hand, simply presenting the way he saw himself.

I was standing with the receiver still hanging in my hand when the light went on, blindingly bright after hours in the dark.

'Jess, what are you doing?'

'I forgot to put the phone down.'

'Are you all right?'

'No.'

'You want to speak about it.'

'I don't know.'

Very gently Pieter took the phone from my hand and hung it up.

'You are very cold. Come, I will make you some tea.' He sat me at the kitchen table and got my fleece from the hook to wrap around me.

'Jess, what has happened? You have been crying.'

'It's all such a fucking tragedy Pieter. It's so long since Martin loved me. He stopped wanting us all so long ago. And now the best I can hope for is some sordid heavy petting session with a tub of lard. A married tub of lard.' At speed, through tears, there was no way Pieter would follow that but I was rather beyond constructing simple sentences without colloquialisms.

He did understand the feeling if not the sense, and said very gently, 'Something good will come Jess.'

'No. It's all done with. I've blown all my chances.'

'Here, drink this dear girl.'

'What is it?'

'Tea.'

I sat gulping, trying to swim in the tide of loss. It had all happened for Martin so long ago, I had been grieving over history, not news.

Pieter watched me drink the tea, waiting to say something.

'I thought you were,' he paused a little, 'staying out tonight?'

'No. He's horrible. And he's married. But mostly horrible. I decided to sleep here.'

'I should not have asked you that this morning. It's not my business.'

'Yes it is. You live here. You're my friend.'

'Am I? Not just boring foreigner lodger?'

'Bollocks.'

'Okay. Bollocks,' he laughed quietly and poured more tea. 'Kath heard today I said that, and she said she knew who had taught that word to me!' He sat down opposite me and looked at me carefully over his mug.

'We talked about you.'

'And what did you all say?'

'That you are very brave.' He looked down at his tea. 'That you will find someone else.'

Everybody said that, as if a human heart cut in half was as easy to regenerate as a worm. I felt the sorrow rising up through me again, filling me like warm water in a bath.

'Yeah. What sort of someone else? Someone who wants an easy fuck on the side, and no more.' I put my head in my hands and sobbed from the soles of my feet. 'Who'll take on a middle-aged woman with two kids and nothing in her future but cellulite and crow's feet? I feel like a bag of smashed china. I had my chance and I messed it up.'

Pieter reached across the table and laid his hand on my arm, hardly touching.

'Jess. You know, this stuff about your "chance is lost",' suddenly his hand gripped my arm, very tight. Tight enough to hurt, 'you know it is bollocks I think. It makes me angry that you feel this.' He let go of my arm and got up. He threw on a jacket.

'Get your coat Jess. We are going for a walk. It's very light in the moon.' He picked up a box of tissues and banged it down in front of me.

'Use these for your eyes and your nose. Then we are going.' He was so fierce that I stopped crying. I blew my nose, put on my coat and we stepped outside.

Dog thought she had died and gone to heaven: a walk with Pack Leader at night when the bunnies were out! She ran off madly, a black shape against the bright lane, a tangle of wagging tail and prancing paws. Pieter put my arm over his and marched me after her without a word.

He walked so fast I was breathless by the top of the hill, almost running to keep up with his long scissor legs. He stopped by a metal gate into one of Mrs E's fields.

'Climb on top here,' he said, banging the gate. Obediently I got up on to the first couple of bars. The metal was very cold and white in the moonlight. New aluminium.

'No, no. Climb up, up,' he banged the top of the gate again.

I got up on to the last bar of the gate with my feet wedged one each side of the top to brace myself. Slowly I stood up.

'I don't feel very safe Pieter.'

'I will catch you. Just stand there and look. Look all around.'

I stopped looking at my feet and spread my arms for balance. Thrust up into the air, the sky seemed very round, pegged down like a tent, tight to the horizon so that blue and silver fields pulled in the same arc as the blue and silver sky. All the plants were breathing out into the night air, so it smelled of green leaves. On the opposite side of the valley, a trio of deer moved across the field, stopping to snack, then moving on again. Down the hill, the yellow light from the kitchen found its way between the branches. At my feet, Pieter's round dark head, and Dog, her nose to the breeze and eyes closed in an ecstasy of smelling. Pieter's face turned up to look at me, 'How do you feel?'

'Alive.'

'So, don't say your chance is gone.'

'All right I won't.'

'Wait, I'm coming up.'

He climbed up next to me, both of us giggling now as we wobbled in the slight breeze. Up against the sky, away from ordinary backgrounds of chairs or flowers he looked more at home. I saw how completely himself he was, with no excuses made to anyone, nor any demands. As natural as a lone tree.

'I love this. To be high. To feel gravity pull me back.' Who else had I ever known who would say such a thing? Who else would notice gravity? Maybe Newton had his moments and stood on gate tops secretly at dead of night, flapping his frock coat in the breeze.

But even standing on a lower bar than me Pieter looked precarious. He spread his arms and flapped and the whole gate swayed,

'If gravity pulls us back suddenly, it's quite a long way down.'

'Okay. I will keep still.'

We didn't move from our absurd position. Almost face to face on top of a metal farm gate in the middle of the night. I wondered what we looked like to the deer on the hill. Not human perhaps. Just unusual shapes against the skyline.

Pieter's face was very close to mine, top-lit with silver and slashed with the blackest shadows. Something felt as if it was about to happen. Heavy in the air, wanting to land and change everything. It made me think of the pictures Sister Ignatia showed us of the Apostles, with the coloured pear-drops of the Holy Spirit waiting to break on their heads. Still, we didn't move, like a pair of infants in the nativity play when Third Shepherd forgets to say 'Let us go to Bethlehem'.

'We should get down perhaps,' I said.

'Not yet, Jess. Last night, when you were out all night, I was surprised.'

'It's not something I do normally . . . being out all night. I mean I didn't, we didn't . . .' I wasn't sure Pieter understood, I wanted him to know that Morgan and I hadn't shagged.

He went on, 'No, not you. Surprised at me. I felt . . . jealous. I'm not a jealous person.' Here was that something, so about to happen it almost was happening, 'I was awake until you come home. I wish I had not said yes to babysit.'

My heart was trying to escape via my throat and my legs began to gyrate at the knees, like girders with metal fatigue. I began to tremble so much the gate shook. At first just enough to be mildly comic, then enough to make balance difficult, and shortly afterwards impossible. I scrambled down before I was bucked off like a rodeo rider, before my legs shook the gate from its hinges. Pieter stood on the gate, bewildered: Third Shepherd about to say his line to an empty stage. He swung his leg over the gate. Missed the bar and the momentum pulled him backwards but left his other leg trapped. He came down like a telegraph pole, banged his head on the ground. I actually heard the snap of his twisted leg, still tangled in the gate.

He came round briefly in the ambulance, still bleeding, and tried to smile at me, but it's hard to smile when your tibia makes a break for freedom through your shin.

'Cryin', 'gain,' he said thickly.

'I'm so sorry. It's my fault.'

'No. No. My flot. Wrong time.'

'What's the wrong time?'

'Please try not to talk,' said the nice paramedic with the red eyebrows.

'Wrong time. Sorry.'

He squeezed my hand weakly and shut his eyes.

Was I imagining it or had something more than a nasty accident just happened? I wasn't sure, but I held Pieter's hand and stroked his forehead all the way to the hospital. Just as a friend. Just in case.

Chapter Sixteen

Summer was lasting to make up for June having been November. Sitting at the back of my border, watching the butterflies coating the iceplants and listening to the bees getting drunk on the echinops, I thought about Dolores again. I thought about her bringing Martin a whisky in the bath, sitting with her feet in the water for a chat, like I used to do. I've pictured this little scene many times, but never before without me running in with a chain saw. The fact is I can think about Dolores now without imagining embarrassing skin complaints for her. I've stopped wanting to see her screaming in the headlights of my car as she is sandwiched between its bumper and a brick wall.

And yet the prospect of seeing Martin and Dolores together was still terrifying. Not that it was part of the plan for the weekend: I knew Martin wanted to drop the kids and run on Sunday night, to avoid any possibility of our meeting, but my imagination kept turning up little scenes of how we would run into each other. Strings of impossible connections and entirely unlikely coincidences. They would decide to spend the weekend in the village and I'd bump into them in the shop. On Sunday night as they returned the kids, Martin's car would break down and he'd be unable to get through to the AA due to the phone lines from here to Edinburgh being down and they would have to spend the night. Dolores would turn out to be pregnant and go into labour on the way here, then have to come in and give birth to twins on my kitchen table.

It went on and on through ever more bizarre scenes in which Martin and Dolores came and enacted scenes from their life together in front of me, so that I was the tortured and unwilling spectator. I never imagined any sort of interaction between us, no scenes of terrible recrimination, no women wrestling in mud over their man. Just being witness to the reality of their partnership was quite horrifying enough.

Of course all the drama of Friday distracted me from the prospect of my first encounter with the 'Woman Who Stole My Husband'. And by the time Pieter had been stitched, x-rayed and sedated, it was well and truly Friday, not just a part of the night really belonging to Thursday. I hung around whilst they tucked him up. Dozy and numbed with drugs, he couldn't speak, but I stayed anyway until he dropped off.

'Are you Mrs Van de Meer?'

'Oh no.' The fat staff nurse raised an eyebrow, she'd seen me holding his hand.

'You're no relation then?'

'No. I'm his landlady.'

'I see,' she said and pursed her lips.

'We need to keep him for a couple of days. He's got a nasty bit of concussion, and he may need surgery on that leg. Can you bring some pyjamas, shaving kit, that sort of thing?'

I sat in the foyer drinking revolting plastic coffee until it was late enough to call Mary and ask her to come and get me. Practical as always, she offered to bring some of James's things in for Pieter.

'There are several pairs of pyjamas that James will never get his tummy into again and a rather nice Paisley dressing gown.'

We stopped briefly at The Court so that I could tell them that Pieter wouldn't be in. I ran into reception, and I was so gobsmacked by how good one of my dresses looked on the girl behind the desk that I almost missed Morgan sitting on the big green chesterfield.

'Jess!' He seemed relieved to see me, it was clear he thought I'd come to find him and apologise. He got up and came towards me.

'Oh Morgan! I'm sorry, I'm in a fearful hurry.' I turned from him to the girl in my frock and told her quickly about Pieter's accident. By the time I was done, Morgan was at my side. He held my elbow and steered me towards the sofa.

'Look Morgan I have someone waiting for me in the car.'

'Okay. But where were you last night?'

'Didn't you get my message?'

'Sure. But just saying you can't make it isn't much of an explanation.' He thought he had the right to be angry with me. I almost laughed.

Too tired to be self-conscious I answered sweetly, 'Would you rather I'd left you a more extensive message? Okay. My message would have been "I can't see you tonight Morgan, because I don't like to fuck other women's husbands".' It was a white lie, after all if I hadn't found out about his wife I'd have had to tell him that I just didn't like him enough to go to bed with him. I didn't look behind him, but I'm sure I heard the sound of a couple of chins hitting the parquet floor. For all the self-deprecating stuff about being a fat bastard, Morgan wasn't used to being refused.

I slept until late afternoon, then drove round to pick the kids up. Mary asked me about Pieter. I felt responsible, as my lodger he was in my care, I told her. And he was so far from home poor chap. I would visit him in the morning after the children had gone, he'd barely be out from the anaesthetic this evening. She quizzed me about exactly how the accident had happened and it was easy to say he fell climbing a gate on a late-night walk. She didn't need to know how late.

But being his host was nothing to do with it. I wanted to find out what had happened between us. I wanted to know if I had the right to feel more than just the concerned host. And of course as the guilty party, it was all my fault that the gate had shaken and he had fallen. My fault that he was up there in the first place.

With Pieter and his accident temporarily out of the way, Dan and Frankie had nothing but a night's sleep between them and Dolores. They were full of bravado at bedtime. Frankie typically saw the whole thing as a straight fight, woman to woman over a man.

'I'm not even going to look at her. I know I hate her. How could she take my Daddy?'

If Frankie were older I might have feared for Dolores's safety. I think Frankie's fantasies about the meeting have been of the single-combat, hand-to-hand, weapons-of-your-choice, variety.

Dan's age and personality mean he always sees the bigger picture.

'I don't want to hurt Dad's feelings. I know how special he says she is, but if it wasn't for her he wouldn't have left us. I'm afraid I won't be able to be nice to her.'

I did the spiel about how nervous she'd be, about how keen she would be to get on with them; about how nice she must be if Daddy chose her. And then I came downstairs and didn't feel like spitting my teeth across the room. I felt too 'in between' to be vicious, an odd kind of pending-tray calm – with Pieter in suspended animation in hospital and Dolores and Martin curled up together in front of Tim's woodburner, Martin whispering into a cloud of red hair, 'Don't worry babe, they're my kids and I love you, so they'll love you too'.

What was I going to feel when I saw Pieter in the morning? What was I going to feel when my kids did love Dolores? I fell asleep downstairs, on the kitchen sofa with Dog on my chest, watching the tiny new moon hanging in the top left-hand corner of the window, like a lemon rind.

The kids were up at six and jumpy. Snarling at each other, sparking with everything from insatiable curiosity to vengeful fury. I kept them busy, walking Dog, feeding the chooks, telling them again that Pieter would be fine, and that I wouldn't forget to take the pictures they'd done for him to hospital.

But anxiety makes you terribly productive. By eight-thirty we had done all the chores. I'd even cleaned the kitchen floor. Packed and ready for their weekend the kids just waited, watching telly in a distracted kind of way. Too debilitated by tension, I sat with them, until a quarter past nine when my fear got the better of me. Supposing Martin had brought Dolores, supposing they walked in now? I checked the kids' belongings one more time, hugged and kissed them goodbye and went upstairs. I locked the bathroom door and ran a huge bath. As I got in, a horn beeped out in the yard and the kids battered the door of the bathroom. Wet and soapy I opened it to give them one last hug.

'Will you be okay Mummy?' said Dan, 'you know you're our only Mummy don't you?'

I'll never know what they've gone through, caught between us as they are. I sometimes wonder about the assumptions we make about the unquestioning, unconditional nature of parental love. I think we get the direction it flows in quite wrong. I'm certain I get more than I give. Dan's parting remark crumpled me. I sat in the bath insensible until I was crinkly as a seventies chip and the water was cold.

The pictures that the children had made for Pieter were on the table in an old torn envelope, for all my promises I nearly left the house without them. They were mostly highly dramatised and gory versions of the accident, plus a few more restful images of Pieter in the garden.

Frankie's gardening scene featured rather alarming giant bees but as she'd written 'Get Well Get Buzzy' over the top I felt it was churlish to offer criticism. Dan's pictures were rather more fanciful, gardens in space was the big theme, aside from huge facial gashes and flashing blue lights on ambulances. Looking at them I saw how much they'd noticed about Pieter. There were his scissor legs, his round head, his long smile. There was his house on stilts, and a bedroom window with a fishing rod poking through. He'd made a difference to them too. Quietly he had got inside their hearts. I think he has a knack for getting into hearts, quietly, without keys or a jemmy.

He was in a different bed, at the end of the ward under a huge window. He was pale and quiet. Apparently asleep. I arranged the pictures round his table with the flowers I had brought, *Lilium regale* for him and a cloud of gypsophila for my benefit. I sat down as quietly as I could and just looked at him. Watching the duvet going up and down.

Unless you're some underpaid night nurse patrolling the wards you only watch children and lovers sleeping. It felt so intimate to hear him breathe after so many weeks of careful friendship. We'd enjoyed each other's company so easily, but in all the time he'd been in my house I'd touched him only by accident. For most people maybe this wouldn't be something to comment on, but I stroke, hug, kiss, hold, compulsively. To have talked, laughed, cooked, walked, watched telly with this man without so much as squeezing his arm must mean something. To have stood so close, madly teetering on the top of the gate must mean something. I wanted him to wake up and tell me what.

The dark fuzz had grown a bit and showed a little patch of silver on one side. Selfishly I found myself rejoicing in that. Perhaps not so terribly young then. Madness had been at high school, or even whilst he was teaching in school. That would make him only a little bit younger than me. No wrinkles though. Lying at peace, his smooth tan against the white pillow, dark lashes like a clipped paintbrush along his lids, he certainly looked painfully young. Someone that young could pull a girl with perfect shell-pink nipples and a straight line across from hip bone to hip bone. A girl without history. A girl to start and finish with. Not a middle-aged woman with two kids, a divorce and more emotional baggage than Imelda Marcos has shoes.

What had I been imagining? That he wanted me? That his kindness had been the start of passion? I had to give up this hoping business, Mrs Termite searching for the wings she ripped off to go underground and lay eggs. Pieter had just felt sorry for me. He's a nice guy and he had found me crying, end of story.

Almost, apart from me making him fall, knock himself out and break a leg. Apart from what he had seemed about to say.

He opened his eyes.

'How are you feeling?' I said.

'Sore.' He smiled. 'The pictures are so lovely.' His eyes were full of tears. 'There are no little kids in my family to do this. Say to them thank you.'

'Of course.' I could barely suppress some embarrassing endearment, this close, this intimate, within the warm aura of Pieter's body.

'The leg is pain. It will be long to mend.' Tired and drugged his English had slipped, his accent was stronger.

'I told The Court what happened. They know you won't be in for a while.'

'Thank you.' He closed his eyes again.

'Pieter, I'm so so sorry about all this. It's my fault.'

'No. No Jess. It was an accident.'

'But if I hadn't made the gate shake and jumped off . . .'

Pieter sighed, opened his eyes again. 'Jess. I am going home to Holland.'

There was that noise again, the whistling sound of life falling down.

'No!'

'Not forever. Just a while.'

'You can stay here.' I panicked. Surely I could stay home and care for him? I could persuade Judith to make a series about my chickens.

'You don't have to go home. I'll make a bed for you downstairs.'

'No Jess. It's better I go home for a while.'

'What about the job at The Court?'

'The landscaping they do to my plan. I can leave. Then plant in the fall.' He closed his eyes. He seemed to sink into the bed with weariness. I'd been right. Nothing had happened but an accident.

'I will call my brother to come, take my things from you, take me home.'

'Let me know when,' I said dully, 'I'll be at work I expect, so I'll leave the door unlocked.'

'I will come back,' he said, then he shut his eyes again. Yeah. He'll come back and stay with Kath and Gerry. No more feeling predated by some sad mad old divorcée desperate for someone to say he might fancy her if she'd just slip this bag over her head. Stop searching for those bloody wings Jess, I told myself.

I didn't cry as I tidied Pieter's room on Saturday evening. There was nothing to cry over except my fantastic ability to construct romantic fantasy from nothing. I'd spent all the years with Martin doing the same, imagining he loved me, so inventing a sensitive and caring persona for Morgan and a grand passion for Pieter was nothing. Peanuts.

I changed the sheets on my own bed, and replaced the two sets of pillows with just one, in the middle. Toast in bed on Sunday mornings, sleeping on my back without a care for snoring, leaving four books under the covers and going to bed plastered in greasy moisturiser. These would be the delights of my bedroom from now on. I took Dog for a long walk in the dusk, then watched dismal Saturday night TV, specially designed to punish all the poor bastards not out with their friends and make them feel even more sad and inadequate than ever. At midnight, I had a bath, went to bed, aware that I hadn't felt anything, anything at all since I had left Pieter in the high pale hospital bed.

I had the same detached numbness, a sensation of being six feet away from my life, on Sunday. It was the skittles tournament at the pub. It gets a better attendance than the village fête: the competition there has to be covert, arriving early to get the best bargains on the plant stall, but at the skittles tournament it can be out in the open and there are lots of chances to be Top . . . best team, best male player, best female player. Except of course they are Gentlemen and Ladies.

It's usually held indoors in their dark little alley that always smells slightly of damp even in the warmest summer, but we're all so entranced with the Indian Summer that this year it was set up outside. The alley was a series of carefully laid boards enclosed in bales, and a couple of tarpaulins slung between the raised bucket of a digger and a parked horsebox made a sheltered sitting area for the barbecue. Everybody brings a pudding and the price of your ticket covers large amounts of charred meat and good beer.

Already at just on midday, the trestle tables were covered with fruit pies and chocolate gateaux, real trifles and treacle tarts and George the landlord – a vast benevolent Bluebeard – was presiding over the barbecue like a blacksmith over a furnace. Alex was marking up the teams on a blackboard, in neat teacher's script – The Mad Cows, The Starly Cross Stompers, The Drunken Chickens, The Bull City Rollers, The Hot Shots – and the serious contenders were getting stocked up on pints of Barn Owl. For the old farming families round here there are one or two solemn scores that get settled at the skittles match. Girlfriends, stolen back in the forties, corners of fields seques-tered by the nocturnal moving of fences, prize bulls mysteriously ailing the night before the County Show. So it's a carnival event, but not to be taken flippantly. There is a serious tradition that one must at least be seen to be trying to hit the skittles.

I arrived with my offering just as Kath and Gerry were getting out of their car.

'Bloody 'ell. I don't believe it. She's made bleedin' profiteroles again. I'll 'ave to force 'em darn like I did last year.'

'Bugger off Gerry. I can only make two puddings.'

'Yeah? So what's the other one?'

'Can't remember!'

'I'm skiving!' grinned Kath, 'I just hope we don't make it beyond the second round because I've got to be in work at two.'

'Who's on our team then?'

'You, me, Gerry, not Alex and Sarah because they're scoring. Alf and Maud, and Susan.'

'Well if Alf's on form, you won't be home before the bitter end.'

And the other serious condition is a kind of social mixing in the teams. For every reasonably young and able member you must have at least one old codger who is either pissed or on a zimmer. But when it comes to it, the 'young and able', which in village terms means people like me, are crap at skittles, and the old codgers, having played it all their adult lives, are demons. Alf and Maud are in their eighties, skinny and frail as sparrows to look at. Wiry and tough as ancient Yogic gurus with a skittle ball in their hands.

'You gonna get the winning team for us today Alf?'

'I shall need a good few pints first.'

Susan is a retired teacher who taught botany and hockey to girls from good families all her life. Having lived for forty years as an example to young people, she let her hair down the day after her retirement. She looks like Ned Sherrin and dresses in an old velvet smoking jacket. An erratic player, but on form she could be our secret weapon.

Martin never made it to the skittles tournament. He was always away or about to go away. I looked round at it all: Susan stubbing out her cigarette and narrowing her eyes ready to shoot, mums with young babies sitting on the bales in the sun, kids tearing around the back of the horsebox in a huge unsupervised gang, big red-faced men licking cream and trifle off their fingers. I wondered if this would have meant anything to Martin anyway, this feeling of having a nice little part in a rural sitcom.

I lined up my shot, and the ball hit the wood with a satisfying clack on the board. Another total miss of course. But Kath and

Gerry were pleased: she could get to work and he could get some more profiteroles. As for the talents of Susan, Maud and Alf, they'd get used on other teams as the strain of five pints of Tawny made sudden gaps in the ranks of the top line-ups.

For quite a while after Kath had gone, I stayed on chatting to Gerry, hindering Alex and Sarah's scoring, but I began to twitch about the children's return. I wanted them to come home to me calm, and to a kitchen full of baking smells and welcome. And I wanted to be a little more sober, or at least not actually smelling like a beer mat.

I walked home across the fields. I could pick the car up in the morning. Even the muddiest corners were dry and hard, the leaves looked crisp with baking but still green, and the hedgerows were full of blackberries. I gleaned and ate like a bird as I walked.

The queue for the loo at the pub had been huge. I hadn't bothered, but I felt I'd enjoy the last two fields a lot more without half a football inflated in my belly. I crouched between two clumps of brambles. You're very still and quiet when you pee, or as a girl you are. Boys make splashing sounds and groans of relief. But women are quiet, low to the ground without a threatening silhouette. So it wasn't surprising to see a fox rounding the blackberries with the late afternoon sun right on her. She looked careworn, her belly had the lumpy look of rows of well-used teats, but her coat was still that glorious triumphant colour: the tartiest redhead at the bar. She was delicately licking the ripe berries from the branches near the ground, and she was so close I could hear the smack of her lips as she pulled them from the thorns. It's great for the pelvic floor, seeing a fox mid-stream. You stop on auto and hold your breath.

But she smelt me, or the alcohol in my urine at the very least, and without a glance or thought she ran up the field and into the hedgerow like a sienna smudge.

I finished my pee and got up. All of the vixen's face, her well-used body and her rough glorious coat had printed right through me like a cookie cutter, straight into the blankness and dark of the last twenty-four hours. For the few minutes remaining of my walk home, that image was all there was of me. I had nothing else to say or remember, so that walking into my house and greeting Dog, I was a clean slate ready for a new thought.

'I've got what I want,' wrote itself over the bright fox picture. 'I've got what I want.' I sat down on the bench outside the back door, with Dog bouncing around me, and I saw it was true. This life in this place with my children was complete enough to sustain me. I might not flourish, but I could at least survive. I might not grow, but at least I wouldn't wither. Nothing Martin had done or could do could take this away. He was an icicle but not a bit of Semtex or a circular saw. I was frightened of him only because he was making all the decisions 'I will see the children.' 'I won't see the children.' 'They will meet Dolores.' 'Dolores won't meet you.' So what if *I* made some decisions? Nothing could be as big as divorcing him.

I cleaned up the kitchen, put a cake in the oven, washed my face and walked out into the yard to wait for Martin and Dolores to bring the children home.

I sat quietly on the dry path looking at the sky change. You could see the break in the summer as the sunset lit up the advancing bank of clouds. As Martin's car turned into the gateway it caught the sun full-on. Blinded, he drove slowly, and I could see him, and Dolores beside him, so clearly, lit by the deep orange light.

She was almost as I'd pictured her. Not so beautiful but kinder. A sweet oval face with a halo of hair like flame in the sun. Martin's face, so familiar in every contour was tense and drawn. As scared to see me as I was to see him. She said something, 'don't worry' perhaps, and he glanced at her and smiled. As he turned back to watch where he was parking she passed a hand over his hair. It was over in less than five seconds, at the very most. But I saw how he looked at her, and the tenderness in the way she touched him. Martin had found his other self, his home universe. I could have no continuing quarrel with that feeling. Love after all is rare and dictates its own terms, but how we manage it and translate that in our lives is what makes us wrong or right.

The car turned out of the sunset's spotlight, and I stepped up to the driver's door. The alarm on all the faces in the car was almost comic. I half expected to see little bubbles with exclamation marks inside them emerge from all the heads.

Martin got out and the children clamoured after and ran to me. Dolores sat rooted, like a fixed figure in a Matchbox car. Someone should remind her to close her mouth, I thought.

'Mummy are you all right? I don't think you should see Daddy!!'

'It's okay Dan. I want to see Daddy.'

'No Mummy. I don't want you to fight. You might hit each other,' said Frankie, pulling me back.

'Poppet, look at me, I'm not cross and I'm not crying, it's okay. Say bye bye and run inside. There's a cake to get out of the oven.' They hung back and watched as I stepped towards Martin, then tore inside.

'This is unacceptable Jess. You didn't warn me. You gave me every reason to believe that you had no desire to see me. I have none to see you. You should have warned me,' he spat the words at me.

'Martin,' I said quietly, 'you are the father of my children. I think we should try and be friendly. Why don't you and Dolores come and have a cup of tea and some cake before you go back?'

Martin didn't say anything. He looked away, then clamped his jaw tighter and breathed hard. 'No. I don't think so.'

I stepped a little closer, thinking about breathing. Speaking slowly and breathing very deliberately I said, 'Okay, then next time you come perhaps. But I'll say what I wanted to say out here. I wanted to say that I accept that you've gone. That you won't come back. Now the decree nisi is through it's just a matter of waiting for it all to be over.'

I'd said all I wanted to. I reached up to his cold cheek and kissed him gently. He stood as rigid as an icicle.

'I wanted to say goodbye to Martin my husband.'

'This is just the sort of emotional circus . . .' he hissed, then lost his voice, and stood breathing very loudly and looking down at his new deckshoes. At last he looked up at me and said very quietly, so that Dolores wouldn't hear I suppose, 'Goodbye Jess,' and for one little moment I saw my Martin, my dear Martin from far away, somewhere there in those blue eyes, in the distance waving to me from the bottom of the long well of our marriage.

It was true then, this end. I could stop fighting. This was the release that families feel when the body of their long missing relative is finally found. At last they can let go, and bury their dead.

'Goodbye Martin. Happy life.'

Then he turned on his heel, and got into the car. I looked at Dolores. I couldn't smile. I raised my hand and nodded and she lifted a finger in reply, and remembered at last to shut her mouth. In a rake and roar of brakes and steering they were gone.

The kids must have been watching and they ran out as the car drew away. We made a totem pole of twined limbs for a little while. Then Dog came scrambling up, barking and wickering in excitement.

'She's learned how to open that back door,' said Dan.

'It's only taken her three years. She so dim!' said Frankie.

'Come on you horrid little children. Let's go in. It's starting to rain. Then we're going to visit Pieter in hospital.'

I didn't even hear the children telling me about Dolores, what they liked and didn't like about her, as we drove to the hospital. I was driven by a 'last reel of the movie' feeling. My instincts had told me I needed to say goodbye to Martin's face. My instincts had told me that screwing Morgan was a bad idea. They'd told me quietly about Martin and Dolores before the Queen tape or the failing magic willy. And now they said 'unfinished business' about me and Pieter. There was one thing I wanted Pieter to know.

It was nearly the end of visiting time when we arrived. The nurses were already beginning to get that Stalag Thirteen look about them, a kind of bouncer crossed with a warder look.

Pieter was sitting up in bed in a white T-shirt, surrounded by a litter of plates, books, magazines, pens and pencils. He looked pleased to see the children, but they were awkward and shy in the hospital atmosphere.

'Why don't you go and find that play area we passed on the way up here? I'll come and find you on the way out.'

'Bye Pieter. See you soon.'

He didn't comment until they'd gone. 'You haven't told them I am going to Holland?'

'No. Not yet.'

'Thank you for coming to the hospital.' He looked at me for a moment, then looked away. The certainty that had driven me running to fetch the car from the pub to get here began to seep away, and the Mrs Termite in a dark hole feeling began to replace it.

And then Martin's voice came into my head, something he'd told me about Dolores, the day he left: 'I know this chance to be with her won't last. If I don't take it, in thirty years I won't be able to live with myself.'

It had hurt so much. So much. What about the chance with me, I'd thought. But here was that feeling. 'Low-flying Life Opportunity. Get your net ready!' Martin had grabbed his net. He had gambled for the first time in his life, on very long odds, with a big stake to lose. But he'd made my gamble easier than his own, my odds were longer, he had taken what I had to lose.

There was something now between Pieter and I but I didn't know what. One of us had to be courageous enough to find out. It was like Gerry always said about bargaining in antique shops, 'Less face it Jess, ve worst they can say to yer is "Fuck orf" innit?'

I put my undrunk hospital tea on the bedside table, and held my own hand for comfort. I didn't know what to say. 'What's happened?' seemed a bit vague. 'Are we falling in love?' too specifically ridiculous.

'Pieter, what were you about to say when you fell off the gate?'

'I don't think you want to hear it. It's not a right time.'

'Why?'

'Because . . .' he sighed. In all the weeks he'd been in my house, I hadn't had Pieter marked off as a sigher. 'Because I'm going back to Holland.'

'But you didn't know that then. Kath thinks you'll be in work next week.'

Pieter was quiet. Apparently finding the top of his blankets fascinating.

A nurse rang a bell irately, 'End of visiting time everybody. Can you clear the ward in two minutes please.'

Pieter was silent.

'Pieter, don't go straight to Holland from here. Come to my house first. Just for a couple of days until you're stronger.'

He looked up at me, my eyes suddenly as interesting as the duvet.

'I said goodbye to Martin today. To his face. I know I don't want him back.'

There was a huge sound of crashing and breaking, for a minute I got the impression that it was inside me. But it was Pieter's plates and impromptu study sliding to the floor as he heaved up the covers and reached both hands to me. He held my hand in both of his, looking at me carefully.

'I will call my brother. I will come to your house tomorrow.'

A last bowl slid off the bed with a terminal crunch.

'Oh bollocks.'

Chapter Seventeen

I don't know how I concentrated on Mrs Mapes's chihuahuas. There were so many, like a plague of mice. I got the impression that if you locked one in a cupboard for more than ten minutes it would divide into four or five more all on its own. Considering how distracted I was I'm amazed that I didn't simply tread on some of the smaller ones. Maybe I did and I'll find them between the treads of my boots in a week or so.

We had to film indoors and it took an age to set up the lights to Rob's satisfaction, by which time we were all getting claustrophobic about being shut in a small room with so many pairs of liquid, slightly poppy eyes: all of Mrs Mapes's children had the day off from school in honour of our filming, and there were about ten of them. I may have one of them stuck to the bottom of my boot too. After a couple of hours they were pretty indistinguishable from the dogs. If you can call something like a rat on string a dog.

After that we had a pygmy goat having a caesarean and an injured tawny owl having its wing set at a veterinary surgery, about forty minutes from home and Pieter's hospital. The vet was brilliant, I didn't even have to think about what to ask him . . . good as a wind-up toy, set him down and off he went. Just as well because by three I was so agitated with nervous anticipation that I'd lost any ability to make grammatical sentences or pay attention for more than four seconds.

'Earth to Jess. Earth to Jess,' said Steve.

'What? Oh sorry.'

'I said, have you got your mike plugged in?'

'Yes. No. I don't know.'

'Jess, I'd like to do the reverses now.'

'What did you say Judith? What reverses?'

'Of the interview we've just done.'

'Did you write my questions down? I have no idea what I said.'

Pieter was mobile enough on his plaster to be delivered home by the ambulance to an empty house. But I hated the thought of him being there alone, still in pain, incapacitated by a plaster and maybe regretting his decision not to go straight to Holland. I imagined him collapsed on a sofa in the dark, too weak to even reach the light switch, Dog licking his hand and whining.

'You're going too fast Mummy,' said Dan as I raced through the lanes from Alex and Sarah's where the kids had been after school.

'I'm sorry, I'm just worried about Pieter.'

'But you said he was okay!' said Frankie, all ready for a drama.

'He is, I just . . . oh never mind.'

'Go faster then. Let's get home!'

He was resting, but hardly collapsed. It was dark enough for the lights to be on, so the kitchen looked yellow and cosy and we could see Pieter, plaster up on the sofa, glass of wine on one side, Dog in blissful ecstasy on the other. All the same, I restrained the kids a little: they'd have jumped on him so hard his other leg would have snapped.

'Well you look better!'

'I am much better.' He looked straight at me again, no sliding glances, no closed eyes. 'I can walk quite well on my crutches. I cooked dinner.' I followed his eyes to the stove and saw a line of teddies, every teddy in the house standing to attention, each with a flower pinned to its paw. He must have killed himself ferrying soft toys down the stairs in spite of his leg. I felt my throat close with tears and something else, some kind of slow explosion of hope.

'I wanted to make a decoration . . .'

'Wow, Pieter, all our teddies.' Dan and Frankie walked along the row as if inspecting the ranks at Sandhurst. Pieter had collected every soft toy from all our rooms, a collection of all our childhoods, Martin's, mine, Dan's, Frankie's. Here was the bear my father bought me when I got measles at seven, here was the bear five-year-old Martin had bathed so much its fur had come off, here was the pink rabbit Frankie had clutched at nine months, and the knitted tiger that Dan refused to be parted from between the ages of two and four. And at the end was a tiny black dog with almost no tail that I'd never seen before, with a freesia on its head: a little fragment of Pieter's life, an almost unknown territory stretching in front of me like an unexplored landscape.

Perhaps this was a first frame of my future, improvised from all sorts of unexpected bits of the past.

'Supper is cooking. Instant from Marks and Spencer.'

'How?'

'I ask one of the nurses and . . .' he smiled and shrugged. I could see him sweet-talking some night nurse into getting him a complete meal for four from the Marks just down the road from the hospital. 'I bring it home with me in the ambulance. It is done in a minute.'

It was a party. Pieter had even brought champagne. He propped his leg on a chair and sat at the table, smiling, relaxed, funny. So much the same as he had always been that I began to fear that there was nothing more to say. That he was just my lodger again. Delightful and easy. That all we were going to have was more conversation about the best way to grow sweet peas, and jokes about eloping with the dog.

I parcelled the kids to bed the moment they showed the first sign of a yawn. But then I lost my nerve, so I cleared plates obsessively and played music until every surface was empty and the only option was to sit down opposite Pieter again.

'Are you comfortable there?'

'Oh yes.' He leaned over and filled my glass. 'The music is a bit loud. Can we turn it down?'

I leaped up as if I'd been connected to the mains and hit the off button.

'Okay.' Pieter took a huge breath. 'Jess I have something to tell you.'

My heart stopped, the last time I'd heard those words sitting in this kitchen, Martin had told me about Dolores. I sat down like an empty sack.

'Oh no! You're going to say that you have a wife and seventeen kids in Holland!'

'No.'

'Then you're gay.'

'No Jess. Listen. You asked what I was going to say, when I did this,' he tapped his plaster. 'Okay, I will tell you. But first a present. On the dresser up there. For you.'

Above the dresser, tucked away beyond the reach of even my most bonkers nocturnal house cleaning, was a little plain cardboard box with a single blue star stencilled on the lid.

I'm nervous about opening parcels, about the contents. If it's something I hate, will I be able to catch my expression soon enough before it gives me away? I must be very hard to buy for because I've almost never received a present I like. Or maybe we all feel that way and we're just in one huge conspiracy to spare each other's feelings.

I lifted the lid and peered gingerly inside. A box like this could conceal any number of horrors: embarrassing sculptures, pieces of pottery the colour of cowpats, novelty doorstops, giant paperweights, ornamental candles, bottles with fifteen different kinds of sand. It was limitless. I wasn't sure I could make the right faces at a Lladro peasant boy.

I pulled out a bulb. White and scaly with a mat of roots like the tentacles of a jellyfish. The box was full of them, each one wrapped in a square of tissue. I sat it on my hand and looked in wonder. No one had ever known me well enough to buy me something I wanted so much.

'Lilies,' said Pieter. 'I choose them very carefully. They all have names in English. Discovery, Bright Star, Bonfire, Journey's End. They are a lyric for you. About you and what you mean to me. I buy them weeks ago.' Tears were standing in the green chameleon eyes.

I looked at him in utter astonishment. Real people don't say these sorts of things. Real people say things like 'S'pose a shag's out of the question?'

All I could do was croak 'thank you' and hold the long brown hand lying on the table top.

'Let's go from the start. You are Jess, who screams at 'er kids. Who walks in the garden with no shoes, feet naked. Who says bugger at the TV. Who kisses her friends. Who listens to me speak about pruning for God's sakes. Jess, who laughs at my jokes. Of course this is the most attractive. This Jess. I love this Jess. I think from the first week here. The first day.'

Looking into his eyes was like looking into a cell with all its little bits of organelles whizzing about. So alive.

'When you jump down from the gate I thought you didn't want to hear this. I thought that night you still want back your husband.'

'But I don't. I really don't.'

I moved across the table so fast I broke nearly all of what was left of my crockery. We leaned over the scrambled cloth and broken plates, holding what we could reach of each other tight, and breathing. There wasn't anything to say, we just clung together in an earthquake of emotion right off the Richter scale. The tidal wave that had been held back by all the times we had choreographed ourselves around the house without even brushing jerseys. We were in a state of shock at what happened as we put our arms around each other. The sort of surprise catalytic reaction you get when innocent pale gobbets of sodium drop into water, and suddenly spit and rage with steam and sparks.

'What do you feel?' I whispered.

'Bit scared. What did we do? What was in the coffee?'

'Milk.'

'Oh. Sugar?'

'No.'

'I feel that I'm home, but I have been away for two million years.'

'No ten million.'

'Okay. Ten.'

'Now I'm scared to let you go.'

'Don't then.'

We bumped Pieter's plaster upstairs to my room, still wobbling slightly, but stopping every three steps to kiss with cartoon ferocity. Then we simply crumpled on to the bed, in an astonished sort of tangle.

Normally, when you fall in love you can't wait for it. You go out to dinner and become irritated because there are three whole courses to get through first. You go to a movie and get angry because they could have just told you the plot in three sentences printed on the screen and you wouldn't have to sit in the warm darkness touching legs for two and a half hours. You invite friends for dinner and just want them all to go home by nine-thirty. Or better, all be ill and not come.

But Pieter and I lay on my bed with most of our clothes still on. We held each other and we talked. Anything more was like experimenting with newly acquired powers of psychokinesis. Pieter would stroke my arm and it would feel so wonderful that I'd start hyperventilating. I'd kiss his fingers and he'd say his head was going to pop.

Sex would risk a kind of core melt-down enveloping the planet.

Pieter constructed a whole world in my head, transferred his vision of his life growing up in a small Dutch town so effectively that I already began to feel the memories were my own. I knew all about his two younger sisters and their various husbands and lovers, about his mum and dad, and about all their friends and relations. I swam around happily in this new ocean of small histories, delighting in the new lifetime of stories he had to tell. Every one of them was perfectly formed with a beginning, a middle and an end. I wished I had grown up in such a place. My upbringing, in fits and starts of places and people, doesn't make a story, just a few vivid snapshots. It's made me a pastiche personality, an improvised patchwork of good and bad. But Pieter's stories have told him, written him to be like Pooh's honey pot, sweet to the very bottom.

We fell asleep in the end. A kind of waking doze. Lucid resting, without dreams but full of light and colour and warmth. We fell into little pools of sleep together, then woke and talked again. I had no idea a night could be so long. It was blue-dark with the stars pressed on to the windows when we woke most times. And then it was pearly grey, with a setting moon silvering everything, thick as paint on a statue. That's when we made love for the first time. Still a little asleep, so the first edge of sensitivity was dulled enough to give us the courage to begin.

'What will happen?' Pieter asked.

'I don't know.'

'In this plaster I cannot move a lot.'

'It doesn't matter. I'll move for you.'

'I love you, is not enough to say.'

'It'll have to do.'

I became aware of everything our senses held. I felt every hair of both our skins. I heard every bird singing in the garden. I smelled every leaf outside, every bead of sweat. I even smelled the furry plum stone I'd left under the bed a week before.

In quite a short time I lost the ability to tell what was my pleasure and what was Pieter's.

We ripped the sheets, kicked the bedside table over. If the kids hadn't been so exhausted the night before they would have rushed in to check on my safety.

'Are we alive?'

'I think so.'

Afterwards I began to cry. Great shuddering sobs. My muscles tightened with each one, then relaxed and let go. Pieter held me and wiped my face with his discarded shirt. He had exorcised me, he had pushed Martin out of my body. All Martin's selves, all his imprints, left me like tissue-paper cut-outs, pulled out one by one like the scarves out of a magician's hat, until they were all gone.

'This is what all that pain was for,' I said, 'I had to lose Martin so I could have you.'

'Like birth pains.'

'Yes.'

'All our lives we were travelling to here.'

This was the Alternative Universe where there were absolutely no rules or expectations that applied to me. I didn't have to drape myself in a flattering light and the right underwear with this man, I could sit cross-legged on the bed in a pair of knickers and a T-shirt, eating fromage frais from its plastic pot. Which I did, just as the sun rose and sent pink and orange under the clouds and into the bedroom. Pieter sat up against the headboard holding the black cherry flavour delicately between a finger and thumb. He stripped the lid off and licked it thoughtfully.

'Jess, in six weeks you are divorced?'

'About that.'

He tossed the lid out of the bed and picked up the teaspoon from the little tray lying between us. He looked at me. 'Will you marry me then?'

It hardly needed to be said. It was obvious, all part of the New World Order.

'Of course. D'you want a taste of this one? Apricot and guava. It's really nice!'

We were sitting up eating and drinking very sweet coffee wrapped in bits of each other's clothing, when Dan and Frankie wandered in sleepily like they always do in the mornings.

Mummy in Bed with a Man who isn't Daddy: the sort of thing that kids spend the rest of their lives recovering from. As they yawned their way to the bed, I remembered Chris telling me tearfully one drunken evening about walking in on his mother breast-feeding his twin brothers. My kids were surely about to experience the same trauma, and I'd made no effort to protect them.

But I had to admit the trauma was pretty subtle.

'Can we have breakfast in bed too?' said Frankie, plonking herself on the end of the bed.

'Yes. Toast okay?'

'Mmm. With butter and Marmite.'

'And jam. And orange juice Mummy please,' added Dan.

'I'll go and make it.'

'Watch out for my plaster Dan,' said Pieter.

I went downstairs leaving them playing cards on the back of an old Rupert annual. Perhaps saving for the therapist wouldn't be necessary.

'Pieter,' said Dan after his last slice of toast,

'Yes?'

'Are you going to sleep in Mummy's room all the time now?'

Pieter looked at me and I smiled.

'Yes, I think so. If you don't mind.'

'Great. Then can I have your room?'

I left Pieter to sleep, exhausted now and dosed with painkillers – too much strain on his plastered leg somehow. I cleared breakfast, chivvied the kids into uniform, and I tootled them to school under the racing sky of grey and blue, with the leaves turning upside down in the breeze. We sang along with the tape of 'Eternal Flame' and counted magpies.

'Two for Joy Mummy!' said Frankie

'No, three for a wedding!' said Dan. And they both giggled.

The New Universe had expanded to include the old.

There was just time to get home and out again for work: tame roe deer in a vicar's garden, a parrot that sings the Marseillaise and a hamster that eats steak. Not too much potential for being savaged. Not that I'd notice if a lion used my foot as chewing gum today. Rob and Steve were going to think I'd finally lost it.

'I'm getting married.' I'd say, and watch their faces. 'Just after bonfire night.'

I slowed down the last hill and opened the windows to the air, the first musty dampness of real autumn on the wind. Spread out below me were Mrs E's prize Charollais crosses with their big blond buttocks gleaming against the green, the gate into James and Mary's field, the crab apple tree where the pigeons nest, the shed with the mad chooks. And my house with the sleeping man held in its arms and beside it the green mounds of foliage promising next years spikes of blue delphiniums.